Shadows Rising

Rohan Monteiro is an amateur chess and poker player, a board gamer, a comic book nerd, a keen consumer of content related to Sci-fi, fantasy, mythology and history, a tsundokuist, an indoor climber, a life enthusiast and last but not the least a dad. His travels have taken him to over fifty countries, ranging from the world's highest free range mountain in Tanzania to shark cage diving off the coast of South Africa, to fishing for piranhas in the Amazon and warding off advances from an amorous orangutan in Borneo.

Shadows Rising is the first in a planned urban fantasy series set in modern-day Mumbai.

CELESTIAL CHRONICLES

Shadows Rising

ROHAN MONTEIRO

Published by Westland Books, a division of Nasadiya Technologies Private Limited, in 2024

No. 269/2B, First Floor, 'Irai Arul', Vimalraj Street, Nethaji Nagar, Alapakkam Main Road, Maduravoyal, Chennai 600095

Westland and the Westland logo are the trademarks of Nasadiya Technologies Private Limited, or its affiliates.

Copyright © Rohan Monteiro, 2024

Rohan Monteiro asserts the moral right to be identified as the author of this work.

ISBN: 9789360450878

10 9 8 7 6 5 4 3 2 1

This is a work of fiction. Names, characters, organisations, places, events and incidents are either products of the author's imagination or used fictitiously.

All rights reserved

Typeset by Jojy Philip, New Delhi
Printed at Thomson Press (India) Ltd

No part of this book may be reproduced, or stored in a retrieval system, or transmitted in any form or by any means, electronic, mechanical, photocopying, recording, or otherwise, without express written permission of the publisher.

Praise for *Shadows Rising*

The only thing thicker than Mumbai's traffic is the plot and action in Rohan's jhakkas debut novel about a semi-immortal chap who gets sucked into a kidnapping scheme. Big, boisterous and absolutely bonkers. Just like the city of Mumbai.'

Sidin Vadukut, author of The Dork Trilogy

'Humour, irreverence and action. This book does everything you don't expect.'

Anand Neelakantan, author of The Bahubali Trilogy

'Myth, magic, mysteries and more than a little hard-boiled noir. It's a potent and exhilarating mix.'

Mike Carey, author of *Lucifer*

'A breath of fresh air in the crowded, elbow-jostling landscape of Indian mytho-fiction. His wry, self-deprecating, ironic style breathes wit, humour and freshness into a classic tale of paranormal investigation.'

Ashok Banker, author of *The Forest of Stories*

'Noir and ancient myth rubbing elbows and told with a reverent purpose—Monteiro has made something special with Curse of the Yaksha.'

Sam Sykes, author of *Seven Blades in Black*

'The crazy, immersive, fantastical debut of the year.'

Kevin Missal, author of The Kalki Series

'An amazing adaptation.'
>Koral Dasgupta, author of The Sati Series

'Not all heroes wear capes. Some swear like sailors and kick ass while doing so.'
>Saksham Garg, author of *Samsara*

'An innovative, witty, page-turner of a spin on Indian mythology. A must read for mythology fans!'
>Trisha Das, author of *Never Meant to Stay*

To mom and dad

*Sorry for all the swearing.
I promise I don't sound like this in real life!*

Yaksha: Male nature spirits, seen throughout Indian art in various religions.

Source: Three Yakshas (Terracotta Exhibit), Asian Civilisations Museum, Singapore
Dated: 1st Century BC or 1st Century Ad

CHAPTER ONE

You know the funny thing about names? Not all of them are created equal.

Some are given in remembrance of a person from long ago. Others have no discernible meaning and are chosen merely to set you apart from everyone else. But then, there are names carefully crafted with the express purpose of influencing who you will turn out to be.

Call them brave or strong or wise in the language of the gods and the meaning will seep into that person's soul. They will imbibe the essence of what those words mean. And the deeds undertaken by that person will forever be remembered and serve as a shining example of what a name can accomplish.

Yes, reader, you are correct. #### (REDACTED) is an unusual name. If these final words of mine should ever see the light of day, they would be dismissed as the musings of a madman. But that is because of the crime I committed. A

deed so terrible, my name was struck from the annals of High Sanskrit. Nobody else will ever take the name of a god killer.
– Last recorded entry by Prisoner ####-###.
Sacred Archives of the Gandharvas, 1361 BCE

PRESENT-DAY MUMBAI

'I need your help.'

I shut my eyes for a moment. Maybe he was a figment of my imagination, and when I open them again, he would be gone. I had been looking forward to this evening all week and now that it was finally here, I didn't want to get involved in whatever problem he was going to dump on me.

No such luck. He was still very much there. The faint musty smell of cigarettes clung to him like a persistent ex, who can't take the hint.

He looked like a walking stereotype of an absent-minded professor. In his mid to late seventies, if I had to put a number on it. His glasses were comically oversized. His clothes looked crumpled like he had been sleeping in them for a few days, the creases in them mirroring the growing wrinkles of annoyance on my forehead.

We were at the Sensex bar in Bandra, which had a cute little gimmick. The prices of drinks dropped with every order of that beverage that came in. Something about supply and demand, which I didn't really care about. The barest smidgen of magic could twist the numbers in my favour.

I had dropped the price of spiced rum to a few rupees. Nobody seemed to notice. It was the only drink I truly enjoyed in this place. It reminded me of a happier time— they called it Soma back then, but, it was really the same thing in a different bottle.

While ordinarily I had no interest in helping strangers who wandered off the streets and came asking for favours, today I wanted to do so even less.

I had a date. My first in a long time. If you think dating is tough among humans, picture how hard it is for those of us who have lived for thousands of years and met all kinds of idiots in our lifetimes. Think of every dating horror story you've ever heard and multiply that by a hundred—that's how difficult it is for us to find a match.

I gave him the nicest smile I could manage without scaring him. Full of sparkling white teeth and dimples on either side. 'Today's not a good day for me. Maybe we can speak tomorrow?'

He shook his head. 'This can't wait.'

'I'm busy at the moment.'

'This is urgent,' he repeated, a note of hysteria creeping into his voice.

Yeah. It always was.

I had no one to blame but myself, really. It started a year ago when I helped find a missing cat. His owner was a regular at the bar and clearly very fond of his pet, given how much he bawled over his loss.

The cat in question was a bleached orange tabby called Nick Furry. Nobody knows if he was blind in one eye to begin with or if his owner being a Marvel fan had something to do with it.

In a moment of weakness and mainly to shut him up, I helped him find his missing pet. His rescue brought me free drinks and a lot of admiring glances from other drunks at the bar. What I didn't put together until much later is how good deeds always come back to bite you when you least expect it.

Slowly word spread. It shouldn't have because, and I can't stress this enough, it was just an ordinary cat. It wouldn't come when called, couldn't sing or dance or predict the next World Cup winner—it was an ill-temprered, feral ball of fur that tried to bite me when I pulled it out of the drainpipe it had gotten itself stuck in.

Yet, somehow, that had catapulted me from another rando in a bar to a local hero who could find 'anything'.

Before you knew it, people were coming to me with all sorts of odd requests, some of which weren't even related to missing items. Vandals who spray-painted someone's car, a couple of poison pen letters, three cases of revenge porn ... that sort of thing.

None of this was my business. I was not a private investigator. Heck, I wasn't even human—though they didn't know that. I had a knack for finding things, thanks to a few unique abilities I possessed. Most of the time when I got involved, I did it because I was bored and needed to entertain myself. When you are semi-immortal, life can get repetitive pretty fast.

This might be as good a time as any to explain the 'not human' bit. There's a reason most jokes don't start with, 'A celestial walked into a bar.' Most of them don't like to live anywhere where you can find humans. I'm not thrilled about the prospect either, but I've had time to get used to the idea. Exile is a wonderful way to make you reconsider your life choices.

Long story short, I happen to be a Yaksha—a semi-immortal, banished for a crime I don't remember committing. It's too long a tale and will make you all weepy to hear it now, so we should probably save it for another day. It's great for killing the mood at parties.

A fun part of being around for a long time is that you can pick up life skills like rare Pokémon cards. We can choose to discard the ones that we lose interest in and hone the rest to perfection over a few hundred years or so. Sure, you can learn to paint and sing and dance till the cows come home—if that's what floats your boat. If you are more like me, then your interests would tend to be a bit more grey than black and white. Picking locks, filching wallets, that kind of thing. Again, strictly because I like knowing how it gets done, not for any actual fringe benefit from the whole experience.

But I had also become better at reading faces and decoding body language. It's a useful trait when you want to leave as little a footprint as you can in the modern world. This man here was telegraphing a whole lot of information. Poor taste in fashion and eventual death by lung cancer went without saying, but there were other more subtle insights. The shrunken, hollow look in his eyes, for instance, meant this problem had taken a toll on him. This was giving him sleepless nights.

'What seems to be the problem?'

His hands clenched into fists. 'My granddaughter. She was kidnapped.'

I stared at him for a moment. 'I don't know what people have been telling you but this is not something you should be coming to me for. Go to the cops.'

'I did. They said they'll look into it.'

'Problem solved then!' I muttered. 'Trust them to do their job!'

Over the years, old people have figured out a way to convey disappointment through non-verbal cues. Looks of reproach, doled out in large doses like a stern parent. Like they had set a low bar and somehow you failed even that.

The old man was doing it now as he stared at me. 'Would you?'

He had a point. In a city with more than twenty million people, the police were overextended and understaffed. A hundred girls got assaulted or groped every day. One more was just a statistic—and not even a significant one at that.

'What's her name?' I asked, giving in to the sinking feeling that I was getting involved, whether I liked it or not.

'Anna,' he whispered, his voice cracking.

'You have a photograph?'

The old man winced. 'I had one—which I always kept in my wallet—but I gave it to the police.'

I don't think of myself as a celestial being anymore, but I could at least hope that people who came to me requesting favours would not be idiots. Is that too much to ask?

'No phone?'

'My battery died a short while ago. I didn't know how to contact you, so I spent the last six hours visiting pubs in Bandra trying to leave you a message.' He gave me a disapproving look as if it was my fault I had a vibrant social life.

'What about her parents? Where are they?'

He shook his head, looking even more sorrowful than before. 'They died in a car accident when she was six.'

Something stirred within me. The annoying old man's story was starting to gnaw through my resolve.

'How old is she now?'

'Twelve. She will be thirteen next month.'

I felt a tug at the edges of my conscience, a flicker of something I thought I had buried beneath centuries of disillusionment.

Most humans are loud, annoying and too talkative for their own good. When they finally become tolerable, they already have one foot in the grave. Over time, it got simpler for me to just not build any long-term relations with them.

But kids? Somehow, that's different. You could argue that thirteen is not exactly a child, but from the few I've met, it's not too great a leap. Their wide-eyed naivety hasn't fully been replaced with the cynicism of an adult. Most of the time, they are just straddling both worlds and trying to manage all the big emotions they are dealing with.

A young girl, snatched away in a city that chewed up and spat out souls on a daily basis?

I couldn't sit here and do nothing. Not when I was able to help. I sighed as I put down my glass.

'Start at the beginning. How do you know she was kidnapped?'

'It happened two days ago. We were both at home cooking dinner. There was a knock on the door, and she went to answer it.'

His lower lip quivered, and I resisted the urge to shake him by the shoulder. A lifetime in their company had made me aware how fragile they were. I could end up either dislocating his arm or making him spasm into further tears. Neither was something I wanted to deal with.

'Three men burst into our home, brandishing knives. One of them hit me with a rod.' He turned his back towards me to reveal a huge bruise on the side of his neck. 'When I came to, she was gone.'

A snatch-and-grab. Someone had deliberately targeted this girl, as opposed to the low risk, low cost option of abducting someone from the street.

Two days were an eternity in victim time. Provided she was still alive, she might not want to be.

'Have they reached out yet? Made any demands?'

He shook his head. 'Nothing at all'.

No ransom note? What kind of half-assed kidnapping was this?

I hadn't dealt with a kidnapping before. Well, there was a pet monkey that ran away that I had helped out with, so I was hoping the principles would be roughly the same.

Figuring out a motive was usually a good place to start.

I didn't think money was the angle here. He looked respectably well-off, but not wealthy.

'Did they take anything else from the house?'

He gave a helpless shrug. 'Nothing looked out of place when I regained consciousness.'

There was one question at the tip of my tongue. One plausible explanation that might explain what had happened.

I hesitated. He didn't look like he would react very well to what I wanted to ask him. I would need to attempt something I hadn't tried before. Diplomacy.

'Did she ever dabble in anything … recreational?'

He frowned. 'I am not sure I understand.'

I struggled to find the right words to phrase this. 'Any medication perhaps that worked for her? Something that made her happy?'

His brow furrowed. 'You mean Vicks? When she has a cold, she uses it liberally, but other than that—'

And this, folks, is why I don't bother trying to be tactful. 'Was your granddaughter into drugs?'

The old man spluttered angrily. A stream of invective followed, each one more creative than the next. I was grudgingly impressed. When someone can string together a colourful description of both your parents, a variety of anatomically impossible positions to contort your body into and a lengthy comparison to the left testicle of a lizard, in a few short sentences, you know you are in the presence of a champion cusser.

I'm betting he was from Haryana.

'Calm down,' I said when he paused to catch a breath. 'I didn't mean anything by it. I just need to cover all the possibilities, yes?'

'It's not a possibility. She isn't into drugs,' he hissed. 'She wouldn't even look at a cigarette. She's a good girl, always has been.'

'Right.' I hadn't realised that was the benchmark for teenage virtue these days. Tactfully, I chose not to say that out loud.

He was still indignant as he glared at me. 'She's a smart kid. Top of her class in every subject. And she goes to the temple every week.'

I tried to avoid rolling my eyes. Praying at a temple made you a good person as much as my aunt growing a moustache would make her my uncle. I never understood why they equated the two.

'Any sudden mood swings over the past few weeks?'
He shook his head.
'Any new friends that she's hanging out with?'
Another mute shake of his head.

I didn't think this line of questioning was getting me anywhere.

'Anything changed about her behaviour recently? Any new places she's been visiting? Does she dress differently? Any new choice of music or reading or whatever it is kids her age are doing?'

The man's eyes moistened with tears. 'No. It isn't anything like that. Anna is just a normal kid.'

'Normal.' I hated that word. As if it was something to aspire for instead of getting away from.

'You don't even have a photograph of her. How are you expecting me to help?'

'I was told you could find people if you had something that belonged to them,' he mumbled.

I started to ask who had been blabbing about me and then gave up. He wasn't wrong. I could trace a residual psychic echo if a strong enough impression was left behind on the object. That is part of the bucket load of charms I can usually cobble together when I'm sober. I'm only guessing here, since I haven't been sober in a while.

Location spells were a form of sympathetic magic. Humans have made strides in understanding it but their knowledge is still flawed. The term they use is 'Quantum Entanglement' which is a crude, unsatisfactory way of describing it. Like calling *Lord of the Rings* a movie about jewellery.

At its most basic level, 'sympathy' worked on the principle of like calls to like. You could use something that belonged to someone to track them down because both parts were inextricably yet intangibly linked and yearned to be together. Voodoo was an entire magical system built on a foundation of sympathy. Throw a drop of your enemy's blood, that they carelessly left behind, on an open flame and you could boil the blood in their veins, even if they were a hundred miles away.

All I needed to do was trace the path between them.

Incidentally, that's how I found the cat. It had left hair all over his owner's coat. Call me crazy but I didn't think this girl had marked her grandfather's coat in a similar fashion.

'Do you have anything of hers I can use? An old sweater or a favourite toy?'

'I wasn't sure if I would find you, so I didn't carry any of those items with me. But I can take you to our place. It's just ten minutes away. Behind the old Lido cinema. Sangeeta Apartments, 2B.'

I drained the rest of my glass in one long gulp. 'Let's go!' I said as I stood up. There was still an hour before my date got here. I could nip down to his house, take a quick look and be back quickly.

To my annoyance, he continued to sit, his lips tightly pursed.

'I heard you were someone who could help more than the police but I know nothing else,' he began. 'I don't even know your name.'

'Akran.'

'Akran,' he repeated doubtfully.

'Yeah, the z and the x are silent.' Let him chew on that for a while.

He took it in his stride, though I had no doubt he would be puzzling over it later.

'How much do you charge? I can visit the ATM if you ...'

I waved him off. 'Forget about money for now.' I meant it. I would charge a small fee, mainly to separate the curious and time-wasters from people who genuinely needed help. This chap qualified.

'I need to meet the cops,' he told me. 'They want me to look at some mugshots. Can you wait for an hour or so?'

He wilted under the glare I shot him.

'I didn't know where to find you, or whether you were even real and would take this case.'

I ignored him as I scribbled a note for Deanne, telling her something had come up. I handed the note to the bartender who knew me well.

'Give me the address and meet me there when you are finished.'

He swallowed hard.

'The key is under the mat,' he said. 'I'll be there as soon as I finish. They just need to ask me some questions.'

Suited me fine. I folded the address he scribbled on a piece of paper and placed it in my pocket. If I had to put up with his company any longer, we would need to call the cops anyway.

CHAPTER TWO

What is a Yaksha, you ask? Think of us as demigods, a level or so below the Devas who, in turn, are a few levels below the Trinity of Brahma, Vishnu and Shiva. They are truly gods. All the rest of us were gnats in their presence.

The Devas held lofty portfolios. Indra looked after the monsoon; Agni was the god of fire; Surya was the sun god; Lakshmi, the goddess of wealth; and so forth.

As demigods, we still had responsibilities, but they were collective. The Gandharvas were singers. The Apsaras were dancers. The Yakshas were warriors.

– Private Journals of Akran

The apartment slouched on the street like a sulky teenager at a family reunion—completely uninterested in impressing anyone. It had a run-down theatre on one side and a women's college on the other. The cars parked in and around the building were mid-tier brands—a sign of an up-and-coming middle-class society. I noticed the location was spitting distance from what could charitably be called a beach. There had been efforts made in the past year to clean up sections of the city, and the more affluent areas always received more attention than others. Garbage-free beaches and a few extra policemen patrolling the area were always popular incentives among the voters. Not a place where crimes could happen openly and brazenly. Whoever had kidnapped the girl was either well-connected or incredibly stupid. Or both.

A bored security guard ignored me completely as I ambled right past him and through the lobby. If you plaster a scowl on your face and refuse to make eye contact, people usually avoid asking you any questions. The security at most private apartments in Mumbai tends to focus on the labourers and delivery boys. As far as they are concerned, well-dressed strangers are incapable of committing any crime.

The apartment was as ugly as I had expected. Full of sharp and angular lines, as if the architect had deliberately attempted to make the space linear and unwelcoming. In the good old days, people didn't have fancy tools to keep the lines perfectly straight. Creatures of magic like myself hate standardised shapes. Our essence, like our realm, is all about chaos.

The smell of incense was faint but still lingered. There were other discernible scents I could make out—musk and sweat; people who didn't understand the concept of deodorant. These were the people who had taken her away. I would come back to them later.

Entering a crime scene, any place really where an incident has occurred, usually gives me a minor headache. There are too many strong emotional residues associated with whatever happened. The more recent the incident, the stronger the echo. I could still taste the girl's fear in the room, just before she was abducted—like bitter lemons. The old man's desperate worry and anger hung in the air too, like a peach gone bad. And something else— an unpleasant taste I couldn't describe but had long been familiar with. Human sadism.

Her room was decently sized, by most standards. It featured pastel walls and smooth sheets, with a hint of a pleasant fragrance in the air. The window on the left overlooked the front of the building.

At the edge of the bed sat a laptop, one of those models that could swivel and turn into a tablet. It was still plugged in. The old man had clearly not touched anything within the room. I started towards it, then hesitated. Laptops were usually a great source of personal information, but I had reasons for not touching it just yet. I would get to it last. It wasn't going anywhere.

A thin layer of dust had accumulated on the dresser. I picked up the photo frame and stared at it for a while. It was a picture of Anna and her grandfather. She was a beautiful girl, wide-eyed and innocent. I studied the picture for a bit longer, committing her face to memory. It was one thing to sit in the bar and listen to the story of her being kidnapped. Now that I was in her room, looking at her picture, this felt more real. Here was a regular teenager, going about her life and minding her own business and then suddenly attacked in her own home.

Gazing upon her picture brought back old memories. A desire to protect and nurture I had not felt since I sat beside a cot and told stories to another wide eyed, innocent child.

I was starting to take this personally. Whoever kidnapped her was going to regret it.

In my admittedly limited experience, detective work is mostly about observation. People assume that it requires deductive reasoning or some specific skill set, but nine times out of ten, it's about paying attention to one's surroundings. There's a certain amount of drudgery in methodically poring over the minutiae of someone's life to see what clues it can reveal.

I started with the dresser. The first two drawers contained makeup—a couple of tubes of lipstick, a hair dryer and a few other cosmetics that I was not entirely familiar with. Another drawer contained underwear—the plain and simple variety. None of the three drawers contained anything worth noting.

The impression I got was that nothing had been moved around since the kidnapping took place. I was expecting some indication that this was being treated as a crime scene. Police tape near the doorway. Chalk marks to indicate testing of fingerprints. None of that was present here. It was sadly a reflection of the city's apathy. Once the police report was filed, there was so much red tape and buck-passing that almost nothing ever got done. Unless, of course, money changed hands. Only then would someone sit up and take notice.

Maybe the old man wasn't used to how this city operated. Or perhaps he was trying to do the right thing by not offering bribes to get the case solved. Either way, nothing would get done, unless I stepped in.

Her bed was in pristine condition. A pink Moleskine diary, which looked fairly new, was hidden under her pillow. The plastic around the cover hadn't been fully torn apart, and aside from her name on the first page, it was blank. I needed something more personal—something with an emotional connection to the girl that would allow me to pinpoint her on a map. A teenager's diary, filled with angst and mushy feelings, would have been perfect, but this one wasn't of use just yet.

I slowly walked back to the centre of the room. No other clues as to why she was taken. That left me with the option I disliked the most—I needed to examine the laptop.

It had taken a while for me to discover that magic and electricity don't mix. Or rather, they mix too well. Celestials born after the invention of electricity became commonplace did not have an antagonistic relationship with toasters, microwave ovens and the like. It's only relics like me who have been around since the Bronze Age who face these problems. After an electric pole nearly exploded when I walked past, I switched to wearing heavily insulated shoes every time I stepped out.

Handling a laptop would require a little more finesse. Luckily, I was prepared. I had gotten into the habit of carrying insulated gloves at all times. They were thin and skin-coloured, so most people wouldn't notice I was wearing them. But since they offended my sense of fashion, I usually put them on only as a last resort. I looked like a chump in summer, and since I live in a tropical country, it's summer all year round. Still, it couldn't be helped. They were a necessity for us fossils when dealing with the modern world.

I knew enough on how to operate them to save my life. The laptop booted up quickly. There was no password needed, which was a relief. I wouldn't know what to do otherwise.

I had spent time with a couple of tech gods who allowed me to pick up some rudimentary tips for situations like this. The first bit involved going through her browser history. There wasn't anything specific I was looking for—it was more about trying to get a handle on who she was and if there was anything that had changed in her interests in the past few weeks.

She seemed like a regular kid. Used Instagram a lot, which was the digital equivalent of attending a never-ending high school talent show, and Facebook, which was the family reunion of the internet—complete with creepy uncles, conspiracy nuts and neighbours with unsolicited advice.

Her search history gave no clues. Clothing, shoes, an environmental rally, that kind of thing. She watched a lot of news online as well as a couple of atheism and history podcasts on YouTube. The only oddity, if you could call it that, was a heightened increase in music-related searches about two days before she was taken.

On her bedside table sat a thumb drive. After a moment's hesitation, I plugged it in. Wouldn't do to leave any stones unturned.

There were two files on it. An mp3 recording and a text file labelled 'READ ME'.

I opened the text file first.

It was a short letter that sounded like a hoax. A sob story about a struggling artist who couldn't afford to pay the bills and so was distributing his music on these thumb drives. If anyone liked it, they were encouraged to write back to the artist and he would share more of his music with them. An email address was also provided.

Definitely a scam. If he was a struggling artist, he should have released this online, instead of buying thumb drives and distributing them. The only way this would make sense would be if the thumb drive had malware on it. That was outside my realm of expertise. I decided I would take it to one of the tech gods I knew.

Still, she had evidently opened the music file, as her search history indicated. So I did the same.

The silence stretched.

Just as I decided it was nothing worth listening to, the music began playing.

Imagine the most evocative, profoundly moving tune you've ever heard. Something that would make you weep buckets when sad or shout out and dance in the rain when you feel alive. That's what I was listening to right then.

The song was soft and melodious with a haunting, familiar strain. A story of unrequited love, yet mingled with hope. But it was much more than a work of art. It was divine. In every sense of the word.

To an ordinary human, it would sound like the call of a siren—hypnotic, rapturous and irresistible. Music like this could drive humans to madness. In the days of yore, they would leap off the prows of ships into a frothing ocean, uncaring of sharks or other creatures of the deep, just to get closer to the source. It could caress you sensuously like a lover, sending you careening into the depths of despair or gird your loins for battle, all through the deft dexterity of a divine minstrel's fingers on a stringed instrument.

With an effort, I shut it down. The haunting melody had brought tears to my eyes. There were many aspects of the celestial world I couldn't stand, namely the petty bickering and politics of the court. Music wasn't one of them.

Granted, people have wide and varied music tastes. 'November Rain' to one of us might sound like 'Inky Pinky Ponky' to the other. But this? This transcended everything I had heard on Earth. There was no doubt in my mind about the music's origin.

A teenage girl, living in Mumbai, somehow gaining access to the music of the gods was baffling to say the least. This mystery was getting weirder by the minute.

A quick check through her mailbox confirmed that she did reach out to the address provided, gushing about the song. There had been no response, but the evening after she had sent it, she had been kidnapped.

So, facts so far. Teenage girl missing. A suspicious thumb drive received with a sob story that falls apart when you study it closely. A music file with a divine origin. A young dashing hero investigating the case.

Could her kidnapping be related to the music file? It sounded like a hackneyed opening of a particularly bad movie plot, but I didn't have anything else to work with.

There were a couple of holes in this theory that were large enough to fly an aeroplane through. People didn't anonymously send thumb drives with the music of the gods to random strangers. There was also no direct link between the music senders and the kidnappers. But the timing of it was suspect. She had vanished a short while after receiving a file she had no business receiving. It was odd, but not necessarily suspicious, like it could be dismissed as a set of unhappy coincidences. My gut, however, was telling me there was more to this story. I also didn't have any other theories at the moment.

If they were linked, the kidnappers' reaction was bizarre. A daylight kidnapping by breaking and entering into somebody's home was stupid. It was an election year after all.

No. The smart thing to do would have been to kidnap her on the streets. There would be outrage, public indignation, all the morons in the government blaming what she was wearing at the time, but none of that would matter after twenty-four hours. It would be dismissed as just another kidnapping, not worth batting an eyelid for.

Nothing else in the room could shed any light on what was going on. This was the point where a human investigator would have been stumped.

I, however, had other tools at my disposal.

Emotions seep into inanimate objects. They carry the weight of attachment that takes a while to dissipate. Crafting a location spell was a fairly simple affair. I needed an item the girl had a strong emotional attachment to. The diary wouldn't work. It was too new and she hadn't yet built a bond with it. Fortunately, I was dealing with a teen. From what I had heard, teenagers tend to be pretty emotional about a whole lot of things.

Sitting on top of the dresser was a stuffed toy. Brown, furry and well-worn around the edges, the bear looked like the huggable sort. I could trace the faint echo of her feelings when I held it. She used to sleep with it clutched to her chest every night, growing up. There was an unmistakable weight of tears and sadness in there. It had grown fainter over time but you could still sense the residual echo of misery after her parent's death. Mingled in there was joy and laughter, along with reassurance —her grandfather was a kind-hearted man, but there was an aching void in her that no amount of love could fill.

Maybe she outgrew it eventually, but it would serve as a decent lodestone. She still felt something for that toy.

The dust on the dresser would be my canvas. I fashioned a crude but effective pentagram with the soft toy in the centre. Some people insist on using black candles, incense and closing all the curtains so no light gets in the room, but they are idiots. Every last one of them.

True magic requires only three elements. The first is a mystic or a person who holds a spark of the supernatural, someone who can access the elemental mana needed to activate a spell. In this case, me. Most practitioners use High Sanskrit or one of the seven languages of the gods, though celestials like myself, who have been around for millennia, can invoke the necessary rites in any language.

The second is an anchor or something to channel magic. Wizards in the old days waved staffs. The more creative ones used pieces of jewellery or swords. In this case, the pentagram served as an effective anchor. Without a channel, calling magic into our realm was like opening a dam. It would gush in without any sort of valve to regulate it. Unchecked, it could blow up the dresser. Or even the building.

The third was the binding. For this spell, the teddy bear, which had a sympathetic connection to the girl, would serve to link the two.

Of these three elements, what's most important is the mana. It's what holds the universe together. Think of it like the life force that sustains every living thing on the planet. It's in the air we breathe, the water we drink and even in the rich brown soil below our feet. Not to be confused with M-a-n-n-a, which was just some leftover food the gods threw to a few starving people in the desert.

Brihaspati once explained mana to me as the elemental magical source that we draw our powers from. He was the spiritual leader of the gods, so he probably knew what he was talking about. All celestials have a pool of mana that they can access.

Thanks to my exile, I was cut off from the larger universal mana pool that other celestials use. Being a Yaksha, my body did absorb trace amounts in minute quantities. It was the equivalent of dipping my face into a raging river—I could taste the water on my tongue, maybe even savour a few droplets, but was unable to drink enough.

The ritual was a simple one. Objects or people with a strong sympathetic bond can be used to locate one another. A handful of words spoken with the right inflection and deference gives you access to the divine map of the cosmos—one that tracks everything and everyone. It's similar to what humans call Google Maps, except this is powered by actual magic.

Location spells are fairly rudimentary. I was expecting either a brief vision of the girl bound and gagged in someone's house or, in the worst-case scenario, an unmarked grave. There were not many other possibilities.

Pretty foolish of me, in retrospect.

Almost as soon as I began chanting, I realised something was wrong. Tucked in within all the emotional baggage of the girl was something else. A tiny coiled black seed of darkness. It did not belong to her—it was as if someone had deliberately inserted something into the stuffed toy. There was a sense of wrongness about it that raised my hackles.

I stopped. What was I getting into? There was no way to use the bear as a location spell without probing that little black seed. It was some sort of countermeasure, designed specifically to prevent someone like me from attempting something like this.

Slowly and hesitantly, I tried again. It was a complicated puzzle to solve, one that connected to the task at hand. At this moment, though, I had no interest in getting sucked into it. Finding her was the priority. I reached out with my senses trying to sneak past the ... seed. Or whatever it was.

It was then that the soft, cuddly and furry toy turned his head to look at me.

My psychic probing had triggered something within. Our eyes locked. His little button eyes gleamed a demonic red.

Then everything went to hell in a handbasket. The soft toy blew up. There's no other way to describe it. The little bear melted like butter in a greasy frying pan before it detonated. The shockwave exploded outwards, slamming into me. I raised my arms in front of my face right before it hit, protecting my head from the brunt of the impact, though I was still flung across the room and into the wall.

I had been stripped of my powers when I was exiled to the mortal world. I could call up simple hexes and use my celestial knowledge when needed, but I no longer possessed magical defences. My aura was a frail wisp of a thing that would shatter easily. Still, Yakshas are notoriously hard to kill, and I was one of the toughest of my ilk.

It was a good twenty minutes before I regained consciousness. My head was still ringing, so I kept my eyes closed and my head down, counting slowly till a hundred, before I decided to open them again.

The room, for the most part, looked untouched. The soft toy, however, was a blackened charred husk. It sat there with a beatific look on its otherwise lifeless face. I stood up gingerly, adjusting my jacket and clutching my arm.

The little dark seed was a psychic booby-trap. This had now gotten interesting. Whoever had taken the girl had placed the fur ball there in an attempt to deter other pursuers. They had at least rudimentary knowledge of magic to figure out that I would use a toy for a location spell.

To humans, it would be just another stuffed animal. This psychic backlash, on the other hand, was specifically meant to deter someone like me. Well, not exactly like me since I was stronger than the average magic user. Clearly, no one had counted on a Yaksha getting into their business.

I sat on her bed as I tried to make sense of what had happened. There weren't too many people who could rig up a custom psychic explosive. It was way too much effort to cover the trail of an ordinary kidnapping. There was definitely more to the story than I had been told.

I considered trying again with another object—maybe the blanket she slept with. But my head was still ringing from the impact. It would take a few hours, possibly a day, before I could try another locator spell.

Spells like this usually had one more hidden layer. That, more than anything, was pissing me off. I had made a rookie mistake by falling for such a crude trap. Magic had its own feel, its own smell, its own taste. You would sense it in the hairs on your arm rising up, in the sinister whispers in your mind, in its lingering malice. If I hadn't been distracted, trying to get back to my date, ignoring the warning signs when I spotted the little seed inside, or been fully sober, I would have detected it. Now, I would face the consequences. Somewhere in this city, a wire had been tripped. The smart thing to do was to beat a hasty exit.

I had been called a lot of names in the past. Pig-headed, obstinate, stubborn... Smart wasn't one of them. Right now, I was pissed off. This city meant something to me. It was flawed, crowded and noisy, but there was no other place I would rather live in. For me, it was home. I would be damned before I let a bunch of criminals kidnap a child in my city and get away with it.

I slipped the photo out of the frame and into my pocket. The sound of a jeep pulling up outside alerted me that I was about to have company. A quick glance through the window confirmed my suspicions. The chain had been yanked, and the hounds at the other end were coming to investigate.

I snuck a quick glance at the mirror in her room. No real cuts and bruises since my healing factor had kicked in. I looked a little roughed up, kind of like that teddy bear but still ready to dish out hugs and cuddles if needed.

There was only one difference though.

Hiding among mortals was like slipping into a second skin. Society had forced polite masks upon us to conceal the darkness within. We smiled and nodded at the stupidity of those in power and gritted our teeth in private, if their idiocy affected us.

But now? I could feel the mask fraying. My face twisted into a vicious smile as I shed my cloak of civility. Something I had tamped down a long time ago, raised its ugly head. Rage.

I prided myself on keeping it leashed most of the time. Now, that leash had finally slipped off.

I shut the door carefully behind me as I stepped out. Anna and her grandfather didn't need any more trauma in their lives. Dealing with the hounds downstairs was my responsibility. I had brought it about by triggering that trap and I would make sure this didn't get back to them.

Not my usual style since I preferred the shadows, but I was feeling reckless. We would do this out in the open, with no heed for the consequences.

I liked disciplining hounds. Especially the two-legged variety who thought swaggering around in a group could protect them. It had been too long since I had administered a whipping.

CHAPTER THREE

To the uninitiated, magic, charms and hexes all look pretty similar. There are actually some fundamental differences.

Let's say I use magic to change into a tiger. I look and smell exactly like a tiger. I sound like one when I roar, and I can charge at my enemies and attack them tooth and claw. Though my mental abilities remain unchanged, I possess the strengths and weaknesses of a tiger. I am essentially indistinguishable from other tigers.

Now, let's say I choose to use a charm instead. That would then be the equivalent of me prancing around in a tiger costume. It might fool you if you have never seen a tiger before or have an IQ under ten.

A hex is like a curse, except its effects are more short-term. It is useful against humans. Use them against others of my kind and it will just piss them off.

Once, I had magic. Bloody good powerful magic. Now, I use charms and hexes to survive.

– Private Journals of Akran

There were eight of them—a minor miracle since they all arrived in a single vehicle. A second miracle was how the watchman and other occupants of the building seemed to have disappeared.

It was an ability unique to the denizens of Mumbai. They can disassociate from anything happening that doesn't involve them. It's the opposite of Delhi where everyone else's business is your business.

As they leapt out of the jeep and moved towards me in a semicircle, I noticed an assortment of weapons, mainly crowbars and knives. One of them held only a lighter. I decided to ask him what his plan was later. I already knew where I was going to shove it if he got too close.

A few moments of awkward silence followed. They were working hard to intimidate me with their presence. It might have worked if I hadn't seen a movie once where a similar-looking group bursts into song and dance. It ruined an otherwise perfectly menacing moment.

Picture the balding paunchy uncles you see on the beaches of Goa, usually the ones with hair coming out of their ears. The ones who are irascible and ill-tempered and convinced that underwear and swimsuits are the same thing. This was like walking into a fucking convention of them.

Despite my many years living among humans, I couldn't get over their appalling fashion sense. Back in my day, men of the ruling classes strutted the streets bare-chested, wearing enough jewellery to put a peacock to shame. And even they had better taste than these idiots in front of me today.

The thought did occur to me that maybe I was the one out of touch with reality. But then one of them stepped closer, and the stench of unwashed sweat wafting to my nostrils put me at ease. I wouldn't be taking fashion tips from someone who hadn't bathed in a week.

He was the leader, based on how the others seemed to defer to him. A stout man with a bicycle chain wrapped around his hand. His eyes were bleary, as if he had been asleep, and I could smell alcohol on his breath.

He stepped forward, close enough that I could count the hairs up his nose.

'I'm going to whip your ass, faggot,' he hissed.

I smiled politely at him. He had interpreted my impeccable sense of style as 'less manly' than desired. Back in my day, we didn't have any particular taboos regarding whom we had sex with. I'm not saying I miss those days, but random slurs about my sexual orientation didn't bother me. Not from this walking, festering pustule, anyway.

'I'm always confused by that term. It's a bundle of sticks, right? Or are you asking for a cigarette?'

He blinked at me, bewildered. It must be frustrating when you've crafted such an epic line, and it just doesn't land.

I held up his wallet, the one I had picked from his back pocket while he was busy staring daggers at me. He gave a little start as he realised what I had done. The fog was starting to clear from his brain as he saw the wry amusement in my eyes and the utter indifference to his threats.

I had met plenty of people like him in my time on this planet. Bullies who got their way through intimidation and bluster. Having a few cronies makes them puff up like bullfrogs. They feed off each other's stupidity and become even bigger jackasses than they are individually.

'Such bad manners,' I murmured as I looked right into his eyes. 'Maybe I need to teach you a lesson.'

For centuries, they had been told never to lock eyes with a celestial. We could mesmerise them, make them see things that weren't there or wish they had never seen. We could mould their memories through the sheer force of our will. This was why they were meant to look down in deference when we spoke.

The barest thread of glamour added to my voice made his throat constrict and his eyes widen. I had learnt this trick from the Nagas, and it worked wonderfully on humans. Nobody could freeze and terrorise their prey quite like a large snake could. At that moment, I had gotten past the pathetic defences of his mind. To his naked eyes, I was a coiled cobra, hood raised, hissing and spitting, ready to strike.

He was prey! A low murmur arose from his companions.

This was not going the way they had expected.

These poor saps had no idea I was just getting started. Now they would really get a show.

I reached into my pocket and removed a deck of playing cards. A regular deck, one you could pick up at just about any retail store, though being in contact with my body had given it a little more oomph. I held it in front of me, on an outstretched palm, and heard the low voices turn into sharp gasps of fear as the cards rose of their own accord and floated between us.

The mortal world is guided by natural laws—immutable ones, like gravity. Objects don't float; fish don't fly; you can't pull off a brown belt with black shoes; and the like.

But the world of the celestials has no such rules. We have guidelines that are subject to interpretation and the rulings of the Gandharva court. Our world intersects with yours often enough, but you don't see us. We live within the cracks of your universe.

Ancient folklore in the Puranas warns humans not to get too close or attached to Yakshas and other celestials. It's certainly good advice. After centuries of boredom with only moths for amusement, we might decide to entertain ourselves by plucking off their wings.

From mankind's point of view, we are capricious, cruel beings. In all fairness, we feel the same way about humans.

But there's another reason that is not often spoken of.

Manipulating objects within two feet of my surrounding is as natural as breathing. The natural laws of the world will bend over backwards to accommodate a Yaksha. It's how the concept of personal space originated.

The cards rose in the air and began to spin around me. Slowly, they picked up speed, and the faces of my audience appeared on each—crude mocking caricatures, yet unmistakable in their resemblance. They leered and winked at the men who stood still, paralysed with fear. True magicians would laugh themselves silly at the thought of this being considered impressive. But to people who had no understanding of the arcane world, this induced raw, gut-wrenching terror.

'Shall I show you how you all meet your untimely end?' My voice had grown deeper as it echoed all around them—a parlour trick to frighten kids. 'Do you want the spirits to read your fate?'

Even as I spoke, one of the cards caught fire. Another one acquired a hole through the centre as if it had been shot straight through the gut. Some of the cards began to moan and cry softly—human sobs and heart-wrenching wailing that slowly began to rise in volume.

The fear was turning real now, tangible and solid. It hung in the air like a noxious cloud of miasma and terror, and all I needed was one final push to send them over the edge.

'Perhaps you've not heard of me, little rats, you who walk around in human skin. Shall I strip it off you? Do you want to know who it is you thought to threaten?' The words were spoken with a sibilant hiss, and the promise of torture was evident in my tone. I wasn't faking my relish at the prospect of some of them putting up a fight.

The first to break was a mousy one in the back. He had wet himself and was slowly backing away, trying to distance himself from his companions as the cards began to spin. The card with his face suddenly began to wail in earnest. It was a plaintive desperate cry, and listening to it wail in his voice was his breaking point. Giving up any hope of a dignified exit, he let out a high-pitched scream and ran. That was enough incentive for the rest of them. They all broke away, screaming in terror, not even bothering to look behind at their hapless leader. Sheer unbridled fear can make mortals lose all sense of their faculties.

In the span of a few heartbeats, the place was deserted once again. That left just me and the leader of the pack, with whom I was very much looking forward to talking.

I released him from my gaze, and he fell to his knees, gasping. I would have held him longer, but his heart was on the brink of exploding out of his chest from the stress of imagining himself in the coils of a sixteen-foot snake. Besides, I too was drained. The psychic booby-trap, plus the use of mana with the cards, had been exhausting.

Stepping forward, I lifted him off the ground by his hair. He thrashed and whimpered as I pulled him up. He was of stocky build, but I was stronger and not particularly concerned about him losing some hair in the process.

'What's your name?'

'A-Akhilesh Kashreshwar. Don't hurt me. I'll tell you anything you want!'

'Of that, I have no doubt whatsoever.' I had learnt early on that enunciating each word carefully somehow made you more terrifying. Like you were a higher-grade of villain.

'Why did you take the girl?'

'We were hired to do so. We don't harm them in any way.' He whimpered in pain as my grip tightened.

'Where did you take them?'

'We only took her and the others to a couple of businessmen near the docks.' He was babbling away freely now. 'They take the girls, make the payment and leave. We don't know where they keep them or what they do with them.'

'Others? How many were there?' I shifted my grip from his hair, which was damp and greasy with sweat, to the scruff of his neck, which I held with an iron grip.

'About a dozen.' He continued to squirm.

Twelve kids? I had signed up to rescue one girl because I was feeling charitable. This was turning into a city-wide human trafficking ring.

I shouldn't have been surprised. The psychic trap that had been laid was quite elaborate; completely out of place for a solitary kidnapping. If this was a larger criminal ring, then they, in all likelihood, had a magic user on hire.

I shook him none too gently.

'How long has this been going on? When did you first start?'

'About two years ago. There are two or three of them. They tell us where to go, and we pick them up.' My grip around his neck must have involuntarily tightened, for his bleating became more pronounced.

'Is it just you and your cronies each time or do they accompany you as well?'

'In the beginning, it used to be just us. The past two or three times, one of them has been accompanying us.'

I had the feeling that the person who accompanied them would be the magic user—the one who left the psychic booby-trap.

'Tell me about the thumb drive,' I suggested, changing tack. 'Where did you get it from?'

'You mean that static sound? They gave it to us. It is one of the tasks they asked us to manage. To every house, we would send a thumb drive and wait. If they responded to the email, telling us they wanted more music or asking questions about it, we were sent to pick them up. We must have sent out over a hundred of these thumb drives.'

'They never asked you to collect these thumb drives back and reuse them?'

'In the beginning, they did. But the last two or three times, after we were sent to take the girls, they didn't seem to care about it anymore.'

He used the word *take* as if the girls were objects. When this conversation was over, I would 'take' a few body parts of his as souvenirs.

Ordinary humans couldn't hear the music of the gods. All they would hear is the hiss and crackle of static—Akhilesh had just revealed that he had no divine blood in his lineage going back a hundred generations. Somehow, that didn't surprise me in the least.

Those who had a spark of divinity would be able to hear the pure musical notes that I had heard. They would find the hypnotic lure of the music irresistible and would reach out to the provided email address asking for more. That's how they were being identified.

What I still didn't know was why they were being kidnapped.

'I am disappointed, Akhilesh,' I whispered softly in his ear. He flinched visibly, unable to help himself. 'I thought that you would have told me something I didn't know by now since I haven't killed you. Instead, you've wasted my time.' I smiled at him in a way that was not at all meant to be reassuring. 'Do you want me to show you how I deal with people who waste my time?'

'Wait! There was one more thing,' he gasped. 'They were after a jewel of some sort. A large ruby, the size of my palm that they said glowed like molten lava. They were very insistent that we find it. We went to jewellers, museums, antique shops, even a few private collectors, but no one had any knowledge about it.'

I nodded slowly. There was a jewel I knew that fit that description, but it had been lost for centuries. It seemed unlikely that they were looking for the same thing. Then again, given that celestials were involved, anything was possible.

His breath was returning to an even rhythm as he began to believe I was someone he could reason with.

'What did they offer you for this?'

Despite his obvious fear, there was no mistaking the flash of greed in his eyes. 'A hundred gold coins for each girl we found.'

There was no way anyone would pay these dolts in gold for such a laughably simple job.

'If you are lying to me …' I didn't need to finish the sentence.

'Here, take it.' He reached into a pocket in the folds of his clothes and pulled out a small transparent plastic pouch. 'This was the payment for the last girl, the one from this building. Just don't hurt me.'

It was at that precise moment that I knew my day had gone from bad to worse.

What he had extracted was trash. Worthless pebbles and bits of scrap. The kind you would find while walking on the seashore. He was holding it out for me to inspect like they were the crown jewels.

When you know what to look for, glamour is usually easy to detect. They had used *maya*—an illusion spell. A complex weave requires more skill, but anyone can cloak an object to look like something else without much effort. The challenge comes in maintaining the weave. Most of such tricks faded away in a couple of hours.

Through his own admission, I was able to tell that he had been doing this for a couple of years. The more efficient way to trick someone for a long period was to directly manipulate the image in his mind. It was a lot more difficult—too complex for the average human mage. It was also highly illegal. Mind manipulation was expressly forbidden by the celestial court.

The mention of gold and the sight of the pebbles put me on alert. He froze as he sensed the sudden change in my demeanour. Any hopes he had of walking away unscathed just took a nosedive.

'Who gave you the money? Describe your employers.'

His eyes widened with fear.

'Please, let me go,' he blubbered. 'It was just a job for us. We never intended to hurt anyone. They'll kill me if they found out I'd even spoken of them to someone.'

I brought my face close enough to his that I could smell the garlic from his last meal. 'And what exactly,' I whispered, 'do you think I'm going to do if you don't tell me what I need to know?'

I could see from the way his shoulders sagged that he had been hoping I wasn't willing to cross that invisible line most mortals stay within. That thin veneer of morality and a fear of reprisals that stops people from taking the most expedient path towards eliminating a problem.

I had no such qualms. The code I held myself to did not apply to kidnappers.

There was no doubt in my mind that Akhilesh would tell me anything at this stage. He was too scared to lie and too terrified to even think about holding back. But even this nail-biting fear wasn't enough to help him recall his employers. His brow furrowed as he tried to remember who they were and it all came up blank. I had been expecting this.

Lifting him off his feet, I slammed him into a parked car. It looked malicious, but it was necessary. I needed him disoriented for what I was about to do next.

Once again, I was inside his head. Except this time, I was not attempting something as mundane as an illusion spell. I was actively shuffling through his memories, tracing back to the identity of his mysterious benefactors. I had seen this look of confusion before. Someone had deliberately obfuscated his mind. If they had gone to such lengths—booby-trapping a toy in the room, tricking him into accepting worthless pebbles as gold—then it was no surprise that they had made a cursory effort to hide themselves.

I should probably emphasise that this was not fun for me. It is like sticking your hand into a loaded diaper—you never know what crap you are going to find in there. And Akhilesh was clearly no saint. His head was filled with enough smut to last him several lifetimes—mostly deviant acts with various popular actresses.

Reaching into someone's mind without permission is a clear violation of their rights. Depending on the severity of the crime, the punishment ranged from exile to a death sentence. In the eyes of the celestial court, I was far beyond the threshold of acceptable behaviour. This would merely reinforce their opinion about me.

Yet, Akhilesh here was a kidnapper at the very least. Worst case scenario, he was an arsehole in all walks of life. I loathed kidnappers. Plus, he had threatened to kill me, so I could make allowances.

There! Tucked deep within his head was an image of the three individuals he had spoken to. But each of their faces was shrouded. Every time he tried to recall what they looked like, a thin misty haze, like a light rain on the windshield would cover their features. It was skilfully done. An artist had woven this illusion, light as a feather, carefully painted brushstrokes to obscure their faces. Akhilesh wouldn't even have realised that someone had spun a delicate little web in his mind.

But that wasn't the only surprise waiting in there. Around those memories were psychic tripwires once again. An entwined mesh of gossamer strands spread over his thoughts, on the off-chance that he would encounter someone like me.

If I wanted to find out who they were, I would have to pull those traps apart.

It took only a few seconds to confirm what I had suspected. The tripwires were rigged to detonate inwards. Whoever had done this had taken great pains to mask their identity. The slightest misstep and Akhilesh would suffer permanent brain damage.

They had assumed rather naively that anyone who decided to investigate this would be one of the good guys. Someone who would hesitate to harm a human.

How trusting of them!

I triggered the trap.

Akhilesh screamed as the psychic backlash tore through his head. The memories of his employers were disintegrated along with the vision in his left eye. He would suffer debilitating migraines for the rest of his life.

I didn't bother to look back as I walked away, leaving him screaming on the ground while clawing at his face. As I said, I had no sympathy for kidnappers.

It was too bad the traps were so well-placed. Triggering them didn't give me any additional information.

But I was also preoccupied with another thought. I now knew who was behind the kidnappings.

INTERLUDE

The ancient world had its own John Connor. Vishnu would send down avatar after avatar, who, like terminators, would eliminate extinction level threats, then with a wink and an 'I'll be back' would disappear into the sunset.

What made them doubly dangerous was how they kept adapting to the situation at hand, evolving in lock step with humans to take down the apex predators on the food chain. Matsya was just a fish, but the next version was a turtle with land and sea within its reach. The boar avatar after that had tusks, and the half-man, half-lion had the human cunning to outwit a demon as well as the animal strength needed to put it into action. Even the entirely human avatars, Vamana and Parasuram were dangerous foes to cross.

So far, so good. These were the scarier, hairier avatars back when the world was a savage place.

But then came Prince Ram, the ultimate poster boy for divine standards. This was the guy you wanted at dinner parties and family gatherings. The personification of every virtue man can possess. The ideal man, or as close to perfect as you can possibly get when patriarchal values are involved.

At this stage, nobody believed an upgrade was possible. When you have achieved the gold standard for all mankind to live up to, those are some pretty big boots to fill. But one avatar was yet to arrive.

The smartest, sneakiest, sexiest God to ever walk the earth. The one with sixteen thousand wives and abilities as diverse as lifting mountains to confounding fashion police and strip-poker enthusiasts with unlimited layers of clothing. Krishna. Who also happened to be my best friend.

– Private Journals of Akran

1358 BCE

The tavern was cold and gloomy. It was right at the edge of the river, and the moisture in the air had taken on a cloying, oppressive life of its own. Three days of rain had turned the whole city into a muddy swamp. Clouds of mosquitoes followed people wherever they went. This particular tavern served the cheapest and most watered-down intoxicants on this side of the river. The choice of poison was limited to *sura*, a beverage brewed from rice, wheat and sugar and a tropical pulpy drink called *mahua*. Both were equally horrible to taste, yet each had a kick like a horse that could make your head hurt for days.

It was a place where the unwashed dregs of humanity could gather together and share a drink. The lowest of the low, the ones that did all the backbreaking work that propped up society, could find a place of comfort here. With other people like themselves, all at the bottom of society through an accident of birth, all hoping that their next life would be better than this one.

In other words, one of the last places people would expect to find someone like me.

I sat in a corner, hungry and miserable. The sura tasted flat and smelt like horse piss. It was a drink of choice among

Kshatriyas, when prepared well. Here it was liquid despair in a dirt-stained glass.

The steaming hot broth had some meat in it that I didn't recognise, though the owner swore it was chicken. The mouldy bread accompanying it was hard as stone. It was already dark and the dim candle in front of me provided too little light to examine the food more closely. I suspect this was deliberate. Beside me sat a handsome young man, his dark face creased with worry.

'How are you doing, my friend?'

I was too bone-weary to reply. The man sighed.

'Here, this will help.' He poured a thimbleful of a golden liquid into a small urn and handed it to me. I drank it greedily, licking every last drop, not particularly caring if anyone was watching.

The crushing sense of despair faded away. The nectar of immortality of the gods was a potent elixir, extracted from the Devas' orchard in *Swarg-Lok*. A few tiny drops were enough to heal my wounds and make me feel as if I had slept for a week.

I took a deep breath as the drink poured life into my veins. 'Thank you, Mas. I needed that.'

He continued to stare at me, with concern writ large over his face.

'I have only a single bottle of amrit left. Use it sparingly. Half a spoon when you are injured, another half to replenish your mana reserves—as much as they can hold at present. Any more and it won't have the slightest effect, given your present state.'

'And then what? I still can't fight them without my powers.'

'Stop fighting them. Learn to cover your tracks instead. They'll lose interest eventually and move on.'

I knew he was right but I hated the thought of having to hide. 'Have you found a way to remove this curse? Maybe a device you can make to fix this?'

He shook his head. 'This was done with the combined might of the court, Akran. I doubt it can be removed by anyone other than Krishna himself.'

I gave a short, bitter laugh. The irony of the situation wasn't lost on me.

'I am destined to die here then.'

'Destiny isn't shaped by the cards you hold, but by the hand you play.' He gave me an earnest look. 'Self-pity doesn't suit you, Akran. Snap out of it!'

I felt a smile tug at the corner of my lips. Mas was a good friend but the platitudes he spouted left something to be desired.

'I need an edge, Mas. Something to make them back off and take me seriously. Right now, I'm a declawed kitten. They need to know that if they come after me, it will cost them. I want them looking over their shoulders, not knowing when I might strike from the shadows.'

'This might help.' He placed an oilskin pouch on the table. Inside were three long knives, black as night, each as large as my forearm. The blades had an odd sheen, like they absorbed light instead of reflecting it. The hilts were simple and unadorned, crafted from animal bone. I recognised the metal immediately.

'Are these what I think they are?' I asked, my throat suddenly dry.

'Forged from the same metal. Each may kill a couple of celestials, maybe more, but they'll all disintegrate eventually after a few times of being used. And tell no one where you got them.'

I nodded, speechless at the gift. At least I had a fighting chance with this.

There was one more item inside. An onyx amulet inlaid into a gold pendant.

'If you are forced to defend yourself, try not to leave any witnesses. Once they start investigating where the knives came from, I could end up on the same hit list.'

'What about the amulet?'

'The amulet hides you from prying eyes. It only blocks magical attempts at scrying your location, so don't go doing anything that will draw attention.'

I nodded, not trusting myself to speak.

'I suggest you find a way to fake your death. After that, wear the amulet and lay low. With luck, they will forget all about you in a century or so.'

'Thank you for this, Mas.' I was genuinely grateful. He was the only one who hadn't abandoned me.

He smiled. 'I've not forgotten what I owe you.' He rose to his feet. 'There's a big world out there, Akran. Lots of people need help. Don't sit here wallowing in self-pity. It doesn't do any of us any good.'

'I thought you wanted me to stay in hiding?'

It was said in jest but Mas considered it seriously for a minute. 'An occasional good deed wouldn't hurt. There's plenty of karma you can accumulate out here, without drawing the attention of those above.'

I smiled at his naïve idealism. 'You still believe in that, don't you?'

'I've cherry-picked the things I like from all the religions they follow.' He grew contemplative for a moment. 'It's a shame they cant learn to do the same.'

'I doubt that will ever happen.'

'Perhaps,' he said. 'But I'll keep hoping. Some ideas are worth believing in.'

I laughed, conceding the point. 'Stay safe, Mas.'

'You too, Akran.'

CHAPTER FOUR

You know the saying about karma being a bitch?

Well, dharma isn't all that much better either.

They are two sides of the same coin. Karma is the fruit of your actions—wave a sword around all your life; you are likely to be impaled by a pointy stick in the end.

Go to your field and find it choked full of weeds? That's karma—your past actions screwing with you.

But dharma? That's about a lifetime of duty and doing the right thing. It's about pain, sacrifice and unwavering commitment based on an accident of birth. It requires you to be true to yourself and never swerve from what benefits society at large.

If you are a teacher, learn and pass your knowledge on to others. If you are a farmer, roll up your sleeves, pluck out the weeds, till the soil and plant crops that feed you and your family.

The worst part? Dharma and karma have plenty of scope to be misused. Your neighbour was an absolute monster to the people around you and nothing happened? Not to worry, his punishment awaits in the next life!

Why am I starving and can't afford two square meals a day while the king lives in a palace and stuffs his face? That's because in your previous life, you were rich and didn't help others while the king was born poor and you chose not to feed him!

There is no arguing with logic like that. As one of the marginalised classes, all you could do was put your head down and hope the line you were being fed was not a load of BS meant to keep you meek and subservient ... which it usually was.

– Private Journals of Akran

He stood there silently, watching the scene unfold.

'Will you do this for me, Akran?'

He nodded mutely. Or, rather, the younger version of himself did. Akran, the older, stared at the two, wishing once again that he could influence the past. His younger self was more impulsive, more prone to mischief and pranks, but this fervent look in his eyes was completely out of character. He had clearly been taken in by the person in front of him.

It had been disconcerting the first time he had the vision. Seeing yourself through another set of eyes is never what you might expect. Especially when the version you are watching is under a spell of some sort.

They stood together in the empty grove. Akran's companion was draped in shadows, and nothing he had done over the millennia had allowed him to penetrate the veil. He didn't know who the mysterious robed stranger was, except that he had subverted the younger Akran's mind.

The sky was tinged with a dull reddish-black sheen. Dark clouds filled the sky, and intermittent flashes of lightning could be seen in the distance.

The weather conditions all around could have been his fertile imagination adding layers of subtext to the conversation itself. He had no way of knowing this for sure. It was irrelevant in the larger scheme of things. Once more, like every single time he had had the dream, Akran strained to hear what was being said.

'First, the curse. Convince Samba it will be a great prank to pull on all the rishis. They will all be sitting together—Vashishta, Vishwamitra, Narada and the rest. The most vital to the plan is Durvasa. Make sure he is present when it happens. His irascible nature will take care of the rest.'

'As you command, master.'

He had had this dream countless times over the millennia, and the reaction it brought within him was the same each time. Akran felt blood trickle from his palms as he clenched his fists in frustration. He knew this was a real incident, not some figment of his imagination. The jasmine grove was real. Before the city had sunk into the sea, this was where he had spent most of his time. But there was nobody he had called 'master' or was subservient to. Even Krishna, would insist he call him by name and not by any titles.

'Then, the weapons. For the next stage to unfold, they need to be lost.'

He moved his lips unconsciously to match what the younger version of him was saying.

'But I am the one in charge of the weapons. How can I let them be taken?'

'You will find a way, Akran.' He guessed the person he was addressing had increased the glamour, for his younger version fell to his feet.

'It shall be done. I will find a way.'

He had no memory of the incident taking place. It was even possible his mind was playing tricks on him, and the conversation was taking place in daylight, with the sun streaming through the clouds. Dreams could be tricky, especially since facts could get obscured by strong emotions. There was no way for him to look dispassionately at the scene unfolding in front of him without feeling like screaming and gouging his eyes out.

Yes, this had happened. He knew it without a shadow of a doubt. Because it was the precursor to all the terrible events that took place soon after.

***

I woke up sober, which is never a good sign. These dreams were the bane of my existence. For the first few hundred years or so, they were about my time as part of the celestial court. The usual run-of-the-mill variety dreams about apsaras I had bedded and enemies I had killed.

It was much later that the dreams took on a more sinister edge. Some, were like the one I had experienced—I had no recollection of the memory I had seen, but I knew these events had occurred. Through a series of actions, I initiated the destruction of the entire Yadava race and kick-started the Kali Yuga. All while under the influence of a demon of unimaginable power. For this stranger, whoever he was, to have breached the walls of Dwarka and gained access to its inner sanctum, suggested abilities that were downright terrifying. Even among my own brothers, there was nobody with such mastery of the occult. Unless—and this was what everything hinged upon—someone had let him in.

Why was the onset of the Kali Yuga such a big deal? It shouldn't have mattered. The four cycles of time, the Satya Yuga (Age of Truth), Treta Yuga (Age of Three Avatars), Dwapara Yuga (Age of Two Avatars) and Kali Yuga (Age of Strife), were supposed to be a natural progression where humankind would get more and more distant from the gods until the cycle repeated.

What angered everyone was the suddenness of how it occured. Yugas typically transitioned peacefully from one to the next. The avatars departed the world fulfilled and content with their accomplishments. They would pass on their divine knowledge and wisdom to the eminent sages of that time. These sages would, in turn, disseminate this knowledge to their students and influence literary and philosophical thought for hundreds of years—codes of conduct, rules of governance, ideas on law, politics, education and philosophy. There was continuity and order in the way their legacy was handled. For a god to die violently was unheard of. Not only did Krishna meet an ignoble death while he was asleep, he also died after being forced to kill many of his kinsmen. A scapegoat was needed to deal with all those unresolved emotions … and conveniently, I happened to be around.

My apartment was a penthouse in a forty-storey building situated at Pali Hill in Bandra. I owned the building, but none of the tenants knew that. Most of them had never even seen my face. They thought I was some sort of eccentric recluse who never stepped out of his home, a reputation I was comfortable with. It was a calculated risk since I didn't want to attract attention. Still, I didn't think I would stand out in a city with over sixty-thousand millionaires.

When you've lived for a few centuries, you get a handle on managing your money well. In my case, I had Sars, another celestial and a close friend, who helped set it all up. Sars was several centuries younger than me and more in touch with the way the modern world functioned. I had taken years to adapt to the idea of paper money. She spoke about derivatives and cryptocurrencies like others would talk about the weather. It was her expertise that allowed me to own this place as well as a couple of other properties in the area without having the human authorities getting suspicious.

The apartment was modest enough in size and appearance to convey an impression of slightly above-average means. All the conveniences of modern life were present, including running water and flush toilets. The rest, I found I could live without, for the most part.

I chose this apartment for three reasons. First, the high ceiling ensured I would not have to deal with lightbulbs exploding every time I walked under them. I had installed wall-to-wall carpeting to make sure I was fully grounded anywhere inside the house.

Second, it was the tallest building for miles around. Having sharper senses also meant I could occasionally pick up on domestic squabbles, smells of cooking, televisions turned on too loud, and other such irritants. Being at the top ensured I could filter out the mundane details of most people's lives, even if they shouted them out from their windows at night.

And finally, I had a private lift. The elevator had an access code only three other people besides myself knew about. It ensured I didn't have to interact with the other people in the building. If it's not clear already, I am not a people person. I can count on one hand the people whose company I enjoy without reservation. I have no particular interest in making new friends.

***

I stepped into the shower and set the temperature to scalding while considering my choices.

We had both made mistakes the previous evening. My mistake was to destroy the minion's mind without confirming where they had taken the girls. Theirs was to let the music of the gods be copied by a fifteen-year-old. Pretty much the only rule that was sacrosanct among my ilk was that we do not draw attention to ourselves. No boons granted, no over-the-top flashy displays of power, nothing with a hint of divinity in an age of science. It was called the 'First Law', and every celestial was bound by the rule. Even exiled celestials like myself. There were specialised death squads who policed our kind and wouldn't hesitate to sanitise an entire city with a natural calamity like an earthquake or a tsunami if it meant killing an aberrant magic user.

That little display yesterday against the gang? Technically, it was a violation of the First Law. If someone had noticed, complained, or posted a video, I would have a fresh squad of assassins on my trail. Fortunately, I think I had gotten away with it.

My, admittedly vague, understanding of social media was that it was one of those fads where people posted intimate and nonsensical details of their lives, in the hope of gaining attention or sympathy. It's usually food and pets, but I've also seen opinions contesting the shape of the earth and the viability of vaccines, which make you stupider by just reading them.

The younger you were, the higher the chance you would be posting stuff online. It was safe to assume that Anna might have done the same. It meant that we would need to shut this down before it attracted too much attention.

I enjoyed hot showers as much as the next guy but today my heart wasn't quite in it. I kept mulling over the missing girl and the identity of her kidnappers, turning it over and over in my head, trying to see if I had missed something.

In case I haven't mentioned it before, every mythos has its own court. A pantheon represents the beliefs and culture of that land. Like Asgard for the Norse or Mount Olympus for the Greeks. Swarg-Lok was the seat of the celestials for the area the mortals call the Indian subcontinent. Someone belonging to this court was behind the psychic bomb that was set up inside the toy and inside the gangster's mind.

I had survived for all these years by staying out of the affairs of the celestials. In over three thousand years of exile, I had intervened only three times, and only when I thought the circumstances demanded it. Each time, the consequences had been dire. If there's one thing celestials do well, it is holding a grudge. I did not want to give up my placid peaceful existence. Not just yet.

I didn't think it was a wilful decision made by Manibhadra or the rest of the celestials. They were known to be harsh but fair. This was more likely the workings of a splinter faction within the court, like the one that was formed shortly after I was cast out, with the express purpose of assassinating me. It had not gone well for them.

The problem was that I was dealing with people who didn't understand humans. Since they had watched the slow progress of evolution before the age of technology, they found it easy to overlook how rapidly science was progressing today. Most of them had never lived here on Earth and continued to assume that humans were stupid. They didn't understand how rapidly information could get disseminated. Thanks to my exile, I was familiar with everything from ghost-to-ghost hookups to six degrees of Kevin Bacon. I knew how fast this could spread.

And once they learned celestials were real, it wouldn't take too long before someone made the connection between them and the scowling drunk in the bar who could find 'anything'. It would be the end of this peaceful little life I was living.

I had no interest in getting involved in whatever celestial scheme was being cooked up. My life was nice and settled, and anonymity suited me. Sure, I was miserable when I first left my heavenly abode, but now? I had carved my own little niche in my favourite city. I had made an insane fortune at games of chance, thanks in particular to my ability to slightly nudge the dice when needed. I could drink enough alcohol to fill a river, and my body would deal with it just fine. Given my rather liberal behaviour in the past few centuries, I knew I was also safe from any venereal disease known to humanity—my unique genetic makeup took care of that. I had wealth, great friends and amazing health. What else could I want?

A conscience that would shut up and let me ignore the coming shitstorm would have been nice.

The kidnappings of the girls gnawed at me. I couldn't bring myself to let go, now that I was involved. There were a couple of sources I had cultivated over the years for all matters of the occult and divine. It would not hurt for me to seek them out and learn some more before making any decisions.

Stepping out of the shower, I dressed in my usual jeans and black T-shirt attire, taking care to dry myself thoroughly before I went to the bedroom safe. It was an old classic with tumblers instead of anything fancy or electrical. Inside was a phone—an old Nokia large enough to bludgeon someone with, and a couple of other objects made for situations like this. I took them all out and placed them in front of me while I debated what to do next.

The fancier phones with silicon chips and cameras that could spot the warts on a frog's ass from a mile away would fizzle out within a week. The older the phone, the better the chance that it would last around me. I needed to alert a couple of people about what I had discovered so far, but I could do so without the phone. Reluctantly, I kept it aside.

I looked at the two other objects. The first was the amulet from Mas. I slipped it around my neck. I never used it because the chain made my skin itch, but a little discomfort was a small price to pay if it meant being hidden from the celestial court.

The second item was a slim serrated blade wrapped carefully in oilskin. It was a nine-inch stiletto, black, as if dipped in tar, yet with a sheen that was best described as unearthly. It was a beautiful weapon, but we had history, and I couldn't bear to look at it for too long without letting my emotions get the better of me.

Still, the sight of it brought back memories. For a brief moment, my fingers slid over the blade's edge, as I recalled the dark history of the blade and how it came into my possession.

This is what most people believe happened at the end of the Dwapara Yuga:

The great dynastic war of the Mahabharata had ended with the Pandavas victorious. Gandhari, the mother of the Kauravas, was distraught when she learnt that all her sons were dead. She knew that Krishna could have prevented the war. She forgot that he had made multiple attempts to broker peace between the cousins. Mad with grief, she cursed him that his clan, the Yadavas, would also get wiped out due to in-fighting among themselves. Their women would experience the same pain and loss that she and the other Kuru women had felt when they lost their sons, husbands and fathers. With the armies of Hastinapur and Panchala devastated in the war, along with numerous other mid-sized kingdoms, the Yadavas were the only serious power in the subcontinent. Krishna accepted the curse since he knew that, if left unchecked, the Yadavas would become a scourge on earth.

Thirty-six years after the curse was cast, Samba, Krishna's son, decided to play a prank on some of the most powerful sages of the ancient world. He angered them by dressing up as a woman, pretending to be pregnant and asking them to guess whether the baby would be a boy or a girl. The sages, not known for their sense of humour, were triggered and cursed Samba that he would bear a weapon that would destroy the entire Yadava race.

Samba then 'delivered' a mace, a heavy iron club with a spiked metal head, which is exactly as painful as it sounds. On the advice of King Ugrasena, the Yadavas ground the mace to powder and threw it into the sea. All except one piece, that was too hard for them to grind, so it was thrown into the sea as is. This piece was swallowed by a fish and then later caught by a hunter named Jara, who fashioned an arrowhead with it.

The powdered mace was washed back to shore and became a kind of grass called *eraká*. At a pilgrimage near the sacred Prabhas sea, the Yadavas got thoroughly intoxicated. Satyaki, who fought on the side of the Pandavas, chose to mock Kritavarma, who fought on the side of the Kauravas, for his actions during the war. Kritavarma, along with Kripa and Ashwatthama, was responsible for the murderous night attack on the children of the Pandavas. They exchanged harsh words, and in a moment of madness, Satyaki attacked Kritavarma and severed his head. The argument then devolved into a full-fledged battle, with the Yadavas choosing sides. In the ensuing battle, Satyaki was also killed.

Krishna arrived at the battlefield and, noticing that his son Pradyumna and Satyaki had been slain, took the eraká grass in his hand, which miraculously became a mace. With this mace, he slew some of the Yadavas who, in their drunken state, tried to attack Krishna. The remaining Yadavas also picked up the grass, which transformed into iron maces in their hands. Inebriated with alcohol, everyone attacked each other with their lethal weapons, resulting in all the surviving Yadavas dying, except for Krishna and his brother Balrama.

After this incident, Krishna found himself a grove to rest in. Jara, the hunter, shot Krishna in the foot fatally with an iron arrowhead, mistaking him for a deer. Shortly after, the city of Dwarka got submerged in the Arabian sea. Like the saying goes, Karma really was a beach.

That is the sanitised version of what happened that day as per the *Mausala Parva*—book sixteen of the eighteen books of the Mahabharata. Even this kiddie-friendly version is a gruesome reminder of how things can devolve when people are drunk and have easy access to weapons.

Now, here is the bit that did not enter the history textbooks:

In some ways, I am glad my part in the story has been stricken from the records. I am ashamed of the role I played in everything that happened. The part where I instigated Satyaki to attack Kritavarma, for instance. But that is a minor detail compared to what's been omitted.

For here's something most people don't think of. What happened to the rest of the grass? Or of the iron maces that were left behind? To be fair, everyone was preoccupied with what had occurred—Krishna dying, the Yadava clan being exterminated, and Dwarka sinking under the ocean. But I knew that at least one bright spark among the Devas, Agni, the fire god, realised that the magical weapons could not be left lying around. Sadly, for the Devas, this realisation came too late.

Two celestials, in particular, were always on the lookout for incidents like this. They were the unsung heroes of our age—remembered only for weapons and fancy buildings. There are very few stories about them because they didn't crave the spotlight, unlike some of the others.

Of the two, Vishwakarma was the more pious one. He was the architect of the gods, having designed their chariots and magical weapons, including Indra's thunderbolt, the Vajra. He was also the creator of the most famous cities of that era, including Lanka, Dwarka and Indraprastha.

The Devas had decreed that any magical weapons must never be left unguarded. This was a smart decision because many of those weapons could do grievous harm, even to celestials. So, Vishwakarma conscientiously gathered all that he could of the iron maces and had them safely secured in the vaults of the gods. The other celestial, however, was not so mindful of the rules of the Devas. Mayasura, the architect of the demons was a close friend of mine. He grabbed as many iron maces as he could and had the whole lot melted down so he could fashion some interesting items out of them.

When the Deva clean-up crew decided to sanitise the area, they discovered to their dismay, that some of the magical weapons that killed the Yadavas were missing. Their first reaction was to blame me for that as well—wholly expected since I was already being accused of far more heinous crimes. Getting everyone to believe that I had stolen several forbidden weapons was not a huge stretch as far as they were concerned. And when every trace of me was expunged from the records—along with my supposed crimes—all mention of the weapons fiasco conveniently disappeared. It was a gift-wrapped solution to their problems.

But now, let's talk about Mayasura, the friend who helped me and to whom I owe my life. Our friendship blossomed much earlier during the Treta Yuga.

Granted, Mayasura wasn't much to look at. He was short and socially awkward with beady eyes and dark, swarthy skin. None of those characteristics mattered to me. But some celestials were racist arseholes. Indra was one of them. He would have been the founder of the original KKK of the previous Yugas. Even his damned elephant was white. He and some of his other compatriots tormented Mayasura, who only wanted to be left alone.

Mas and I bonded quickly over our mutual hatred for Indra. Seeing how he harassed Mas constantly, I decided to lend a hand. Someday, I shall tell you how I managed to humiliate Indra and teach him a lesson he would never forget. Suffice it to say, I helped Mayasura and shielded him from the worst of their petty barbs and insults. My efforts ultimately succeeded in getting the Devas to back off and leave him alone. Mayasura never forgot that. His weapons kept me safe when I was exiled and had to fend for myself. That and the bottles of amrit he managed to smuggle away from the Devas' larder.

This was one of those three blades Mas had given me that I now held in my hands. The years had done nothing to dim its power, though I knew from experience that it had a limited life. With each use, the knife would grow more and more brittle before it finally shattered to dust.

Two of the earlier blades had already been destroyed in previous clashes between me and the remaining celestials. Every few hundred years or so, a few Celestial shitheads crawled out of the woodwork, thinking I would be an easy mark since I had been shorn of my powers. After I killed nearly half a dozen of them using the blades gifted by Mas, they finally backed off.

I slipped the knife into a specially-made sheath onto my back. If the price for rescuing the girls was to cull the celestials of their more hare-brained brethren, it was well worth paying. I had lived for too long in the shadows.

It was time to remind them why shadows were feared.

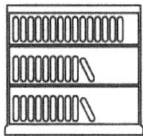

CHAPTER FIVE

Maybe I am being a little harsh on Indra. The truth is more complicated.

A lot of people assume there is only one Indra. That isn't true. Indra is a position. A title: King of the Gods. Most agrarian societies that depended on rain believed that the god who controlled the weather would be the most powerful and hence would be king. Zeus and his thunderbolt among the Greeks. Thor, God of Thunder and heir to the throne of Asgard. Indra, God of Rain and, therefore, King of the Gods. Along with the title came a portfolio of responsibilities, such as ensuring adequate rainfall and leading the rest of the Devas in battle. But at different times, there were different Indras. The one who helped Uttanka was not the one who harassed Mayasura. The one who killed Vritra was not the one who antagonised Krishna. The father of Vali was not the father of Arjuna. You get the idea.

While some Indras weren't too bad once you got to know them, others were extremely insecure about their position. Human sages could tap into the cosmos through their austerities and gain powers of their own. It put them on an equal footing with the gods. That didn't sit well with most celestials. To hinder sages from growing too powerful, the Devas—mostly Indra—would find ways to distract them from their penance. The most common method was to disburse celestial hotties, like OnlyFans subscriptions, to any sage that was gaining too much power.

Said hotties would primp and preen; the sages would perk up like Energizer bunnies. And once they began the pants-off, dance-off routine, the fruits of their penance— would slowly drain away.

When they finally came up for air, still ready to give it the old college try, the Apsara would vanish, leaving the sage standing with a tree of his own, forced to take matters into their own hands.

Were you expecting these stories to have a happy ending? They don't. In every sense of the phrase.

It's strange how people hold the gods up to a higher standard when they also believe they were created in their image. That's why I admire the Greeks—very few expectations of good behaviour from their gods.

– Private Journals of Akran

The tiny library in Churchgate, where I was headed, rarely received visitors. In large part, this was because its existence was not widely known. Access to the place was through a board gaming café named Creeda that had opened recently in the area. The owners of the two establishments had a rent-sharing arrangement since the city was getting more expensive with each passing day.

Making yourself more attractive was the popular option when using spells of glamour. But you could also use it in reverse. Make a person or a place less interesting and more non-descript. A couple of glamour wards, reinforced every night, ensured that most people didn't even notice the library's presence. Unfortunately, it hurt the business of the café, but that couldn't be helped. If anyone managed to stumble upon the library despite the glamour, they would discover it was surprisingly well-maintained despite the shabby exterior.

I had been here before. Several times, as a matter of fact. Because the mousy little librarian with ugly ass spectacles was someone I knew very well.

One of the amusing oddities of my favourite means of transport in Mumbai is how rickshaw drivers never sit with their butt firmly in the centre of the seat. They aways occupy one corner of the seat cushion with one ass cheek dangling in the air, while the other squirms uncomfortably as it tries to support their entire body weight. I discovered the reason for it when one driver confessed that most of them had to share the seat with an instructor while learning how to ride, and hence most of them just got into the habit of sitting in that manner even when they were driving the rickshaw by themselves.

For some reason, Shukra sat on chairs and desks in much the same manner, like he was never comfortable giving both cheeks a rest. His nose was buried in a musty old tome, and he studiously ignored me. Either that or he was so absorbed in his reading that he had no idea I had walked in. Knowing his nature, it could easily be the latter.

It could also be because he was blind in one eye, thanks to a diminutive dwarf and a straw, but that is a tale for another day.

The book he held looked ancient. Bound in leather with thick vellum pages and spindly writing cramped tightly across each page, the book looked like it had been inked in blood. It was just the kind of tome I knew I would hate reading. *The Necronomicon*. The last time we met, he was offering fantastic sums of money to anyone who could procure it for him. He had finally got what he wanted. Good for him.

I cleared my throat pointedly.

'The library is open, but I'm busy. Feel free to explore it by yourself,' he said without looking up.

I raised one hand, and blue sparks crackled across my fingers. 'Will the librarian be free if I burn the book he is so deeply immersed in?' I enquired.

He looked up, startled. For a second, something flashed across his face—too quickly for anyone to notice—and then he went pale.

'Lord A-A-Akran!' he stammered. 'How may I be of service?'

'I need a quiet spot where I won't be disturbed,' I told him.

'N-No trouble, Lord. Please, anything you want. Just leave the books alone, I beg you.' He started guiding me towards a secluded corner of the library, looking meek and helpless as he did so. I followed with a sardonic smile on my face.

'Did you finally recall the Sanjivani mantra, Shukra?' I asked, pronouncing his name with care.

He looked like he had swallowed a bitter pill. 'No, Lord. As I mentioned the last time, it was purged from my memory. Ever since you ... you —' he stammered.

He had meant to say 'Ever since you managed to get Krishna killed on your watch.'

'Choose your words carefully, Shukra. I'm not in a patient mood.'

'My apologies; I meant my powers have diminished and the mantra remains out of the reach of my memory.'

I smiled at him. 'Well, it is a good thing I don't have a use for it now, else I would be most interested in seeing if I could coax it back into your mind.'

Shukra made a strangled sound as we finally turned a corner and reached a spot between two large cupboards. He then turned and punched me hard on my arm.

'You idiot!' he hissed. 'Why didn't you tell me you were coming? I almost smiled at you back there.'

I winced as I rubbed my aching arm. 'Sorry about that. Time was of the essence.'

Shukra and I were old friends. The act in the main library hall was for the benefit of anyone who may be watching. Officially, this place was neutral ground. Shukra cared more about books and gathering knowledge than the political machinations of the celestials. The library was hidden because he catered only to beings like us. Plus, the occasional few humans who had shown the appropriate thirst for knowledge.

Everyone needed a watering hole, a home outside of home with an informal atmosphere. The library, by unspoken compact, was treated as neutral ground. There were many like me who had not adapted to the changes in technology and couldn't always access information through digital means. Officially, it was meant as a place of sanctuary for all celestials. Unofficially, several unsavoury elements had cast spells of listening or left orbs of seeing, in different locations within. As one of the library's founding members, Shukra had decided some time ago that it was best to let them remain. Their suspicions would only be heightened if we removed them. This way, they would be convinced we were harmless and would ignore us.

My hostile behaviour with him in public was part of an ongoing deception on both our parts. The truth was, I couldn't really burn anything as large as a library with just a few sparks crackling from my fingers. Like most of my other talents, that skill had been severely diminished from the good old days when I could conjure up enough fire and lightning to turn the building into a smouldering ruin of smoke and ashes. I had survived for all these millennia primarily through a mix of bullshit and bravado—by not letting my enemies see how weak I really was.

Shukra was one of the few people I trusted. I would never approve burning of books, so my threat was hollow and he knew it. Also, his books were magically warded against fire, dust, milkweed, termites and dampness, so I couldn't damage them even if I tried. In ages past, both the Devas and Asuras decided they needed spiritual advisors from among the sages who could guide and advise them. The reigning Indra at that time chose Brihaspati to be the spiritual advisor for the devas over Shukra because the former was tall and fair, while Shukra was short and dark. It was a colossal blunder. Shukra knew the mantra to bring the dead back to life, something even Brihaspati couldn't accomplish. Realising his mistake, Indra decided to level the playing field by killing Shukra. He screwed that up as well and had to be rescued by Vishnu. In the battle, Shukra's mother was killed.

The fallout from that story had two major consequences. First, it pushed Shukra firmly into the camp of the Asuras and away from the rest of the gods.

Second, it led to Shukra's father, Rishi Bhrigu, cursing Vishnu to live multiple lives on Earth as a mortal so that he too could experience pain and loss like a human. One of those lives on Earth was as Krishna.

It might seem strange that he and I could be friends. Shukra hated Lord Vishnu passionately because of his mother's murder. At the same time, he recognised that Krishna, the incarnation of Vishnu, was very different from the god he hated. To the Asuras, the Trinity were terrifying, ruthless and powerful gods whose attention you very much wanted to avoid. Krishna, on the other hand, was charming and funny when he wanted to be, sly and cunning when required and a matchless warrior if provoked. It was impossible not to admire him.

In my initial days, after my exile, Shukra was one of the few who had helped me survive with no ulterior motive of his own. As far as I was concerned, he was one of the good guys.

Shukra, like a few other celestials, mostly the curious kind, with imagination and wanderlust, had decided to spend his life on Earth. After the Kali Yuga started, the endless battles between the Devas and Asuras ceased. Both sides had grown increasingly irrelevant in the Age of Science—not enough people worshipped the Devas, choosing instead to focus on the Trinity. A few continued to hold their sway, such as Ganesh and Durga, but those were localised to specific areas. Nobody really worshipped Surya, Vayu, Agni, etc. anymore. For the most part, it was a brand-new world, and people like Shukra, Sars, Mas and a few others were all the more happier experiencing life among humans than among other celestials.

***

'What are you working on at the moment? Anything interesting?' I asked.

He frowned. 'Interesting to me, yes. I just looked at crime statistics in India over the past ten years and they all seem to spike on one particular day each year. Here, take a look!'

He pointed at a screen where a brightly coloured chart showed a pointed spike upwards. I hated looking at spreadsheets of numbers but even I could make sense of a colourful chart.

I peered at the screen. 'Unless I'm mistaken, the date changes each year.'

He beamed. 'Exactly. Yet, it's always in this narrow time band. Which means it's not related to the standard calendar. Instead, it's based on a particular planetary alignment that corresponds to...'

'Naraka Chaturdashi,' I finished. 'A festival that occurs one day before Diwali every year, the date for which changes based on star positions.'

Shukra looked miffed. 'Well, yes. That is the point I was trying to make. How did you deduce it so quickly?'

I shrugged. I was fairly familiar with events involving Krishna. Naraka Chaturdashi was a festival celebrating the defeat of a demon lord named Narakasura (Narak: hell and asura: demon).

'The veil between our world and the demon realm is said to be at its most porous on that day,' I said.

'Yes, of course, but don't you see what that means?' Shukra said impatiently. 'It means for the first time, we have a concrete link between human behaviour in this world and the demon realm, and its impact.'

'In other words, another reason for humans to absolve themselves of responsibility for their actions,' I said.

'I don't think it means that,' Shukra protested. 'Co-relation doesn't indicate causality after all.'

'True,' I agreed. 'After all, humans are known for reading the fine print and not jumping to conclusions, aren't they?'

Shukra was looking more and more dismayed. 'This isn't what I wanted at all. What should I do? Shall I delete all this research?' He began pacing up and down, a look of panic on his face.

'Shukra, relax! It isn't that big a deal!' Seeing his worried anxious face, I clarified. 'People will believe a lot of stupid things. You aren't responsible for their actions!'

'But ... But…'

'But nothing. If your research is sound, then you should let the world know. What they do with it is up to them.'

'I guess.' Shukra looked a bit mollified.

'Enough about my work. You don't look well. Was the date that bad?'

In all that had happened, I had completely forgotten about my date last evening. I was going to have to call and apologise.

Briefly, I explained what had happened so far, including my suspicions about the celestial court. Shukra listened carefully, neither commenting nor changing expression as I spoke.

'So that's it,' I concluded. 'Somewhere in the city, we have a kidnapping ring, an oddity involving heavenly music and a group of celestials. The toy, the coin illusion, the psychic trap—whoever these people are, it looks like a well-organised racket.'

Shukra said nothing for a long moment.

'I'm going to tell you what you should be doing,' he said at last. 'Knowing you well, you are going to ignore my advice anyway, but ...'

'I wouldn't ignore sensible advice,' I interrupted.

'Good. Here it is then. Walk away from this.'

I stared at him, nonplussed. 'I don't understand.'

'Walk away,' he repeated. 'You have got yourself tangled up in some kind of celestial web, the girl and her grandfather mean nothing to you, and you have spent the last few millennia avoiding precisely the kind of attention you seem to be courting now.'

'Walk away?' I said, still struggling with the concept.

He pantomimed a shuffling motion with two fingers as if they were legs making their way across from me. 'Like that. It's easy.'

'I can't let it go.' To my surprise, I found that I meant it.

Shukra smiled but said nothing.

'I can't,' I repeated. 'If I had not taken up this case, then yes, I could walk away. Now that I've heard his story, been to her house and been attacked, twice, no less, I am involved.'

'Why should that matter?'

'Because my mind is now running amok with every gruesome possibility that could be happening to this kid I've never met. The time for me to walk away was yesterday. Not now. Not anymore.'

'If I may say so,' Shukra said gently, 'it feels like you are taking this a little too personally, are you not?'

He was right. My hands were clenched into fists and my knuckles had turned white. I had never felt like this about any case ever before. I took pride in myself on my detachment when it came to humans. Having lived with them for thousands of years and not made any meaningful attachments was something I was exceedingly pleased with. Now this girl and her fate were getting under my skin, I could feel it like an itch at the back of my brain, something that I couldn't quite scratch. Memories of paternal affection, of nurturing a child that I had refused to think about for so long were now in the forefront of my mind. Wearily, I rubbed my temple and tried counting backwards to ten. The pounding in my head, which I hadn't even noticed a moment ago, slowly began to ebb.

Shukra patted me awkwardly on the back. He looked distinctly ill at ease and I could sense his discomfort. Like me, he wasn't a people person. The only time he expressed any emotion was when we did our little act in public or when reading a rare text of some sort from his library.

'What is it about this case that's gotten you so riled up?'

I took a moment to reply. Briefly, I considered telling him who she reminded me of. But no. Some things were best left buried.

'I had thought for a while that I was finally free from the webs that are spun by the celestial court, that they had given up on tormenting humans and chosen to leave them alone. But no, it's starting all over again. Or maybe it never ended and I was just too blind to notice.'

I shook my head. 'I don't know how many times they have intervened in the past to manipulate the human world either.

As long as I was far away from their schemes and intrigue, I could ignore it.

'But now, it's happening in my city and I've been roped into this. It isn't even like these were people of any consequence—just an old man and a kid, minding their own business. What does it say about them that they are picking on people without abilities of any kind? What does it say about me if I let this slide, if I don't do anything despite knowing what is happening?'

'It would tell me you are finally being smart and not drawing attention to yourself,' Shukra muttered.

I leaned back on one of the bookshelves, exhausted.

'How do you do it?' I asked softly. 'How are you able to stay with them, all the time, get involved in their routines, integrate yourself into their lives and not lose your mind when something like this happens?'

'For one thing, I'm not a Yaksha,' he said calmly. 'My life's calling is the pursuit of knowledge and teaching others. The fact that I spend most of my time in a library should tell you that this is what fulfils me. You are affected because you are not meant to be a bystander, wasting your life, drowning in self-pity and alcohol. You need to follow your purpose and be what your instincts are telling you to be.'

'A basket case?'

He smiled. 'A compulsive do-gooder. Defined by a need to protect others, be it a stray kitten in the sewers or a world that needs saving.'

'I don't want to save the world.'

'Saving a little girl is much easier than saving the world. You are more likely to succeed. The world is too far gone for you to save all by yourself anyway.'

His eyes misted over like he was lost in thought. 'Somewhere out there, might be someone who is the exact opposite of you. A person who looks at the big picture and tries to save the world but not the smaller issues like protecting a child that has been kidnapped.'

'What's your point?'

'My point is that maybe this case is tailor made for you. A sign from the universe that you need to do something with your life. Everyone is but a thread in the weaving of the world and this may be the one you need to unravel.'

'A minute ago, you told me to walk away. Now you want me to go after them. Which is it?'

He shrugged. 'It's not about what I want you to do. It's about what you can do. Walk away if you can, solve it if you can't. Sitting here and moaning about how unfair the world is won't save the girl. If this is what you've decided, drop everything else you have on your plate and give this your full attention. Close this case and rescue her before you draw any more attention to yourself.'

'I was planning on doing exactly that.'

'Making plans is not the same as acting upon them.'

I scowled. Shukra wasn't to be deterred.

'Aren't you thinking a drink would feel really good right about now? To take the edge of all this despair perhaps?'

I gave him a sheepish look. That was exactly what I was thinking.

'Pleasant as that might sound, it is nothing but a distraction. A way to make you forget about this problem. You need this girl's fate front and centre of your brain. Find her, get her back to her guardian, then leave the city and lie low for a few days.'

'I don't know how to find the girl.'

He looked at me kindly yet his words were unsympathetic. 'Then I suggest you figure it out. The alternative is a slow descent into madness as you run yourself ragged, worrying about her while a new set of death squads pick up on your trail.'

I nodded wearily. 'I need your help. I need the entire Rat Pack's help. I'm in over my head at the moment. I can't see round the corner and it's obvious there are angles I haven't worked out yet.'

Shukra said nothing for a moment.

'This jewel he described—it seems familiar,' he said at last.

'I know. There is a story of Krishna and a large ruby that seems similar.'

'Yes, that's the one! I have forgotten its name, though. Let me check.' He reached over and tapped a few keys on his computer. 'Here it is. The Syamantaka.' He gave me an owlish look. 'I don't think they want it for the wealth it can provide.'

I nodded. According to legend, the jewel supposedly produced nearly a hundred kilograms of gold daily, from thin air. Personally, I had never put much stock in such stories. It is all very well to claim you can pull gold out of your ass, but that made no sense. There would be so much gold that its price would fall, rendering it worthless. Just because people didn't understand economics when they made tall claims didn't mean its laws were somehow suspended.

'A lot of people have been searching for it for thousands of years. There were reports of it being sighted in Surat, then in Jaipur, even England for a brief period.' Shukra grinned as he scanned his laptop screen. 'Listen to this. Some people believe it is the Kohinoor diamond. Imagine that. They hope to find it but don't even know what stone it is.'

I snorted. 'It wouldn't be found around here, at least. From what I recall, the land it is in will be forever prosperous. I think we can safely rule out any country where most people don't have access to clean water and sanitation.'

Shukra smiled. 'We all see through a mirror, darkly.'

'Their mirrors are a bit murkier than ours.'

'Quit being so cynical,' he chided. 'It's not their fault they lead short lives, and the Age of Gods was so long ago. Stories get embellished over time. It is the natural order of things.'

'Shouldn't it be up to us, with all the years we've got under our belts, to set the record straight?' I shot back. 'Someone whose dharma is to educate, perhaps?'

Shukra laughed. 'I'll update Wikipedia right now,' he said. 'It's a ruby, not a diamond,' he typed in bold. He turned to me, still grinning. 'Happy now?'

'I suppose it will do until the next idiot decides he knows better. Can we put out feelers of our own, though? Just in case someone might know where it exists.'

'I might know someone already who claims to have it.'

I stared at him. 'One of us?'

'Correct. A Naga, to be precise.'

The Nagas were a race of snake-people who lived underground. They had the ability to change shapes between snake and human form. There were plenty of stories about the Nagas in ancient times but the one consistent thread across all those stories was this—they were collectors of gems and other shiny items.

The Nagas were all prosperous merchant families and jewellers in the modern world. A keen sense of business and focus on wealth accumulation had led to the establishment of several successful businesses.

'I've met him online. He is very discreet, but he has been hoping to meet you for a while. He has offered a lot of cash for an introduction. Call it a finder's fee. Seems to think you might be able to point him in the direction of some exotic weaponry that was lost around a few thousand years ago.'

'I take it you told him exactly where he can stuff that money?'

Shukra gave me a long-suffering look. 'No, I told him I will see what I can do, because it never hurts to be polite to people. And someday, we might find his connections useful. Like today.'

I shrugged, conceding the point. 'When can I meet him?'

He tapped out an address. 'You can go right now. He lives close to Doolallys' at Malabar Hill. I'll tell him you are coming.'

'Tell him I'll meet him at the pub. I need a drink. That is the place with the craft beers, yes?'

'That's the one. He would probably insist on meeting there, anyway. Just because he wants to meet you doesn't mean he trusts you not to kill him and steal his stuff.'

'Speaking of people I want to kill, can you get a message across to someone in the celestial court that rogue elements are wandering about here kidnapping humans?'

Shukra shook his head.

'I don't keep in touch. They are a bunch of prickly, arrogant snobs. But I know others who do. I'll ask around.' He hesitated. 'If you've chanced upon an officially approved mission, it is going to raise a shitstorm.'

I shook my head. 'Call me naïve, but I trust Manibhadra. From the little I remember of him, he followed a rigid code of dharma. He would never sanction something like this.'

Shukra looked uncomfortable. 'This is probably a conversation we should have had earlier, then ... I thought you knew Manibhadra is no longer king of Swarg-Lok.'

'What? When did that happen?'

'A while back. They've changed with the times. Now there is a ruling council that decides what actions are to be taken.'

'You think the council sanctioned this?'

'I doubt it. They have grown increasingly isolationist in their ways. It doesn't sound like them. I'll alert the rest of our friends and tell them to be on the lookout.' He paused for a moment as he read something on his screen and then turned to me, his face grave.

'There is definitely something going on. I tried cross-referencing the girl's age with other kidnappings in India, and it seems this has been going on for some time now. Quite a few similar kidnappings.'

That sounded suitably disturbing. 'Since when and for how long?'

'Since the past year.' He walked over to another computer and began punching keys. 'At least forty girls have gone missing in Mumbai.'

'That doesn't sound too bad. As in, don't get me wrong, it's terrible, but I somehow expected the numbers to be much higher.'

He shook his head. 'No, you don't get it. All forty that I am talking about are girls plucked from their homes, not from the street. All in the age range of eleven to thirteen. The number is more than two standard deviations beyond the mean, which at ninety-five per cent confidence level and a standard error of …'

'It's fine, I get it,' I interrupted. I didn't but I didn't have time for a course in statistics either. If he said it was a significant increase, that was good enough.

Unlike me, Shukra had embraced technology and figured out how to work with it. He believed that the internet was too important a source of knowledge for us to ignore. I suspect the vast quantities of freely available porn online also played a 'significant role'.

See. Who said I couldn't talk in Nerdinese when I needed to?

'Such a spike can't be explained easily. And there is more.' He beckoned me over with a wave of his hand. 'I think you need to see this.'

I peered at the screen. He was on Anna's Facebook page. The recording had been uploaded a couple of days ago and had received a hundred and fifty comments. Most had been of the 'WTF is this?' variety. But there were at least half a dozen readers who had shared the post, claiming how wonderful it sounded.

This was bad. These were the kind of idiotic stories that the media focussed on. The last thing I wanted was to draw attention to ourselves.

'Can you shut it down?'

Shukra looked thoughtful. He had picked up many skills in his long time on Earth.

'I'll need to speak to Sars. Working together, we might be able to do something about this. It's a good thing Anna wasn't, what you might call, the most popular kid in school. Her circle of friends was small. We have a window of opportunity before this blows up in our faces. We need to involve a few more people to contain this.'

'Do it,' I said, with an edge to my tone. 'This was the fault of the celestial court. Let them clean up their own mess. And send a clean-up crew to pick up the laptop from her place. Have it sanitised to make sure no other traces were left behind. Tell her grandfather you are a friend of mine and you need to search the laptop for clues as to her whereabouts.'

'Will do,' said Shukra, his mind already lost in thought about the problem in front of him. This was what he lived for—engineering solutions to the various crises that threatened to engulf us. Cleaning up the messes of monumental stupidity other celestials had made. I left him to his devices as I walked out.

CHAPTER SIX

Uttanka, a disciple of Sage Gautama, was once asked for a pair of celestial earrings by the guru's wife as a form of guru dakshina. The earrings belonged to a mortal queen (the stories differ as to who it was). She gave them to him but warned that they were coveted by many celestial beings, so under no circumstances should he allow them to touch the ground, or else they would get stolen.

As expected in stories like this, the earrings did touch the ground. A Naga chanced upon them, stole the earrings and escaped into an anthill. In grief and rage, Uttanka dug into the anthill with a stick for thirty-five days, trying to find a way into the underworld to recover the earrings. Indra and Agni, taking pity on him, decided to help. Indra used his thunderbolt to help Uttanka carve a path into the realm of the Nagas. Agni, in the shape of a horse, met Uttanka below and instructed him to blow on his behind. Despite the oddity and sexual overtones of the request, Uttanka did as he was asked. Doing so released massive clouds of *smoke that engulfed the underworld and choked the snakes in their lair. The king of the Nagas, Vasuki, humbly asked for forgiveness and returned the earrings.*

There's one tiny detail that the stories missed. The Naga who stole the earrings? His name was Virach. That little kleptomaniac is the one I'm about to meet now.

– Private Journals of Akran

Doolally's was a wonderful little pub. Their quiz nights were some of my favourite events in the city, especially since the prize was a bucket of beer and through a couple of charms, I could peek into the answer sheet in the quizmaster's hand. They also had a mango-flavoured craft beer which was better than any alcohol I've ever tasted. All in all, it was a great place to set up a meeting.

Virach was already waiting for me when I arrived. Like all Nagas, he was a shapeshifter, though most of them had only two shapes they could choose between—a snake form and a human form. The more powerful Nagas, however, had a wider repertoire of shapes and forms they could take.

My first impression when I saw him was that he was not a very powerful Naga. Why else would someone look the way he did on purpose?

If you are picturing Nagas as tall and handsome, then stop. Like humans, they came in all shapes and sizes. Virach was a pudgy man, and I suspect he had those shoes with in-built heels to make himself look taller. He looked inordinately pleased to see me, which was a little disturbing. It could be construed as charming if you were feeling particularly charitable. If you weren't, we could call it creepy and leave it at that.

He was dressed in a suit that was clearly custom-made for him. Everything about him, from his suede boots to the expensive Rolex on his wrist, was meant to communicate a sense of wealth.

He leapt up to greet me as I approached him.

I motioned him towards a seat.

'Thank you for coming,' Virach started. 'It's a rare honour. You don't know how much this means to me. I've been waiting for so long. Thank you again.'

He seemed eager to please. Like a Eureka Forbes salesman.

I smiled politely. Most people don't believe that I can be charming when I want to be.

'I understand you've been looking for me?'

Virach bobbed his head vigorously. 'Yes, alright, straight to business, then. As Shukra may have told you, I am a collector of rare and divine artefacts. Items from the Treta or Dwapara Yuga are highly prized. I always pay far better than anyone else for such items.'

I resisted the urge to smack him as he blathered on about himself. Maybe this restraint on my part was the 'personal growth' people had been telling me I would eventually achieve.

Virach seemed slightly disappointed that I wasn't more impressed with his hobby.

'Recently, I've come into possession of a few items. I was hoping you could take a look and confirm their authenticity.'

'Why me?'

He coughed, embarrassed. 'Some of these items belonged to, ah … the eighth avatar of Lord Vishnu.'

Most people seem to think there were only ten Vishnu avatars.

The truth is, there were hundreds of avatars. Even Gautama Buddha is regarded as an avatar in some parts of India. Mohini, for instance, was a female avatar of Vishnu who played an important role in acquiring the nectar of the gods and the subsequent killing of multiple demons. Despite her contribution, she isn't considered important enough to be included among the ten primary avatars—one of the early examples of sexism.

Still, I knew whom he was referring to. My friend Krishna, whose death I inadvertently caused.

'I am prepared to compensate you handsomely for your services,' he said.

'Keep your money. As it turns out, we may be able to help each other. Do you happen to have in your possession a large red ruby? One which glows brightly and is supposed to possess divine powers?'

His face immediately became guarded. 'I may know the gem you are speaking of. Why do you ask?'

I studied him quietly for a moment. There was a chance that Virach was an unscrupulous businessman who wouldn't really care about the kidnappings, but I doubted it. The Nagas were a well-respected and honourable clan. Part of the reason they had survived so long is that they would usually operate on the right side of the law. That and they usually had friends in high places. Virach seemed venal and selfish, but he also didn't seem the kind who would survive long in an Indian jail—that alone is enough to make most people avoid any trouble with the law.

I gave him the abbreviated version. Girls being kidnapped, local hoodlums, possible celestial involvement, large ruby being searched for. He took it all in, looking more and more dismayed as I spoke.

'You are the second person to ask me about it. Of course, I didn't know anything about these kidnappings.'

'Can you describe the other person?'

Virach shook his head, looking embarrassed. 'Unfortunately, I cannot. My business relies on discretion. I don't talk about my customers.'

Briefly, I imagined grabbing Virach by his neck and doing what I had done to the hoodlum earlier. I indulged in that fantasy a bit longer than I should have before letting it go. I had a code. I would not invade someone's mind without permission unless they threatened or intended me harm in some way.

'Besides,' Virach continued, 'it wouldn't do you any good. The people I spoke to were intermediaries. I don't know who the buyer is. All I know is that he is in possession of multiple divine ornaments, which he will give me if I can procure the jewel for him. He wants to borrow it for a few days.' He wrung his hands anxiously together. 'You think the ornaments also might be stolen?'

'I would stake my life on it.' Actually, no, I wouldn't, but it was an expression I enjoyed using. 'Did they give you any indication why they wanted it?' I asked.

'No, but it is obvious, isn't it?'

'If it were obvious, would I be sitting here asking you about it?'

He blushed, embarrassed. 'Sorry. According to legend, it can provide a lot of gold every day, if you know the right mantra to activate it. I suspect they know the mantra and want to use it for a while.'

I wasn't too sure of that theory. As I had mentioned to Shukra, most celestials don't obsess over gold. There's more than enough hidden under the earth that they could get to if they really put their minds to it.

'I would like to keep the jewel out of these people's hands for a while. I don't think they intend to use it to get rich. It is more likely they have some sort of ritual sacrifice, a yagna, in mind, which means—best case scenario—a time-based request. Would you be willing to keep this off the market for some time?'

Virach's eyes gleamed. 'I run a business. If you want me to do this, maybe there is something you can offer me in exchange?'

I knew what was coming. 'What do you want?'

He coughed delicately. 'Before your fall from grace, you were entrusted with the sacred weapons.' Seeing the look on my face, he hastened to add, 'I'm not asking you to sell them to me, though that is a possibility if you are interested. I thought I could hang on to one of them for a while so I could examine it while you borrow the jewel. When we are done, we can each take our respective items back.'

It kept happening. Every few centuries, someone or the other would track me down and offer obscene amounts of money for locating the weapons. For some reason, they seemed to think that I would prefer hoarding them in secret over living on the celestial plane without being accused as a thief and god killer.

'I don't have the weapons. The knowledge of their location was lost.'

He seemed disappointed. Can't say I blamed him.

'Can you speculate as to where they might be?'

I could but it would make this conversation last longer than I cared for. Most celestials came into being before pockets were invented. What we did possess was a little intra-dimensional fold in time and space that was exclusively ours. It is how the gods would grant certain gifts—not by conjuring them out of thin air, but by extracting the appropriate elixir, weapon or ornament when chanting a specific mantra keyed to our wavelength. I would guess that I had done something similar—extracted the divine weapons from the armoury and placed them in my little mystical pouch for safekeeping. And thanks to whoever clouded my mind … I had forgotten how to access it again.

'No, I have no idea.'

He seemed to deflate a bit. I debated telling him about the little sword that was sheathed on my back, under my clothes, but decided against it. It was my only magical weapon. Giving it up now would be like sitting down to pray in the middle of a frigging battlefield. Who would ever do something as stupid as that?

On an impulse, I asked him, 'Which weapon were you looking for?'

'The Chandrahas.'

I frowned. That was a rather obscure weapon. Of all the requests to date, nobody had ever asked me for the Chandrahas.

'What makes you think I might have it?'

Virach laughed nervously. 'Among the artefacts in my care is a personal diary written by Vibhishana a few years after he ascended the throne. Your name was mentioned in it.'

That made sense. My name had been struck from all official records. But a private diary? That could easily slip through the cracks.

The Chandrahas was an indestructible sword given by Lord Shiva to Ravana. According to legend, Ravana tried to uproot Mount Kailash because it was in the way of his flying chariot, Pushpak. As he was lifting it, Lord Shiva placed his toe on the mountain to put it back in place, crushing Ravana's fingers. Realising his mistake, Ravana offered obeisance to Lord Shiva and sang the 'Shiva Tandava Stotram', a song that describes Shiva's power and beauty. Impressed, Shiva gifted him the weapon, cautioning him to use it only to uphold righteousness.

That is pretty much the only reference to the sword in official texts. The sacred archives of the Gandharvas had a few more details.

When Ravana abducted Sita from the Dandaka forest, a giant eagle named Jatayu tried to save her. Ravana used his sword to strike the bird down. As he had used it for a selfish cause, one that diverted from the path of righteousness, the sword lost its power. It remained inert until Ravana's death. After his brother Vibhishana ascended the throne of Lanka and took possession of the sword, it regained its powers. It landed in my care through a series of adventures.

Until I lost it when I lost everything.

'Call me if you hear anything further,' I said.

He bobbed his head like a fish. 'Let me know if you ever, uh, find any of those missing weapons.'

I didn't deign to reply.

CHAPTER SEVEN

We are not immortal; we are long-lived. There is a crucial difference. We wouldn't die of old age, hunger or disease. In case we are wounded, our bodies can use mana to heal.

But if someone was really determined to end our existence, then there are ways to accomplish that. Most of the time, people assume they need a fancy badass weapon like a spear infused with a god's holy essence or some such thingamajig. But if anyone's been paying attention, they'll see that nearly all magical weapons have one element in them.

Silver.

Silver is the weapon of choice of the gods. It acts as a magic dampener that can cut through defensive spells like a hot knife through butter. Stab us with a silver knife or something sharp made of silver and the wound won't close. If we bleed long enough, we will die. That's what it really boils down to. Cause damage at a faster rate than the speed at which our mana can heal us.

> *Merely stabbing us won't do, of course. Yakshas especially have a most unreasonable tendency to fight back.*
>
> *So why did Jara's arrow cause such grievous harm to Krishna? Mas had an interesting theory. According to him, the metal wasn't from earth. It came from a meteor which had crashed onto the outskirts of Dwarka. The mineral ore within had the dull sheen of raw iron and the same magic nullifying properties of silver. But tell people that and the story of a pregnant male prince birthing a mace and you know which one they would rather believe.*
>
> – Private Journals of Akran

I was on my way back to the library, lost in my own thoughts, when I first sensed them. The air crackled with power as two Yakshas emerged from the shadows.

They were young and cocky, full of the arrogance of youth. I didn't recognise them, but that was hardly surprising. It had been a long time since my exile, and more than a few matings would have occurred in the past three thousand years.

Celestials balanced their long lives with an insidious form of impotence. Everything would function as you might expect, but most of the time, we ended up shooting blanks. Only once in every hundred years or so could we have progeny. It kept the population down. If only they had implemented it for all humans, the world would have been a better place.

These two were dressed like a pair of American gangsters from the eighties—torn jeans, faded metal band t-shirts, and way too much bling. I made a mental note to let them know there were other shows out there besides *The Fresh Prince of Bel-Air*, if I survived whatever this was.

One of them stepped forward with a hard look on his face. I think he was going for menacing. I gave him points for trying.

'Are you the one who attacked our people last night?'

They didn't know who I was. Which seemed like a pretty basic failure on their part. 'Know thy enemy.' I had taught an ancient Chinese dude named Sun Tzu most of my wisdom and that fellow even wrote a whole book on it, but these idiots hadn't even bothered to do their research. To them, I was just some street-level magic user.

Despite my disdain for their attire, I found myself mildly impressed. Someone had figured out pretty quickly that their little errand boy's brain had been turned into quivering jelly. Knowing that it was someone with knowledge of the arcane, they had staked out Creeda. It couldn't be these two morons, of course. It had to be someone else—the brains behind the operation.

'Who wants to know?' I enquired.

His brow furrowed. Clearly, he wasn't used to answering such complicated questions. In response, he raised his hand, and flames crackled over them. It was similar to what I had attempted when Shukra and I were doing our little bit of playacting. Except all I could produce then were a few measly sparks.

'Do you want to be burnt to a fucking crisp?' he sneered.

There was a quaver in my voice as I tried to sound whiny and scared like the hoodlum from yesterday. 'I'm sorry for the trouble. Please, don't hurt me!'

The younger of the two smirked. How did I know one was younger than the other? I didn't, really. But one of them was pissing me off more than the other. I would lay good odds that he was the younger of the two. I can't stand kids.

'Now, what sort of message would it send if we don't avenge our people?' he drawled, even as he raised his hand to throw a fireball.

I don't like to brag, but ... Wait, who the hell am I kidding? I love to brag. My reflexes made this younger generation look like a bunch of geriatrics. His hand was still coming up when I stepped closer, palming the deck of cards from within my sleeve and flinging them out like razor blades. The cards slashed through the air between us, hitting their auras and exploding, sending them staggering.

Akran – 1, Arseholes – 0.

I had three decks on my person, each one painstakingly charged with my limited access to mana every night. The throw had bought me a limited window while they were still trying to recover. Each exploding card also released thick smoke that camouflaged me for a few seconds while I flung the second deck within my personal space and began chanting as I threw. The deck flew forward and then rearranged itself into a familiar form. My own. A shimmer of power passed within them as the illusion knitted itself into a remarkable likeness of myself while I used a solitary card of shadow to fade into the alley. It was a pretty little glamour, but weak. It could be dissipated easily, and I held my breath as I waited to see what would happen next.

They reacted predictably and with outrage. Two more fireballs smashed into my illusion, shattering it completely.

There was a moment of disbelief as the duo realised it was an illusion. They closed in, frowning in disbelief, half expecting to see my ashes on the ground.

'Who the fuck is this guy?' I heard the younger one say.

'Whoever he is, he couldn't have gone far,' the elder one snarled. 'Let's take him alive.'

Despite my impressive performance so far, they had a massive advantage over me. They were drawing from a large mana pool while I was fighting for scraps. I couldn't sit in the shadows for more than a few seconds, tops. The only way I could level the playing field was to get inside their aura and use my fists.

There's a reason why Yakshas don't creep up and pat other celestials on their back. Think of a celestial's aura like a personal energy shield. We can allow someone into our personal space or we can repel those who get too close. I was hoping that given enough momentum, I could charge at one of them and knock him out before his aura sent me flying ignominiously across the alley.

I was reluctant to use the sword on my back since that was my last line of defence. If I could disable them without killing them, then maybe I could find out where the kidnapped girls were.

I settled on the younger one. I had no idea whether I could get past his aura with my pitiful mana levels, but the choices were fight or flight. They were blocking my only exit from this place. So, fight it had to be.

Springing forward with the remainder of my deck in hand, I slammed into his aura.

And was lifted off my feet and crashed into a wall ten feet away.

Turns out I should have chosen flight.

All my fighting skills and experience counted for nought when I had barely enough mana to fill a teacup. I had hoped for a few seconds where I could do some damage. But doing that required me to have at least some level of power, to begin with. This was like Yudhishthir going up against Shakuni in a game of dice—a disaster of colossal proportions.

I rose from the floor even as two more fireballs smashed into me.

The blue flame that Yakshas use doesn't always burn. It is a manifestation of our will. You can use it to asphyxiate someone, just as you can use it to burn or physically push away an enemy. In my case, it felt like a vice around my heart and lungs, squeezing them both and bringing me to my knees.

In their minds, my value had risen from 'annoying insect to be crushed' to 'interesting specimen the boss will want to meet, so let's take him alive.'

My last thought as I passed out was how incredibly embarrassing it was to have been taken down by two idiots who weren't even old enough to shave. By celestial standards, I mean.

***

While unconscious, I dreamt again. Another of the not-so-pleasant dreams that I despised. Once again, it was a disembodied experience, as if I was floating above everyone else:

The courtroom was packed. It was the trial of the Mahayuga. A god was dead. And the ramifications were being felt throughout the world.

A portly Yaksha stood up to address the crowd that was baying for blood.

'The Age of Gods is over. The Age of Man has begun.' He paused for dramatic effect. 'And it is all because of him.' He pointed accusingly at Akran, who stood silent.

The crowd seethed. All around were celestials of all races. Gandharvas, Apsaras, Yakshas, and even a few sages. This was the largest gathering in millennia. And I was the guest of honour. Or rather, him. Akran, the younger.

Manibhadra waved the crowds to silence and motioned for Akran, the younger, to speak.

'Do you understand what you have done, Akran?'

The younger Akran stared back, a hollow glazed look evident in his eyes. It was hard to not feel sympathy for him. Then again, maybe it was just me. Everyone else seemed perfectly content hating him.

Manibhadra sighed.

'First, you convinced Samba to anger the sages. We dismissed that as a prank. Then you lost the sacred weapons that were entrusted to you. Again, we attributed it to carelessness and not deliberate malice.'

His voice was slow and sombrous as it echoed in the halls. I respected Manibhadra. His disappointed parent routine was annoying, but he was also known for his fairness. Justice, I mean, not skin tone.

'Twice, you were forgiven. But then you suggested the Yadavas go on a pilgrimage to the Prabhas sea. You plied Satyaki with drink and encouraged him to attack Kritavarma. When all of this was done, you led Jara, the hunter, straight to Lord Krishna disguised as a deer.' He had a pained look in his eyes. 'Help us understand. What could possibly motivate you to do something like that?'

Put that way, it was certainly damning evidence. It almost looked like a deliberate attempt to undermine the Yadava clan.

There was only one problem.

I didn't do it.

I remember goading Samba to tease the sages. I also remember urging Satyaki to attack Kritavarma. They had fought on opposite sides during the war and were never friends, to begin with. The memory of both these incidents hung over me like a storm cloud, as if my head was heavy with drink. I can't remember why I acted the way I did or even the words that I spit out of my mouth. If I had committed these crimes, they were only ever intended as mischief, but now it seemed as mischief gone horribly wrong.

But prancing about like a deer? No way would I do that and not remember. Krishna and I had joked about it a couple of times, how in a previous incarnation, a demon disguised as a deer had helped him fulfil his purpose. We had wondered back then at how hard it seemed for humans— from Dasharatha to Pandu—to tell apart a deer and humans.

I was in charge of the sacred weapons, so I had only myself to blame for their loss. But to lose something so valuable and not even remember how, I had to be under a spell of some kind. None of this added up.

Predictably, no one believed me. My peers were veterans of a hundred wars. Big names with powerful epithets. Aswakranda of the great war cry, Rainuka the fearless, Chitrasena of the dazzling dance, Uluka of the swaying testicles—though that may have been an error in translation—Swasanaka, Nimesha, Praruja ... and right now, every one of their faces was filled with hostility and dismay.

There was genuine puzzlement in Manibhadra's eyes. 'You were regarded as the best of us, Akran. The favourite of the lord. Why would you betray his trust and ours?'

Akran, the younger, stood silent. I watched the proceedings with a peculiar sense of detachment. I knew exactly what was going through his mind. There was bewilderment and an inescapable sense of loss. He had lost the only true friend he had, failed his most sacred charge and stood accused as a traitor, all in the span of a single day. He couldn't fathom what had happened.

Mankanaka, the gatekeeper and the only Yaksha who had never left his post and so never interacted with any of Vishnu's avatars, stepped forward and bowed low. He was one of the pitiful few in that chamber I could still call a friend. At a nod from Manibhadra, he spoke up.

'Learned sages and my fellow Yakshas, please help me understand. The Kali Yuga was destined to happen. The great war is over and the Pandavas are the rightful rulers of Hastinapur. Lord Krishna defeated all the major threats that were present, including Kamsa, Jarasandha, Narakasura, Sisupala and Dantavakra. He thus completed all that he set out to do. Maybe this was part of his plan. Why are we then blaming Akran?'

A chorus of boos and hisses greeted his words. Swasanaka, of the fiery temper, stood up.

'It is not for us to judge when an avatar's work on the mortal plane is completed. Akran' actions were malicious. They have hastened the Kali Yuga and destroyed the Yadava clan in its entirety. Dwarka was supposed to be a centre of learning and wisdom that would guide the world in these troubled times. Instead, it has been swallowed up by the oceans.'

'That was due to the curse of Gandhari,' Mankanaka pointed out. *'You can hardly lay the blame for that at Akran's feet!'*

More boos and cries echoed in the halls. Swasanaka called for silence. He fancied himself something of an orator and enjoyed the opportunity to show off his oratorial skills.

'A curse by a human! Not even a sage but an ordinary woman! You think something like that could destroy Dwarka?' he snorted contemptuously.

A misogynist as well. I chose to say nothing. This rabble had already decided I was guilty.

'We are left bereft, without guidance as to what to do next. We are left defenceless since the greatest weapons of our age were also entrusted to him for safekeeping.' Swasanaka paused to catch his breath and pointed dramatically at Akran. *'I demand he be put to death!'*

Loud applause greeted his words. Once again, I scanned the court, searching for anyone I thought might have an ulterior motive, someone who looked overly pleased with himself at my downfall. But the look on everyone's faces was a mixture of contempt and loathing. I had turned overnight into the most hated celestial.

'Furthermore,' Swasanaka continued, *'while interrogating him, we probed his mind and found that he was indeed acting on someone else's orders. His memories are fragmented, and we were unable to determine who it was, but this person appears to be hidden in the shadows. Akran refuses to reveal anything about who he was in cahoots with and how this demon even got into the inner sanctum. We can only conclude that this is part of something they hatched together.'*

The calls for my death became louder and more insistent, and Manibhadra finally had to stand up to quiet everyone down.

'Akran is guilty. There is no doubt about that. But I am hesitant to have him killed, given his long record of service to the gods. Therefore—' he raised a hand to forestall more protests, 'I'm going to strip him of his powers and cast him down to Earth. Let him live like a human and see what his actions have wrought on us.'

He looked at me, and for a brief moment, there was something akin to a flicker of sympathy in his eyes. 'Someday, perhaps you might find a way to redeem yourself.'

This was a punishment crueller than death. What could possibly be worse than knowing you had committed the worst crime in history and then been exiled to live for eternity in shame?

***

I awoke to find myself seated on a chair with my hands cuffed behind my back. A couple of mosquitoes buzzed angrily over my head, trying to penetrate my aura. They failed.

I was inside a large warehouse. It was well-lit, and the faint smell of the sea told me where I was. I could hear the two idiots who had captured me laughing uproariously, along with two more people. They were playing dice, a favourite pastime among celestials. The world had moved on to games like *Assassins Creed* and *Fortnite*, but not them. Most celestials who didn't live on Earth were the same. Old habits die hard.

I continued to study my surroundings, trying to gather as much information about the place as I could. The sword had been left untouched in the sheath on my back. Either they had naively assumed I wasn't armed, or they just didn't care.

My movements were deliberately slow and sluggish, so I didn't attract their attention, at least until I had a better idea of what I was dealing with. To my left was a row of beds, well over a dozen of them. I reached out with my senses and realised they were occupied. Each bed had at least two sleeping children on it. I had found the kids!

Three of my captors got up. From their conversation, it was apparent that they were heading out.

'Three more days till the ceremony,' one of them was saying. 'The planets will be aligned for at least six hours. After that, all of this will finally be over.'

The other one snorted. 'We should have done this a long time ago—why did we wait until now?'

'Multiple reasons,' answered a third voice. He sounded older, and his voice reeked of power. I couldn't quite place him, but I knew he was the leader.

'The stars align in this configuration once every couple of hundred years. Each time they did, they were too far from the auspicious date. And each time, something was missing. The earrings took six centuries to locate. Not to mention the umbrella. This time, we have all of the required elements.'

'All except one item,' said the first voice sourly. 'We still don't have the jewel. '

'We will have the Syamantaka very soon,' the leader replied, and his tone brooked no room for argument. 'It is only a matter of time before the Naga gives it up.'

There was a murmur of agreement from the other three. I tested my handcuffs by giving them an experimental twist.

As expected, they were made of silver—enough to dampen any thoughts of escaping through magical means.

A brief creaking sound indicated that one of them had left. I hoped it was their leader, who probably had better things to do than sit and play dice.

'What do we do with him?'

'We could rough him up a bit.' I recognised the voice of the younger Yaksha, the one I had tried attacking. 'Get him to tell us everything he knows.'

'Not yet,' said the other one. 'We need to go back to the library. See if anyone else comes by.' There was a rasp of command in his voice, a voice used to being obeyed.

'Guard him well. We will be back in a few hours.'

Clearly, there was a pecking order even among these three. And the one at the lowest rung of the totem pole was being relegated to guard duty.

The younger one chuckled nasally. 'Yes, keep him safe. I have something special planned for when we return.'

That was a cheery thought. Exactly the kind of motivation I needed.

I felt the air crackle and burn once again. The two of them had gone, leaving me with just one solitary guard. This would make my escape easier. I had hoped for some more time, but that wasn't going to happen. The celestial who was left in charge of me decided to come closer, no doubt curious about who I was.

He was young, as far as our kind goes. Maybe eight hundred years old, give or take. That made him almost a teenager. His powers weren't in full bloom yet, but they would still be vastly superior to mine in my current state.

He stood a few feet away from me, whether out of fear or caution, I couldn't quite tell. He looked unafraid as he locked eyes with me, studying me silently.

Let him feel he's in control. Build a rapport, so you are harder to kill. I knew all the little things I should be doing.

'Can we talk?' I asked politely.

A hate-filled glare was his only response.

'I'll go first. I'm Akran. What's your name?'

He continued to stare wordlessly. I sighed. Not a chatty Cathy, then. It looked like I would need to carry the conversation forward.

'Ok, I'm just going to call you Bob, so this can go easier. So, look we aren't supposed to be interfering in the affairs of mortals. These girls,' I jerked my head to point in the direction of the beds, 'have families. We don't want to bring attention to ourselves.'

He continued to stare without speaking. I found myself liking this kid. He would have made a good interrogator. Two minutes with him, I was already talking my head off.

'I know you are afraid to talk to me. They've probably told you all kinds of stories about all the crazy shit I can pull off with both hands tied behind my back, huh? But it is not true. Why do you think they didn't gag me? It is because they are hoping I'll spill something of significance. And the only way I can do that is if we have a dialogue. Now, what do you say?'

'I'm not afraid of you,' he spat. 'You are just an old relic who can't see which way the world is turning.'

Attaboy, Akran. Be sure to give yourself a pat on the back when this is over.

'Kid, I've been on this planet for a lot longer than you have. This is a different world from everything they've told you. Humans are a lot smarter than you give them credit for. That music you sent them? It is already circulating over the internet.'

He gave me a blank look. From his expression, I realised he didn't know what that was. In some ways, it was like the old problem humans talk about when it comes to new technology. How do you explain the internet to your great-grandmother? Even worse, how would you explain it in a situation like this, where your grandmother was born nearly eight hundred years ago?

'The point is,' I said hurriedly, not wanting to get dragged into a discussion about the internet, 'there's a significant chance of being detected. Or even killed. They've got big satellites up in the sky watching everything. They've got machines that fly in the air. People don't fight with clubs and spears anymore.'

He gave a derisive snort. 'It doesn't matter what weapons they have. We will pull all their big machines out of the sky and send them crashing down on their seats of power. The barracks of their soldiers, the schools of their children and the marketplaces of their commerce. They will lose the will to fight after our first demonstration.'

'You might kill a few thousand of them,' I conceded. 'Tens of thousands even. But then what? They breed like rabbits. You can kill a million of them for every one of us, and there'd still be many more.'

He waved his hand dismissively. 'Their numbers won't help when they don't know where we are. We can strike them down from behind. Kill their leaders. Burn their crops. As long as we have the power and they don't, we will ultimately win. We can turn the earth into a wasteland while they are still cowering in fear and wondering where we will strike next.'

He spoke with the casual arrogance of youth—the cocky little youngsters who've never had blood on their hands or had to wade through mud and excrement to kill their enemies.

'Is that what you want? A wasteland to rule over?'

He sneered. 'I don't expect you to understand.'

'We've kept the peace. All these millennia, peacefully co-existing together. What's changed now?'

He gave me a disgusted look. 'That was our benevolence. They should be falling to their feet and worshipping us. Thanking us for the kindness we have bestowed by not exterminating them all these years.'

This guy could have a good alternate career as a troll on Twitter. He was full of stupid ideas and moral outrage. Typically, that's all you need.

He also couldn't answer a single direct question without a rant about the people who had offended him in some way.

I had seen this before. Simple minds could be whipped up into a frenzy with a fiery speech and by giving them a target for their frustration. All they needed was an external enemy to hate and blame for all their problems. If you didn't have an enemy, you made one up. After that, they lost the ability to reason and simply parroted what others told them.

'Who put you up to this?'

He scowled. 'What do you mean?'

'You met someone recently who fed you this bullshit. Who was it?'

He took a step forward glaring at me. 'You calling me stupid?'

Yes!

'No, I'm saying you didn't answer my question. What's changed? What's different now since, oh, I don't know, roughly the last three thousand years give or take? What makes you want to go postal on a bunch of humans who don't even know you exist?'

Another blank look. I decided I would have to start quoting slightly older metaphors. 'All the world's a stage' or some rot like that.

'There's a reason why we co-exist,' I began again. 'The humans pray to the gods. Their belief in the supernatural keeps us alive. It is a symbiotic relationship. By killing them, we are shooting ourselves in the foot.' He sneered. 'That's a bedtime story we tell children. To frighten the sheep into good behaviour.'

'Ok, first of all, that's a really sad childhood you led if those were the stories you were told, but I'm not making this up. Nobody wins in a fight between humans and celestials.' I paused, seeing that there was no getting past his thick skull. 'Except,' I added, with a sudden burst of inspiration, 'the Asuras.'

He had been ready to dismiss whatever I was going to say, but my words stopped him short. 'What about the Asuras?'

'They have a plan to take over the world.' I was clearly bullshitting at this point, but it was the best I could come up with at short notice. 'Fighting against the humans weakens us and splits our forces. We need to work together. Like in the past.'

He looked like he was thinking it over. 'Who are these Asuras that are planning this?'

I really couldn't tell if this was working but I couldn't give up now. 'Umm … Harold,' I hazarded. 'That was one. And Kumar was the other guy. Regular run-of-the-mill chaps.'

'Uh huh'. He didn't look convinced and I couldn't really blame him. 'I've never heard of them.'

'No reason why you should,' I extemporised. 'They have their very own private castle. It's white and overlooks a …'

'Enough,' he snapped. 'I knew you were weak but now you have proved you are a liar as well. The Asuras are on our side.'

It took an immense effort not to let my jaw drop. A random shot in the dark had suddenly revealed a new piece of information.

'You are a fool to trust the Asuras.'

He shook his head. 'They want the same thing we do—the end of the Kali Yuga.' His face took on an expression that I've seen on humans before—it's either fervent fanaticism or constipation. I get the two mixed up, but if I was betting, given the circumstances, it was the former. 'We don't need to wait for a pre-ordained time. The stars will finally be in alignment. We can push the event forward.'

His words sent a trickle of sweat down my spine. With crystal clear clarity, I knew what they were planning. I also knew that this was not something I could stand by idly and let happen.

'Kid, listen …'

'Don't call me that!' he shouted. 'I'm not some child. I've killed plenty of humans before. Call me by my name. Varunn.'

'Varunn, please. Listen to me,' I said, trying to speak to him as slowly and calmly as possible. 'It is still not too late. Walk away from this now, and no one needs to get hurt.

Inform the council about this, and they will forgive you. You might even get a reward.'

He spat on the floor. 'I am no traitor to the cause.'

'Don't betray them. Walk away. I give you my word; I won't tell anyone about your involvement. This is a stupid plan that is bound to fail and will end up killing millions. I can't let you do this. If you persist, I will be forced to kill you.'

Even as I said it, I knew it was futile. Just like the younger version of myself, there was a light of fanaticism in his eyes. A sense of implacable conviction that he was right and the rest of the world was wrong. Nothing I was going to say would convince him otherwise.

I really didn't want to kill him. He wasn't old enough to know better. He had fallen into the wrong company and been easily influenced by them.

He sneered. 'You are going to kill me? Tied up in that chair, you mean? How exactly do you plan to accomplish that?'

'Like this,' I said as I brought my hands in front of me, showing him the unlocked handcuffs.

I couldn't use magic because they were made of silver. But they were still regular single lock push pin handcuffs. I had lived several human lifetimes among the riff-raff that dabbles with the occult—the diviners of your fate, be it tea leaves or crystal balls, the stage magicians, the escape artists. It was safe to say I had picked up a few things … like escaping from a straitjacket while submerged in a glass tank that was locked from the outside.

Or, as just demonstrated, a pair of handcuffs. Something I could do in my sleep after having been arrested so many times in the past decade alone.

He gaped at me, bug-eyed, obviously taken aback by the sudden change in circumstances. I saw his fist clench as he began to cast a spell, but it was too late. I plunged the black blade from the sheath at my back into his abdomen. They hadn't even taken the basic precaution of searching me for weapons. This is what happens when you get too arrogant and underestimate your enemies.

I would have preferred giving fair warning. There was, after all, a code we followed. But unlike me, he had access to actual magic. All I had was the element of surprise.

A shudder ran through my arm as the blade absorbed his essence. Even as it did so, it turned milky white, indicating its power had been drained once again. One more celestial and it would turn to dust, having run its short life.

Varunn collapsed onto the floor, the look of shock never leaving his face. Taking his leave, I made a quick circuit of the warehouse. The girls were all asleep. They looked peaceful, as if under a deep spell. There was nothing to indicate that they had been molested in any way, which was a relief.

Unfortunately, the girl whom I had set out to find, Anna, was missing. Either she had been moved or this was only one of the many locations where the victims were kept. I suspected the latter. Shukra said there were at least forty abductions. From what I could see here, at least a dozen girls were still unaccounted for.

A large safe sat in one corner, similar to the one I used—all tumblers and no electrical safeguards. On the side was taped a combination, which I keyed in. Yes, a lot of celestials did idiotic things.

Inside were multiple objects, most of them divine. A few precious stones and jewellery pieces were also present, though one particular set of earrings caught my attention. I had seen them before on two separate occasions. They had once been worn by Ma Aditi, the mother of the Devas. After they had been stolen and recovered, Indra gave the earrings to Surya, who gave them to his son, Karna. They were supposed to prevent disease and ageing, and combined with the sun god's armour would make the wearer invulnerable. Knowing that he would be invulnerable with the armour and earrings and seeking to protect his son Arjun, Indra disguised himself as a Brahmin and asked Karna for the earrings and armour as alms. Karna recognised Indra but honoured his moral code and gave the earrings and armour as requested. Pleased, Indra gave Karna the Vasav Shakti, a weapon that could be used only once but would kill any single enemy once deployed.

Ancient history to most. Nostalgia for me.

I slipped the earrings and the remaining contents of the safe into my jacket before I made one more circle of the room. There on a large wooden desk lay a sheaf of papers listing the names of different girls and addresses. I skimmed through them briefly before shoving the whole bunch of papers into my jacket.

Once I was certain there was nothing else of interest lying about, I returned to look at my latest victim.

Varunn lay glass-eyed on the floor, his life force ebbing with every heartbeat. Despite my reputation, I took no pleasure in killing—celestials or humans. Bending close to him, I briefly touched his head and examined his memories. A red mist was slowly erasing them from existence as his vital functions shut down. His thoughts were unfiltered and full of pain as he opened his mind unwillingly. I saw, in a span of a few seconds, what was essentially his existence in centuries, living in the celestial realm. The runt of his litter. A group of bored, disaffected celestials with purposeless lives stretching to eternity—a bleak existence to look forward to. Plenty of teenage angst and awkwardness as he struggled to be acknowledged. Falling in with a group of celestial incels, similar to human incels, yet even bigger tools, for in their heads, their divine birth made them the chaddiest chads who ever chadded. An audacious madcap plan suggested to give their lives meaning. Being offered a chance to make a difference and his leaping at the opportunity—even if doing so violated the rules of dharma.

In these last moments, he felt fear. Death is a scary thing for us all, the uncertainty of the unknown. There was also regret. Me getting the better of him would lower his image in the eyes of his 'friends'. It was such a big part of who he was—his desperate need to be seen as competent.

Gently, I closed his eyes and said a prayer over his dead body. It had been a while since I had someone's blood on my hands.

Somehow, I knew it was going to happen again … and very soon.

CHAPTER EIGHT

*T*he Syamantaka was a ruby worn by Surya until King Satrajit asked the sun god for it as a boon. It was said to be so bright that it blotted out the wearer's face. That bit was an exaggeration. Still, it was pretty shiny.

During a meeting, Krishna requested Satrajit to give the jewel to Ugrasena, the leader of the Yadavas. The jewel supposedly conferred great sums of gold on the owner and Ugrasena could use it to benefit everyone. Satrajit, however, refused and gave it, instead, to his brother Prasen, who was killed by a lion while hunting. The bright shiny object attracted the lion, who took it back to his cave. Jambavan, one of the heroes of the Ramayana, fought and killed the lion and recovered the jewel.

Meanwhile, Satrajit accused Krishna of killing his brother to steal the gem. To clear his name, Krishna ventured into the forest and tracked down Jambavan. The two fought long and hard since Jambavan couldn't be killed because of a boon that granted him immortality, and Krishna was ...

well, Krishna. The two made peace when Jambavan realised that Krishna was an avatar of Vishnu. As a devout follower of Ram (the previous Vishnu avatar), he offered Krishna the jewel and his daughter Jambavati in marriage. Krishna then took the jewel back to Satrajit. Filled with remorse, Satrajit offered both the jewel and his daughter Satyabhama who was described as a 'jewel among women' to Krishna in marriage. Krishna accepted Satyabhama's hand in marriage but refused to keep the ruby.

– Sacred Archives of the Gandharvas

The café in Bandra was small and unobtrusive. Named 'Tea Room,' it looked like most other cafés in a premium location—tiny, overpriced and full of pretentious snobs with fancy laptops, mooching off the internet.

What made the place marginally different was the basement, where gamers, magicians and groupies hung out. It was a little slice of the hidden world—a secret society for the ones who don't belong, misfits who decided long ago that starched shirts and suits didn't work for them. They rubbed shoulders with another group of misfits—people who enjoyed board games, comic books and other esoteric hobbies that people with limited imagination turn their noses up at. During the weekend, the crowd slowly expanded into a wide variety of geeks from all walks of life. Hackers, musicians and pickup artists all eventually found themselves drawn to the little store, thanks to some experimental feng shui that the owner had implemented while setting up shop.

Most people didn't realise that there was another hidden level within the basement. A subterranean nook that was at least three times the size of the café upstairs. The nook was off-limits to everyone except those who could tap into the world's mana stream. True magic users, not card sharks and stage magicians.

Yes, even here, there was a hierarchy. And the Rat Packs were at the top of that little pile. This was our slice of heaven. A home away from home where we could relax and hang out in each other's company without accidentally revealing who we were to the humans upstairs.

The room was heavily warded—more than any other place in the city, including the library.

Besides the standard spells of confusion and doubt encountered by anyone who tried to scry our location, there were multiple layers of defensive magic as well. We could conceivably repel a full-scale assault if anyone was stupid enough to attack us here. I had been reliably informed that twenty-seven possible doomsday scenarios were likely to happen within the next century, including a nuclear winter, a worldwide famine and a zombie apocalypse. We were prepared for all three in our den. This was where we would make our heroic last stand.

Shukra was already there when I arrived. He had a smug smirk on his face—the satisfaction of a job well done. The dispersal of the heavenly music had been contained using some tech gobbledygook he had strung together. It was good news. The date for the world to learn of our existence had been pushed forward.

K was the next to make an appearance. He sauntered in without a care in the world, whistling a happy tune that I recognised from the soundtrack of his latest obsession. Something with wolves and lions and a whole lot of people dying.

K was my nickname for Kama, the god of love. I meant that, literally. He really was a physical embodiment of love, except if you are picturing him as a fat, ugly cherub, shooting arrows, you are doing it wrong. K was good-looking. By that, I mean he was literally corset-popping, panty-dropping gorgeous. Especially when he turned on the charm.

K had been a rising star in the celestial community until he was asked to help hasten the relationship between Lord Shiva and his would-be consort, Parvati. A demon had been terrorising the heavens and had received a boon that he could only be killed by a son of Shiva. The rest of the gods convinced Kama to shoot a flowery arrow of love into Shiva's heart to inflame his passion when he saw Parvati.

It worked out well for Shiva, Parvati, the rest of the gods and the world in general. All, except Kama. Furious that he dared to use his powers on him, Shiva burnt him to ashes.

After a long and painful recovery, K decided he would not get involved in the politics of the celestial court anymore. He chose to stay here on Earth, which is where we met, once I got exiled.

K was an interesting character. You would expect the god of love to have more gravitas, given how seriously most humans take love and how much effort they put into finding a soulmate. But no, K was mischief and mayhem personified. He possessed the curiosity of a child and the impulsive, reckless attitude of a teenager in love.

An unexpected benefit of his immolation was that he had no physical body and his natural state was being invisible. It made him a half-decent spy, that is when he wasn't distracted by good-looking women. Incidentally, he was also mostly useless in a fight. But he balanced out my cynical, depressing and mostly pessimistic worldview and was always there when I needed him. Of all the people in the room, he was my closest friend.

Sars was the next one to enter. She was the owner of the café and also the tech genius who handled all our finances. Unlike the rest of us, she was the aspect of a true goddess, still worshipped by millions. Aspects were like goddesses-in-waiting—daughters and handmaidens that represented a unique facet of their progenitor's power.

Her mother, the goddess Saraswati was the embodiment of knowledge, music, flowing water, abundance, art, speech, wisdom and learning.

The Goddess was typically clad in white, bedecked in white ornaments, holding a book and a pen in her hands, and usually sitting atop a lotus. Sars wore black from head to toe, even going so far as to wear black pearls and onyx earrings. She walked around with a laptop in her backpack, usually listening to something on her wireless Bluetooth headphones that were, you guessed it, black.

Sars was the resident hacker in the group. It tied in with the aspect that she symbolised: hidden knowledge. Goddess Saraswati encouraged hard work and penance to access the learnings mortals craved. Sars was of a different bent of mind. She represented the idea that information should be free—a philosophy that had been gaining more traction in the real world, which had thus brought her into being. Part of her talent was her prodigious capacity to decode the written word—just about anything ever put down, be it on paper, pixel or stone, could be translated by her. She could speak languages that were dead for years, gain flashes of insight by merely looking at a person and hack military-grade encryption once she put her mind to it. There were no secrets from the aspect of the Goddess of Knowledge.

Sars was also sweet and helpful, which made her one of my closest friends. Shukra was no slouch in the brains department, but Sars was another level altogether. If you think of Mas as the Tony Stark of the group and Shukra as Dr Pym, then Sars was Shuri, Bruce Banner and Mr Fantastic, all rolled into one. She didn't really like her name, not after it got associated with a disease, but we weren't going to let a little thing like that get in the way of us having some fun. So, she was stuck with that name for a while … at least when she was with us.

The last and final person in the room was Deanne, the date I had cancelled yesterday. I had pegged her to be an Etruscan— most of her kind went extinct when the Roman empire rose, leaving her with no home to go back to. Living for thousands of years had instilled wanderlust, and she had roamed the Earth, seeking new adventures and pursuits. K had befriended her at a bar, and she had hung around with us for a while, amused at his antics and my roguish charm. As far as I could tell, she was a psychopomp—a guide to souls who were journeying to wherever their next destination would be.

And that was the Rat Pack: my little gang of compatriots who I knew would stand by my side when the world came to an end. The only one missing from today's gathering was Mas, who had saved my life with those swords of his and was also hands down the greatest engineer the world had ever seen. Unfortunately, he often took off for a few years at a stretch while trying to solve some knotty problem. The last time we saw him was nearly twenty years ago.

There is a good reason why most of us chose to hang out in Mumbai instead of the traditional 'holy cities' like Ayodhya or Varanasi. Humans hadn't yet reconciled with the idea that you didn't need altars or physical places of worship to commune with the gods. A heartfelt unspoken prayer could achieve the same result as loudly thumping your chest and screaming out your devotion. Places of worship today were built primarily for stroking the egos of humans, not gods. And, to launch political campaigns.

Sars and Shukra both gravitated towards technology, and both Mumbai and Bangalore were excellent for that particular reason. However, Mumbai also had a vibe that made it cooler. That, plus the fact that there was no maddening traffic every waking hour of the day. Also, much better food options.

The mutton raan at Persian Darbar, the kosha mangsho at Oh Calcutta, the prawn pulao and apricot custard at Martin's Corner, the thandai milkshake at Bachelors'—it was a culinary orgasm of mind-bending flavours and tastes. The most mouth-watering delicacies and sensuous food delights from every corner of the subcontinent were brought together in one single city. Millennia had passed, and I still couldn't quite get over how delicious and inventive human food could be. Don't get me wrong, Amrit is delicious. But when you are having it for breakfast, lunch and dinner, it starts to get a bit old.

Back at our table, I briefly told my friends what had happened so far, omitting no details. They all listened attentively, choosing only to interrupt occasionally when required.

'Who do you think is behind this?' Shukra asked. 'A Chiranjivi?'

Kama frowned. 'The Telugu actor?'

I would have throttled him if he wasn't being serious. 'No. A Chiranjivi is another word for an immortal. Well, not an immortal exactly. More like a long-lived.'

K exchanged a quizzical glance with Deanne. 'You're going to have to explain that slowly,' he said.

'Sars, can you weigh in here?' It's not that I didn't know the answer. She was just able to explain it without swearing and in a way that everyone else could understand as well.

'Celestials aren't the only ones walking the earth for all these years,' Sars explained. 'Sages can do it as well by tapping into the cosmos and healing their bodies. Also, ordinary humans who have been granted boons from the gods may live for several centuries. They will die eventually; it will just take a longer time for it to happen.'

'Why will they eventually die?' asked Deanne.

'Because nothing in this Universe is truly immortal. Entropy is a given. It's just the rate of decay that can be sped up or slowed down. So much that it is unnoticeable in some cases.'

I shot Deanne a reassuring smile. 'We are all bound by the myths of creation of our own existence. Yours might be something else entirely.'

'So even you …?'

'Even me. Assuming nobody tries to kill me first. Given the past few days, I'm not liking my chances.'

'So these Chiranjivis are sages?' she asked.

'Not all of them, no. There are nine in total including a bear, who, thanks to the boons from the gods, cannot die until the end of the Kali Yuga. Don't …' I warned K who had just opened his mouth to make a bad pun on the situation being 'un-bear-able'. He pouted but said nothing.

Deanne nodded thoughtfully. I was just about to speak to Sars when she spoke again.

'They mean to end the Kali Yuga? Isn't that a good thing?'

'Also,' K drawled, 'isn't that technically similar to what you did? Trying to end the Dwapara Yuga early? I'm surprised they didn't try to recruit you.'

I scowled at him. 'I didn't deliberately end the Dwapara Yuga. You all have known me long enough to have heard my side of the story.'

K grinned and motioned for me to continue.

I turned to Deanne. 'We aren't supposed to interfere in the way destiny unfolds. We are the guardians of the human race. Their watchdogs and their shepherds. We don't invite the wolves to feast on the sheep.'

'But you are not a Yaksha anymore,' Shukra pointed out. 'Any responsibilities that came along with the role also ended when you were exiled.'

'Also,' K added, 'I think that's a pretty good idea for shepherds to try out—keep a sheep out as bait and kill the wolves when they arrive.'

Sars elbowed him hard in the ribs as I shot him a glare.

'It is not about what they are doing. It is how they plan to do it. People are going to die. Thousands of them.'

I glanced at Sars, 'You know what this means, don't you?'

'There is only one way that they can end the Kali Yuga early,' she said, rubbing her jaw thoughtfully. 'They'll need to raise a demon. I think I know who they are going to resurrect.'

Of all of them, I knew Sars would be the one to put it together first. 'I think so too. Narakasura.'

'Wait, how could you possibly know that?' K asked, puzzled.

'It might not even have occurred to me if it wasn't for a conversation with Shukra this morning. Of all the possible demons they could raise, he represents their best chance. Two days from now is Naraka Chaturdashi.'

Deanne looked perplexed, so I told her the condensed version. Narakasura was a powerful demon whose reign of terror caused a lot of suffering. The Devas couldn't stop him as he conquered the heavens. In that time, he stole Indra's elephants, sixteen thousand maidens, Varuna's umbrella and, most notably, the goddess mother Aditi's earrings, grabbing them straight off her ears. This last act was the final straw, and Krishna decided to intervene. He attacked Narakasura's stronghold, and a fierce fight ensued. Eventually, Narakasura was killed and all his possessions were returned.

'Weren't there more powerful demons than him? What about Ravana? Or Hiranyaksha? Or even his brother?'

'They were definitely more powerful. Compared to some of the demons from the earlier yugas, Narakasura was a lightweight. But the other demons were killed with no possibility of them coming back.'

Deanne did a double take, 'Demons in your mythos return to life after they get killed?'

I grimaced. 'Not all of them. Narakasura is a special case. Before dying, he earned a boon that everyone should celebrate his death.'

She frowned, 'I don't understand.'

I thought for a minute how best to explain it. 'We are made from the memories and worship of people through the ages. When they call out to us in times of need, when they yearn for someone to aid them or someone to ease their suffering, that was the spark that brought the gods into being. We remain here because in some way, these memories keep us alive. As long as these stories remain unforgotten, some spark of life remains—a tether that binds us to the mortal world. Narakasura presumably made this connection before most others did. Rather than fading away into obscurity, he requested that his story not be forgotten, that people celebrate his passing.'

Deanne listened with rapt attention. 'So, if people don't remember your name, you eventually fade into obscurity. Nobody worships you anymore or makes offerings or sacrifices in your name or beseeches you for help. Even worse, your deeds of valour get attributed to someone else.' I paused. I had expected talking about this would bring back unpleasant memories, but saying it aloud no longer brought a dull ache to my chest. 'That's what happened with me. My name was stricken from the records. It was a way of excommunicating me. Now, no one remembers me anymore.'

'Which means,' said Sars. 'Narakasura's popularity in folklore makes him a likely candidate for resurrection. Someone who was remembered for years on end would theoretically continue to have a foothold on this plane of existence.'

I nodded. Hearing it laid out methodically made me look at this in a new light. Maybe this had been planned centuries ago and was only now being set into motion.

K had a question. I knew it was something idiotic, but I nodded. It was best that he got it out of his system.

'Why does Varuna, the god of the sea, need an umbrella?'

I ignored him and turned to Deanne, who had a more pertinent question.

'What does this have to do with the girls they kidnapped?'

'All reincarnations of the women Narakasura had captured. Since they had been forcibly abducted, nobody else was willing to marry them. To restore their honour, Krishna married them all and raised their status to nobility. Their closeness to Krishna's divinity gave each of them a spark that has continued through their reincarnations. The ones with the strongest spark had been able to perceive the music. That's how they were being identified.'

'You are saying these Gandharvas or Yakshas or whoever else is in this conspiracy may have kidnapped thousands of women?'

'Sixteen thousand maidens,' Shukra mused. 'If Narakasura decided to visit just one every evening, it would take more than forty years before he made a second visit.'

This comment was so off-field that it derailed everyone's train of thought. Randomness and sex jokes in the middle of a serious conversation were completely in character for K. Shukra carried himself with a bit more gravitas.

'Where are you going with this?' asked Sars.

'And before you answer,' K interjected, 'I know how to cut that number down to twenty years.' He had a dreamy look in his eyes. 'I'm pretty sure I can cut it further down still if I put my ... mind to it.'

Everyone gave that comment the amount of attention it deserved, which was to say, none at all.

Shukra looked embarrassed. 'Sorry. Was thinking aloud. Even a virile and lusty demon would think twice before kidnapping sixteen thousand women. He would be hard-pressed to house and feed them, much less attend to each one. If I had to guess, I think that number has been grossly inflated. You are probably looking for a pool of fifty, maybe hundred girls at max.'

That made sense. I had seen a lot of liberal use of poetic license as far as the epics were concerned, be it in the number of soldiers or years between events.

'If they conduct a blood sacrifice, they won't even need so many. A dozen perhaps?' I turned to Sars, who nodded, with her lips pursed tightly.

An anonymous tip to both the cops as well as two national media outlets ensured that there were plenty of witnesses when the girls got rescued. The footage was being telecast over and over across news channels. Loud-mouthed, obnoxious TV anchors were screaming at each other till they were blue in the face about how the nation wanted to know how this had happened. Predictably, lines had been drawn, and both political parties were blaming each other. It was the same bullshit that had been going on for decades. Nothing would ever change until these morons found a way to work together for the common good of all the people in the country.

As my cursory examination had indicated, none of the girls had been molested or harmed in any way. They had been put into a magical sleep. and remembered nothing beyond the abduction itself.

'So, it's done. You've saved the girls and stolen back the ornaments or whatever they had ... that should be enough, right?' K asked. 'They can't raise the demon without the sacrifices and the remaining items!'

'I'm not too certain. I never did find that girl I was looking for—Anna. Which means, there are a few more missing girls out there. I don't know how many components they need or what the exact threshold of sacrifices they require for the yagna to succeed. My guess is that just because we've foiled them, they won't simply let the rest go. They might attempt the yagna anyway, which means they are still in danger.'

'Raising a demon to end the Kali Yuga sounds counter-intuitive,' mused K. 'Wouldn't that just prolong it?'

I sighed. 'Here's the scary part. Their plan could actually work. The Kali Yuga supposedly ends when the final avatar of Vishnu, Kalki, descends with a flaming sword atop a white horse as he cleanses the world. Kalki is supposed to arrive when wickedness and evil are at their peak. Raising Narakasura may trigger the Kalki avatar and bring this yuga to a close.'

'You can't get more evil than bringing a top-notch demon into this world,' Sars agreed.

'I thought your yugas were supposed to be longer,' Deanne mused. 'Four hundred thousand years or some such?'

Sars rolled her eyes. 'That's bad math. Someone decided that a day in heaven is the same as a year on earth. So, everything got multiplied by a factor of three hundred and sixty-five. The last yuga really ended in 1183 BC.'

Deanne blinked. 'Huh! That ... actually makes sense.'

'Also known as the Collapse of the Bronze Age,' I said quietly. 'And the Fall of Dwarka.'

A moment of silence followed.

K was the first to break it …

'So, after years and years of just sitting idly, this coalition of Yakshas and Asuras suddenly woke up and began plotting the end of the world?'

'There are certain planetary alignments necessary for the coming of Kalki. And I suspect they need a similar alignment to best guarantee their chances of success with the resurrection. That, plus locating all the items, might have been what took so long.' I paused. 'There might be another reason. Someone brought them together and organised this whole plot. Whoever the brains behind this operation is—I didn't get to see his face and I don't think he bothered looking at mine—that person might be the reason why it's all happening now. The others are just the muscle in this operation.'

'What I don't get,' said Deanne, 'is which side of the coin does one believe in? Either something is destined to happen, in which case nothing can change it, or nothing is written in stone and one has free will. How can you be banking on some future avatar while also thinking you can flip fate the bird?'

'I don't think they are two sides of the same coin,' I said slowly. 'You ever played Housie? That game with little bits of paper with numbers on it. If your numbers in a row match with the numbers that are called out, you win a prize.'

'Not that game specifically,' she responded dryly, 'but I'm familiar with the concept.'

'Okay, good. So now imagine instead of using the ticket that was given, you decide to write up your own ticket. Nobody's going to stop you from playing!'

She looked puzzled. 'What's your point?'

'The point is, you are free to choose any ticket you wish to use. Or decide the game is for schmucks and choose not to play. That's free will. Your ability to choose. In the end, though, the winning numbers and jackpot remain the same. The rules that govern the game also remain unchanged. That's fate.'

She frowned.

'I believe an avatar will rise. That's set in stone. Whether his rising is now or later, the number of people who die and what happens to the world ... those can change. Our actions will determine that.'

Shukra looked puzzled. Almost like he couldn't fathom why this was a problem.

'Many humans will die, true. But once that is over, we will be in a new age of peace and prosperity, right?'

'Presumably,' Sars said. 'The yugas are cyclical, which means the wheel of time will circle back to where we once were.'

'Back to an idyllic peaceful world,' Shukra finished. 'Sounds like a good outcome to me.'

I opened my mouth to answer, but Sars spoke first.

'That's a very simplistic way of thinking how the yugas work. People assume that it would be similar to the world we have now, except the gods would walk among us and people would be more honest, kinder and charitable.'

K frowned. 'That doesn't sound so bad!'

'Exactly! But that's the best-case scenario. The paradise that the ancients envisioned when the scriptures were written is very different from what we might imagine it to be today.'

K shot her a blank look. Judging from the expressions on Deanne and Shukra's face, they weren't clear either.

'Back in the past, when the gods walked among us, science had not yet evolved. Going back to that age might mean a complete wipe-out of everything we have here today. Think of it like a post-apocalyptic world with bows and arrows instead of nuclear missiles. A pre-industrial civilisation, like Vedic times. Similar to the aftermath of Ragnarok in the Norse myths. The earth cleansed. Bronze age settlements instead of cities. Small pockets of humans left behind to repopulate the earth.'

'I'm not seeing any scenario where I need to repopulate the earth as a bad thing,' began K with an amused look on his face.

Sars rolled her eyes. 'No Netflix. Or the internet. Horses as the main means of transport. Cold water baths in streams. Rubbing stones to make a fire. No restaurants, malls, taverns, bars, brothels, strip clubs ….'

'Aah, okay,' said K hurriedly. 'Got it.' He gave her a reproachful look. 'You really should have led with that.'

Shukra still didn't seem convinced. 'That's a very pessimistic way to imagine paradise.'

'It's actually the only way that makes sense. We don't unlearn technology unless there's a catastrophic system failure. With every new spin of the wheel, we've discovered or invented even more powerful weapons to destroy the world. If we are expecting a new Golden Age after the Age of Darkness, that's the most realistic possibility.'

'Like I said, that's one way to interpret it,' said Shukra, 'I doubt it would be that drastic. But even if it were so, I'm fairly certain we would survive. This isn't something we should get involved in.'

This was what I was worried about.

'Maybe nothing will come of it. Their ritual won't work, and everything will go back to the way things were. Or maybe it does work, and the world will be a better place if we let them succeed.'

Shukra nodded approvingly. 'Exactly what I was thinking. It's not a decision we have to make. We only need to sit back and do nothing.'

I shook my head. 'Sitting back and doing nothing is still a decision. We can choose to wash our hands off this whole affair but if we have a chance to stop it and we deliberately sit on the sidelines, we are we are making a choice. A choice to let these events unfold with every consequence that follows.'

Shukra made a non-committal sound. I ploughed on nevertheless.

'Maybe I could let this slide. I've never had any sort of affinity with humans. The whole world can go up in smoke tomorrow and I wouldn't shed any tears. Everyone I care about is already in this room.' I paused. 'There is only one problem.'

I made sure I looked at every single one of them as I spoke. 'These people plan to murder children to get their ritual to work. I don't care how much good this yagna might do. If it involves sacrificing a child, even a single one, then this has the taint of evil in it. I refuse to believe something like this would lead to a better world. And I for one, am not going to sit idly by when such an act is perpetrated, no matter how fucking wonderful the end result is.'

Nothing quite brought home the stark differences in who each of us was than to have them stare blankly at me after what I thought was the most eloquent speech I had made in a while. I seemed to be the only one taking this personally.

Sars, as mentioned earlier, was an aspect of a true goddess. She thought in terms of millennia, not centuries. Humans would die and more would be born. In the long run, it made no difference.

Deanne was not even of our realm. Psychopomps remain detached from the souls they guide to the afterlife. I did not expect her to get involved either.

K might crib and complain, but he was a survivor. He would find a hole and wait out whatever apocalypse took place. No matter who was ruling the coop, I knew K would find a cosy corner to hibernate in and pop out when things were right and rosy again. Shukra was once the guru to the Asuras. While he was warm and friendly towards me and our friends, his patience and empathy for humans was limited. He was used to making cold, rational decisions. If anything, he would be the hardest to convince.

What did it say about me that my closest friends in the world didn't get that this mattered?

After what felt like an eternity, K stirred. 'I agree with Akran about the children. I will not sit by and let this happen either.'

I released a tiny breath of relief I hadn't realised I was holding. Of course, he wouldn't. I had known him the longest.

Sars nodded slowly. 'You are right, Akran. The wisest course of action here is to nip this in the bud before it spreads.'

Deanne and Shukra both seemed to be on the fence. Shukra had this mulish look on his face. I knew what he was thinking. That I was being too emotional about the whole thing.

I could understand Deanne's reaction—we had only known her for a few weeks. Getting involved in a conflict with a bunch of celestials in another land wasn't what she had signed up for.

I didn't want to frighten them into helping me. I had hoped they would do so out of purely altruistic reasons, but I didn't have the time to persuade them. I played my final card.

'There is one other possibility that you all haven't considered. What if the ritual works, but it doesn't trigger the end of the Yuga?'

Deanne frowned. 'What do you mean?'

'We don't know if unleashing an evil on this world would necessarily activate the final avatar. For all we know, the avatar may still arise only at a pre-ordained time.'

'But if the ritual works,' Shukra said slowly as he saw my line of reasoning, 'we could be looking at a few thousand years or more of slavery under a demon.'

I was right. They hadn't considered it. It was, quite frankly, the worst possible scenario.

'What do you need from us?' Sars asked softly.

I turned to her. 'Somewhere in this city, they plan to raise a demon. I doubt it's going to be on a crowded street or even a backstreet alley. There'll be infrastructure set up for this, most likely to host the other kidnapped girls as well. Find out where the location is and who is pulling the strings. You can start with the warehouse. Find out who owns it and what other locations they own.'

Shukra's eyebrows furrowed in concentration. 'I would imagine the place of his death would be the best possible location to raise him. Modern-day Assam.'

'Not necessarily. Power congregates at the points where they have the largest number of devotees. All of the major metros would be far more potent locations. Given that they stashed the girls here, I would suspect it would be somewhere in Mumbai itself. Look for factories, mills, warehouses or even farmhouses. Any place with plenty of space within while being far away from traffic or any public roads.'

Sars nodded thoughtfully. 'I can write up something that will help narrow this down. Points, where ley lines intersect, might show other phenomena or signs that may not be obvious in isolation but might throw up patterns when studied at scale. Lusher fields, purer water streams….'

'Extra fertile chickens,' put in K helpfully.

Sars rolled her eyes. 'Yes, ok, maybe that too. Give me a few hours.'

I turned to Shukra, 'Set up another meeting with Virach. I shall give him the sword I have in return for just a few days with the jewel.'

'I'm not sure that's the best course of action,' Sars objected. 'Now that they know who you are, they will be looking for you. Just lie low for a few days, giving up the only protection you have is—'

'Foolish,' I agreed. 'I don't really have a choice though. I suspect it will disintegrate with one more use anyway, so at this point, it really is more of a collectable rather than an actual weapon.' I glanced at K. 'I have need for your special talents.' Watching him perk up, I added hastily, 'Not those. I mean your invisibility. Stick with me for a while. I'm going to paint a target on my back and see who comes to attack.'

'You know what I just realised,' K said suddenly. 'What you have is a Death-Star wish!'

Don't ask, don't ask, I beseeched the rest of them with my eyes. No possible good would come of asking.

'What's a Death-Star wish?' asked Sars innocently. Despite being the goddess of knowledge, she was often the naivest when it came to K's nonsense.

'You remember that scene in *A New Hope* where Luke Skywalker flies his X-wing into a trench full of blazing laser cannons and drops his proton torpedo into a tiny exhaust tube and blows up the whole thing?'

I was aware of the scene. I knew it backwards since K had made me and Sars watch the movie at least once every year on the 4th of May. We had even done the *Star Wars* sandwich and with nine movies, it took up most of the day. It was a good thing he didn't consider the new ones worth mentioning or watching.

'I know the scene!' I growled. 'What's your point?'

'That's what you want. You aren't looking to just die. That would be too pedestrian—you want to go out in a blaze of glory. Maybe against an enemy that is a hundred times stronger than you, and even when you are completely outclassed, outmatched and utterly useless against them, you are hoping you will somehow pluck one final proton torpedo out of your ass and blow the whole thing sky high!'

Credit to K, he wasn't wrong. I just wasn't going to tell him that or he would be insufferable for the next hundred years.

'What are you trying to say? That it's too dangerous?'

K's face split into a wide grin. 'Heck, no! I love Death-Star wishes. Let's go and blow some shit up!'

With that out of the way, I could now tie up the final pending issue.

'Deanne,' I said, 'our lives really aren't as chaotic as this. Usually, we aren't embroiled neck-deep in people trying to kill me or whatever.'

Her eyes sparkled. 'Are you kidding? This is the most fun I've had in ages. Kidnappings, attempted murders. Foreshadowing for a big dramatic battle.' She gave a wolfish predatorial grin. 'I will gladly lend my sword to this cause.'

I hesitated, wondering how to put this across delicately. I didn't know much about her except that she was good-looking and we enjoyed her company. She had a fascination for Indian myths, and given that we had lived through most of them, when she was around, we usually did most of the talking. We did trust her, just not enough to put her on the front lines in a shadow war that was about to erupt into raging violence.

'Um, maybe you should sit this one out?' I spoke carefully, hoping she wouldn't take offence. I didn't really think I was being unreasonable here. What's wrong with wanting to protect your potential girlfriend from a battle with the bad guys? She should be delighted that I cared so much about her.

Right?

It turns out, that despite being alive for thousands of years, I knew very little about women.

The temperature in the room dropped by a few degrees. Her face darkened. 'Why?'

Thin ice, Akran, my man. Very thin ice.

'Um... I-I thought you would prefer to s-stay safe?' I bit my tongue. It sounded even worse when I said it out loud.

Because I'm a woman? Her voice had lost its normal cadence and taken on an icy tone. Even her eyes had turned flinty as she spoke.

I knew in this case, what the wrong answer to that question was.

'Of course, not,' I stammered, pouring as much sincerity into my voice as I could. 'I would never imply that ..that...'

Deanne stepped closer. There was something sleek and dangerous about the way she uncoiled as she came forward. With almost deliberate slowness, she stepped closer, until she was less than an inch away, daring me to pick a fight.

'Are all you Yakshas really this misogynistic?' she said softly, her words somehow even more menacing when she spoke in a lower timbre.

I did expect us to be up close and in each other's personal space. Just not in this manner.

K made a loud snickering sound like a cartoon dog I had once seen. You could always count on him finding a way to make things worse.

Shukra looked amused as well though he had the grace to stare at his feet, refusing to get involved. Sars was the only one kind enough to not make fun of my predicament. She gave me a disappointed look like I had failed some sort of test. There was also a bright shiny intensity in her eyes.

I knew that look. There was something there, some clue that was blindingly obvious and right in front of us the whole time that I had overlooked. There is a fine line between what sounds chivalrous in your head and what comes out of your mouth. Particularly when you are dealing with strong, confident warrior women.

This was what came from not taking the time to get to know her enough. Furiously, I ran through every topic of conversation over the past few days. She had mentioned how her role was in guiding souls once they depart this realm to the next. I had assumed because of her name; she was an Etruscan psychopomp. I had also assumed that I sounded gallant when clearly, I was being a jackass.

I asked her to sit this one out when she offered me her sword and that annoyed her.

The sword.

Why would a psychopomp need a sword anyway?

It struck me then.

I was a fool. I should have known what she was.

'I apologise, Deanne,' I spoke formally and humbly, my right fist enclosed within the palm of my left hand, a traditional gesture of respect among warriors I had known.

She glared at me, expectant, waiting. Given the enormous power most celestials wield, there are a great number of protocols and rituals for every kind of encounter, engagement or interaction between us. An apology usually required suitable abasement and gifts to soothe wounded pride. A half-assed 'oops' from my end wouldn't cut it.

'I intended no disrespect. It was out of misplaced concern. If you wish to join us, we would be delighted to have a warrior of your calibre in our midst.'

She looked mollified. A slight smile played on her lips. 'A wise decision,' she murmured.

I had hoped this embarrassing little moment was over and we could put it behind us, but Deanne wasn't done yet. She leaned forward and put her lips to my ear. 'Among my people, rejecting an offered sword is a terrible insult.' Her voice was sharp as a blade. 'And insulting my honour would leave me no choice but to fight you right here and right now.'

I nodded warily. Message received.

Sars broke the awkward silence that followed. 'Deanne,' she said sweetly, in a voice I recognised all too well. It was the one she used when asking questions she already knew the answers to.

'That place that you would guide souls to, what was it called again?'

Deanne erupted into a deep, throaty and full-bodied laugh.

'Valhalla.'

CHAPTER NINE

While it sounds harsh to blame the mother for the faults of her children, it does seem like Gandhari deserves some of it. The sane thing to do when finding out your spouse is blind would be to support him through the use of your perfectly functioning eyes.

If you are really pissed, give him the cold shoulder, tell him you have a headache every time he is feeling amorous, sigh deeply and tell him, 'I'm fine' when you are clearly not. Maybe even re-arrange the furniture.

She chose instead to blind herself – which has got to be the stupidest way to demonstrate love or passive aggressive behaviour.

Granted, a hundred children born simultaneously meant someone would get the short end of the stick. After all, you could only throw about twenty of them in the air before your arms started to hurt.

But having both parents sightless? That deprived them of any meaningful relationship with their kids. Having two

> *blind parents, one by choice, one by stupidity, played a role in shaping the Kauravas into insecure brats as kids and sociopaths when they grew up.*
>
> *Honestly, if there's one thing, we can learn from Gandhari, it's that love may be blind, but deliberately keeping yourself in the dark makes things a lot worse*
>
> – Private Journals of Akran

I spent another miserable night with a dream full of painful fragmented memories about the past. I had naively entertained the hope that rescuing the girls might have cut me some slack—that the Universe would ease off on the constant stream of unpleasant memories like a leaky drip faucet.

No such luck. The dreams were as vivid as ever. I tossed and turned until four a.m. and when I finally fell asleep, the buzz of the intercom sounded like it had just gone off.

Blearily, I checked the time. It was already nine a.m.

I pressed the button to let Shukra and K in, as I poured myself a cup of scalding hot coffee, one of the mortal world's few comforts.

K walked in, sporting his usual cheerful look. He smelt like he had been pimping himself out in a perfume factory. He gave me an expectant look but I ignored him. He would gladly tell me stories of his sexcapades if I indicated even the tiniest bit of interest. I had decided long ago that I didn't want to know.

My eyes were bloodshot from lack of sleep. If you live on the mortal plane long enough, you experience all of their frailties. The need to sleep and eat, to incessantly grumble about the government—even the occasional need for intimacy, though that I could manage by myself.

Shukra looked like he hadn't slept well either.

'Virach called. He wants to set up a meeting. Says he can give you the jewel.'

'That's good. What time and where?'

'No, you don't get it. I didn't call him. He contacted me.'

A moment of silent understanding passed between us. Neither of us had lived this long without good instincts. It's only paranoia if they are really not after you.

'It's got to be a trap,' said Shukra.

'I wouldn't dismiss that possibility.'

'But you are still planning on going, aren't you?'

'If there is a chance to keep the jewel away from them, I'm going to have to take it.'

'You managed to take all that other stuff from the vault. That should slow them down. Why does the jewel still matter?'

I grimaced. 'I'm guessing every little bit helps. Narakasura was killed a long time ago. Bringing him back requires a lot of effort. Every little thing that ties into the legend and to him will help.' Besides, none of the other items in that vault are directly connected to him. For a successful resurrection, you need items related to him or the people around him when he was killed. In this particular case, there are only three points to the triangle. Krishna, Satyabhama and Narakasura himself.'

Shukra nodded, listening intently.

'We don't have any belongings of Narakasura. We have next to nothing of Krishna's belongings as well after all these years,' I said. Most of his worldly possessions sank, along with Dwarka, under the ocean. 'The jewel, however, is connected to both Krishna and Satyabhama.'

'I never heard her name in association with the jewel before,' Shukra observed.

'She was the daughter of King Satrajit, which meant she did spend time with the jewel. When Satrajit gave his daughter's hand for marriage to Krishna, he offered the jewel to him but Krishna declined.

'Another thing, and this is more interesting, Satyabhama had another link with Narakasura. She was an incarnation of Bhumi Devi.'

Shukra gave me a blank look.

'Bhumi Devi, the original, not the incarnation, was the mother of Narakasura. This familial bond is why she granted him the boon of being remembered every year on his death.'

He snorted. 'They do have complicated family trees, don't they?' He grew contemplative for a moment.

We had been friends for a long time, but everyone had skeletons in their closet. There are some topics we didn't talk about out of respect for each other's personal demons.

For Shukra, the moment had finally arrived. I couldn't put it off any longer.

'I need to ask you something. The Sanjivani mantra, it can bring someone back to life, yes?'

Shukra gave me a wary nod.

'Anyone else knows how to use it?'

A shadow passed across his face. 'The hymn was a secret. There is nobody else besides me who knows it at present.'

'They will need the mantra, or something like it, to serve as a binding when resurrecting Narakasura.'

'There is nobody else out there who knows the mantra,' repeated Shukra firmly. 'Anyone who did has either forgotten it or is now dead.'

Dead is good. But forgotten? That could be a problem.

'Among the many abilities of the gem is an obscure one that Krishna once told me about. It's supposed to provide clarity of mind. I'm not sure what that means. Could it be that if someone knew the hymn once, it could help them recall it again?'

Shukra looked sceptical. 'I have no idea what is and isn't possible with a magical gem. In theory, yes. It still requires an enormous amount of power. Maybe a sage who has been doing penance for over a thousand years could conceivably pull something like that off. There aren't that many of us left who might be able to wield the gem in this fashion.'

'I don't know enough about the jewel. But I have another theory about it,' I continued.

Shukra shot me a quizzical look.

'Satrajit's brother died while wearing the gemstone. He was killed by a lion while on a hunt. The lion died at the hands of Jambavan. Jambavan lived because he was a semi-immortal, a Chiranjivi, but I have no doubt that if he were anyone else, he would have met a similar fate at the hands of Krishna.

Satrajit was killed by robbers seeking to steal the stone. Kritavarma who was one of the robbers was killed by Satyaki. Krishna got the stone and was killed by the hunter. We already know what happened to Dwarka.'

'Yes, you obviously don't know enough about the jewel,' Shukra said dryly.

'You are missing the point. Every single person who came in contact with the gem died before their time. The bodies just kept piling up and nobody noticed because they were too focused on the jewel I don't think it is a wonderous magical item at all. It represents the greed of humankind. Surya gave it to Satrajit to teach him a lesson. For daring to reach for something so far above his station. Maybe it does create gold out of thin air, and everything else it claims. But for all its fabled magic, I'm convinced the stone is cursed.' I paused as something struck me. 'I just remembered. That annoying little prick, Samba? The one who made this whole mess by teasing the sages? He's the son of Jambavati—the bear that Krishna married and whose hand he received in marriage because of the jewel. Maybe that was another way in which the curse manifested. And ultimately destroyed Dwarka in the process.'

Shukra nodded grimly. 'A cursed jewel might also make an attractive lodestone when calling the soul of a demon. How tough do you think Narakasura will be?'

'Reincarnated? No clue! This is not something I've ever dealt with before. But the last time he and Krishna fought, he was a major threat. He was able to knock Krishna unconscious in combat. I know of no other demon who has ever done that. Krishna was only saved thanks to the interference of Satyabhama, who picked up Krishna's bow and arrows and fought him off.'

'Not a battle I would expect you to be fighting. This is out of your league,' Shukra said quietly.

'Perhaps. But nobody else seems to be stepping up to get involved.'

I shook my head. 'If we all stand back and wait for someone else to take action, nothing will ever get done.'

'You realise how you sound? Like nobody else can stop this from happening. The responsibility for saving the world doesn't lie only on your shoulders. You sound like a ... a ...'

'Yaksha?' I asked raising an eyebrow.

He raised a hand to forestall any protests on my part. 'I'm not saying you are being arrogant. Although knowing you, it might apply…' He trailed off as I glared at him before continuing.

'This is reckless. You've killed one celestial already which means the next time, they won't take you so lightly. There are, at least three more of them involved. You only escaped through sheer luck. Without your mana, you don't have a chance!'

'I am afraid, Shukra,' I admitted. 'In fact, I've never been as afraid. I had been away for so long that I forgot what it was like fighting a celestial without mana. I actually thought I could beat them for one instant before I was knocked out. What you are saying is definitely the sensible thing to do. But…'

Shukra scowled. 'Has anyone ever told you when the next word out of your mouth is "but", you've negated everything you said until that point?'

'But,' I repeated. 'Doing the sensible thing can only get you so far. Look at the humans we live with. Every story they revere, every action of theirs is guided by emotion. Their greatest acts of heroism have always been when they chose to follow their hearts instead of their heads.'

'That can be said about their greatest acts of stupidity as well,' Shukra pointed out.

I shrugged. 'I vowed a long time ago never to give in to my fears. Mas suggested that I fake my own death back then. But even at my lowest ebb, I knew I couldn't do it. I want to go out being true to who I am. To do what my conscience tells me is worth standing up and fighting for.'

'It's also what's going to kill you.'

'Death comes for us all and if this is my time, then so be it. Saving a child from whatever evil they are planning? That's a good death no matter how you look at it.' I gave him what I hoped looked like a confident smile. 'Besides, despite the frikkin' odds, I did win. So maybe I was meant to do this. The big difference is I'm not going about this alone. I've got you guys with me this time.'

Shukra sighed heavily. 'If I can't change your mind, then let me help you improve the odds.' He handed me a small black device with a chrome finish.

I looked at it curiously. It looked like a child's water pistol though it was too well-crafted to be something so mundane. It fit snugly into my gloved hand, and its aesthetics appealed to my sense of style.

'What is it?'

'A gift from Mas. It's meant to be like a human weapon—you point and shoot at any one trying to kill you. He described it as a fusion of human ingenuity and celestial magic. He told me to give it to you in case I thought you were about to do something stupid.'

Mas was forever tinkering with human gadgets trying to make them better. Of all of us, he was the one who appreciated human technology the most.

'Why didn't he just give it to me?

'He was afraid, having it would tempt you to go out and do the stupid thing you aren't supposed to do. Just remember, you may only get one shot with it before it needs to be recharged, so make it count.'

I nodded. 'I will.' Placing it on my dresser table, I shook his hand. 'Thanks again.'

'I'll be at the café. Good luck, my friend.'

K entered the room all scrubbed and clean. He had been busy in the kitchen, making himself a plate loaded with cheese sandwiches and green chutney and was wolfing them down as he spoke. 'I'll take care of him. Don't worry.'

Shukra was almost out the door when he turned back suddenly. 'I forgot to tell you. Sars identified who the warehouse belonged to. Andor & Sons Shipping. It is a large multinational conglomerate. They deal in shipping and logistics.'

The name sounded familiar.

'The name sounds like a board game. Where have I heard of them before?'

'There is a board game "Legends of Andor" that we have played but this has nothing to do with them. These guys are the ones who won the bidding contract from the Indian government a few years ago for excavating the ruins of Dwarka. From what I understand, theirs was the lowest bid by a large margin.'

It was too much of a coincidence for them to be connected to Dwarka. They were definitely involved in what was going on.

'Find out who owns the company. And let me know if we can find any other places owned by them.'

'Sars is working on it. They have multiple shell companies and a pretty tangled web of financial transactions. She'll keep me posted.'

K and I waved him goodbye and left. And without realising what a terrible mistake we were making, we let him go back, alone and unguarded.

INTERLUDE TWO

*T*here were three primary codes of conduct, or neeti, as defined in the scriptures. The Brihaspati Neeti said that in order to achieve an honourable end, the means must also be honourable. 'Fight fair, do it with class', that kind of thing. The first ten days of the war under Bhishma were fought abiding by this code of conduct. An example of this was how a group of warriors could not gang up to attack a single warrior, or how the battle would end at sunset and could not resume until daybreak.

The Shukra Neeti could be summed up as, 'Forget honour, just get it done!' This was the Wild West of moral codes, where the means didn't matter as long as the end goal was worth striving for.

The Kanika Neeti said that if you have an enemy, use any means at your disposal to defeat him. Your neighbour's dog is pooping on your lawn? Kill the dog, burn his lawn, call him an anti-national, maybe even stab your neighbour a few times for good measure.

Shukra Neeti was frowned upon, but you could still justify the results to yourself and others. Kanika Neeti, on the other hand? That was a 'scorch the earth, burn the bridges and take no prisoners' policy with long-term consequences that you couldn't walk away from.

The next time you're in a sticky situation, ask yourself: What would Brihaspati do? Or maybe Shukra? Just ... maybe not Kanika.

– Private Journals of Akran

1361 BCE

I should address the elephant in the room—the true story of the Mahabharata and the role I played in the events that occurred all those years ago.

The voluminous epic has been described by a lot of people in a lot of different ways. As a dynastic struggle, a battle of good vs evil, a story of greed and empire building. But at its core, a lot of people believe that it was a war for justice. Of young, honest, upright Kuru princes being pushed around by big bad bullies until they pushed back. Of the underdogs triumphing against impossible odds. And how, ultimately, those who stuck to the path of righteousness defeated those who did not.

Meh. Not really.

The story was a classic example of sibling rivalries extending too far. And also, a shining example of why history needs to be written by a neutral third party instead of the victors. Today, we have unambiguously assigned the Pandavas as the heroes and the Kauravas as the villains of the epic, though things were not so black and white back then, and for many centuries after.

As someone who lived through the entire saga and had no active stake in either side, here were my two copper pieces.

It all started with Kunti, a Yadava princess.

Kunti had been a gracious host to a wandering sage named Durvasa. Pleased with her devotion, he taught her a magical hymn that could be used to invoke any god to 'bless her' with a child. It goes without saying that dishing out boons like that to a teenager wasn't a smart idea.

Curious whether the boon would work, she invoked Surya, the sun god, who gladly rose to the occasion. 'Consent' was still an evolving concept at the time, so once the god appeared, she couldn't leave him hanging.

It turned out that sex with a god was divine in more ways than one. Once Surya was done illuminating places where the sun didn't shine, a baby appeared. With a couple of magical gifts to assuage his guilt for the upheaval he was going to cause in her life, Surya wrapped his shiny bits and made a hasty exit.

Kunti was still unmarried at the time, and even in those days, people frowned upon such dalliances. To hide the shame of being an unwed mother, she placed the baby in a basket and set it afloat down the river, where it was found by a charioteer.

Does this story sound familiar? It should. The tale of a child floating down a river in a basket is also told as the story of Moses in the Nile, Sargon of Akkad in the Euphrates, Romulus and Remus in the river Tiber, Taliesin in Celtic folktales and, in its most recent incarnation, the story of Superman. It is one of the most familiar routes to claim divinity—mysterious origins, incredible luck and a cosmic destiny that allows the kid to survive and ultimately realise their greatness.

But I digress. A couple of decades later, in nearby Hastinapur, the mighty Kuru dynasty was about to face its greatest crisis.

The king had passed away. Dhritarashtra, the crown prince, was the rightful heir by virtue of being the eldest son, but he was born blind and hence deemed unfit to rule. His younger half-brother Pandu thus inherited the throne. Pandu's queen was none other than Kunti, the Yadava princess with impulse-control issues.

One day, while hunting, Pandu shot an arrow at a sage in the throes of lovemaking. In his defence, he thought it was a particularly randy deer. Getting confused between people and deer seemed to happen a lot in that era. A few decades later, the exact same thing would happen again with a hunter mistaking Krishna's foot for a deer and shooting an arrow through it.

Some accounts suggest that Pandu got confused because the sage in question had a fetish for deer and was either dressed as one or having sex with an actual deer. Regardless, it was the last time Pandu assaulted anyone with a loaded weapon, friendly or otherwise.

Furious at the interruption, the sage cursed Pandu. If he ever slept with a woman, the sage decreed, he would immediately kick the bucket.

It left Pandu with a rather stiff … predicament.

The sage could have ended his curse with 'No hard feelings,' but that would have been a lie. Pandu would have literally nothing else for the next couple of years.

One of the few pleasures kings had in those days that took away from the tedium of administering a kingdom, was the vigorous lovemaking they could indulge in. Being a king, there was no potential shortage of willing bedmates, but now this was no longer an option. Hunting was also another favoured pastime but he had already proven that he couldn't even distinguish between a deer and a man. *'If I cannot get laid, I will pursue a life of austerity and meditation,'* seemed like a perfectly reasonable reaction at the time. Certainly, no mention has been made of it being seen as too extreme.

Renouncing his kingdom made Dhritarashtra, the elder but blind prince, the king.

At this point in time, Pandu was effectively written out of the succession. The Kuru line, already shaky because of a prior incident involving a fisherwoman and a couple of terrible oaths by the rightful claimant, Bhishma, was on its last legs.

It was then that Kunti revealed she knew a magic hymn that was a wonderful solution to their problems. Almost as if the fates had conspired to bring this perfectly planned sequence of events into place.

Kunti used her magical hymn to deliver three kids—Yudhishthir, Bhim and Arjun—through a prevalent practice called Niyoga, whereby a widow could sire a child through a male relative. Kunti wasn't a widow at the time, but the circumstances were unusual enough that an exception was made. She claimed that all three sons were sired by gods, and as any student of history knows, a link to divinity never hurts a royal succession claim. Everyone, from Roman emperors to Egyptian pharaohs, have claimed to have divinity in their ancestry.

Of her three offspring, Yudhishthir was the son of Yama, the god of death and dharma; Bhim was the son of the wind god, Vayu and Arjun was the son of Indra, the god of thunder and also the king of the gods.

On Pandu's request, Kunti also taught the hymn to his second wife, Madri, who soon delivered twin sons, fathered by the twin Ashwini Kumaras. These five children of Pandu collectively were known as the Pandavas. Mark their names well, for this story really is all about them. Everything before this was just background noise.

Despite his good intentions, Pandu was unable to keep it in his pants. Long story short, he got handsy with Madri; one thing led to another, and soon, Madri and Kunti became widows.

'Probably realising at this point that her part in this story was merely as babymaker (and not even very important babies in the larger scheme of things), Madri decided to exit stage left. In my personal opinion, a very irresponsible thing to do when you have kids.

Inch for inch, a burn is the most painful form of injury one can inflict upon oneself. Despite numerous other available options available in the forest including hanging, drowning, being eaten by wild animals, stabbing and poison, Madri decided to go out with a bang and immolate herself.

Around the same time, Dhritarashtra's wife, Gandhari, bore a hundred sons, collectively known as the Kauravas. Yudhishthir, the eldest of the Pandavas, was older than Duryodhan, the eldest of the Kauravas.

And now, we arrive at the billion-gold-mohur question. Who would inherit the throne?

A case could be made that the Pandavas had a claim to the throne as the sons of the rightful king since Dhritarashtra was the regent. But there's something very important to keep in mind. Namely, they were *not* Pandu's sons.

By her own admission, Kunti's kids were the children of Yama, Vayu and Indra. Most people accept this as true today. We also know that through the ages, many women have claimed their children were birthed by gods. One such case (involving a divine birth and a virgin mother), has even become the cornerstone of a massive religion encompassing more than half the world!

Claiming your kids are semi-divine beings to woo the ignorant populace is relatively easy. Also claiming that they are the sons of Pandu … and hence deserve the throne was a bit harder to swallow. The circumstances around the succession were nuanced enough that either side could bring valid arguments to the table. From Yudhishthir's point of view, Dhritarashtra was never the king, which meant that his son should not inherit the throne.

However, it was also true that when Pandu handed over the reins of the kingdom to his brother, he was childless and had no expectation of being able to make any kids, thanks to the sage's curse. It was only after he became an ascetic that Kunti revealed to him that she had a convenient little boon that allowed her to sire kids from any of the gods. From a succession standpoint, Pandu had thus effectively written himself out of the story until the Pandavas inserted themselves back in.

To muddy the waters even further, there was not a single shred of corroborating evidence that Yudhishthir was older than Duryodhan. Dead men tell no tales and at this point, each and every witness was conveniently out of the picture.

Pandu? Dead as a doornail.

Madri? More gruesome but similar fate.

Sage who loved deer a little too literally? Also dead!

Deer who was the object of the sage's affection? Could be alive but not really a great witness.

Kunti was the only one whose word they could take, and she had a vested interest in propping her son as the heir. The magical hymn that summons gods? Nobody had even heard of it before Pandu and his wives went to play 'Tarzan and Jane' in the woods.

And that was essentially the crux of the disagreement. Exacerbated by jealousy, vindictive insults, an impossibly melodramatic game of dice, a humiliated wife, multiple attempted murders and a whole host of other nasty actions, the original dispute finally became a full-blown war. The Kuru empire had many vassal states and allies as well as a fair share of enemies, all of whom joined the battle. It lasted eighteen days, killed hundreds of thousands of soldiers and redrew the geographic and political maps of ancient India.

It's not like people didn't expect this to happen. Anyone with half a brain could have seen, given the animosity between the cousins since childhood, that war was inevitable. Dhritarashtra attempted what he thought was a fair and equitable solution by splitting the kingdom equally between both sets of princes, only to have the Pandavas stake their kingdom, wife and freedom on a game of dice. At this point in time, it looked like the Pandavas didn't even deserve the throne.

Or maybe, keeping how these stories have been retold over time, the narrative was designed to make their redemption arc all that more impressive. The Pandavas returned from exile, refreshed, rejuvenated and ready to fight. They had acquired magical weapons, made new allies and gone through heroic transformation arcs so epic that even Joseph Campbell would've traded his monomyth for a front-row seat and some popcorn.

Yudhishthir made a final appeal to Duryodhan to let him have five villages to rule. This offer was also rejected.

While some may have called Duryodhan a dumbass for not granting the five villages as requested, he was fully in his rights to refuse them. Besides, if he did give the Pandavas five villages, it would legitimise their claim further. The Pandavas were a popular bunch. They said all the right things in public, made obeisance to the sages and were friends with Krishna. They also had a very powerful public relations campaign going that they were the sons of gods. So, while jealousy, hatred and anger certainly influenced Duryodhan's actions, he also made the rational decision to go to war right away rather than wait for their supporters to swell.

To fight against the mighty army of Hastinapur, aka Duryodhan's army, the Pandavas needed external help. The Mahabharata details the army compositions and troops on both sides. The Kauravas had twelve divisions. The Pandavas had seven. Those seven divisions were all external kingdoms—Magadha, Virata and even Hastinapur's greatest enemy, Panchala. So, despite the Pandavas being loved by the people, it was not a civil war. It was a full-fledged invasion by the Pandavas attacking the kingdom of Hastinapur using a coalition of foreign armies. The Pandavas also had a very powerful ace in their hole. Krishna, nephew of Kunti and Avatar of Vishnu, supported them. He chose not to fight but instead serve as Arjun's charioteer. The honourable grandsire Bhishma and the wise sage Dronacharya fought on the side of Duryodhan to defend Hastinapur from the invading forces of the Pandavas. Both of them had, at different points in time, expressed their feelings of support for the Pandavas and hopes for their success. Yet when it came to following the letter of the law, both men chose to support Duryodhan. That, if nothing else, should show who had the stronger claim to the throne.

To be clear at this point, the Kauravas were no saints either. There are several incidents that show them in a terrible light. But the narrative that eventually emerged later after the war, that this was a war of good vs evil, i.e. a dharma *yuddha*, is not an accurate representation of what happened. A better way to think about the Mahabharata is like a crisis where each person's adherence to dharma was put to the test. As we know from the story, very few people stayed on the narrow dharmic path when faced with a difficult choice.

Now, remember that baby in the basket? His name was Karna, and he was a friend of Duryodhan's and fought on his side during the war. Of course, he had no idea he was

Kunti's son and thus the eldest brother of the Pandavas. He found out on the eve of the battle when his mother told him, but by then, it was too late. Duryodhan had treated Karna honourably when no one else would and raised his status by making him a prince of the Angas. In contrast, the Pandavas had been dicks to him, Bhim, in particular, because he believed that Karna was the son of a charioteer.

Karna could have been the compromise candidate everyone would accept—the eldest of the Pandavas and a close friend of Duryodhan. Alas, the Pandavas only found out the truth at the end of the battle, after Duryodhan had died. Although upset that his mother had kept this a secret from him, Yudhishthir decided it wasn't really her fault. The entire female gender was to blame. He thus cursed them that henceforth, women would never be able to keep a secret. Feels like a dick move to me, particularly since he is seen as a beacon of good morals and justice—but what passes for wisdom among humans is as perplexing to me now as it was then.

As for the Pandavas' claim of righteousness? Well, that, too, was a little problematic. Many of the Pandavas' actions were a bit dubious—not just by today's standards; even at that time. Yudhishthir gambling away his kingdom in a game of dice and staking Draupadi in a last-ditch attempt to win it all back, Arjun slaughtering the Nagas in the Dandaka forest, Bhim abandoning his wife Hidimba, Arjun sharing his wife Draupadi with the rest of his brothers, collectively judging Karna and Ekalavya because of their caste. The list goes on and on. And these were just their actions before the war.

It got progressively worse. Each of the leading Kaurava commanders was killed in a dishonourable fashion. Bhishma was killed by Arjun as he hid behind Shikhandi, because it was known that Bhishma would never attack a woman. Drona was killed after he was tricked into laying his weapons down, even though the Kshatriya code forbade the killing of an unarmed man. Karna was killed by Arjun while fixing the wheel of his chariot. When the Pandavas finally cornered Duryodhan and offered him single combat, he chose Bhim, the only Pandava whose skill with the mace was equal to his own. Bhim won the fight by striking Duryodhan on his thigh, which was against the rules of mace fighting.

None of the Pandavas' victories could thus be described as honourable. You might argue that these tactics were necessary, but neither side can claim the moral high ground here. It was war, and both sides wanted victory—whatever the cost may be.

Why am I reminiscing about this now, after all these years?

Maybe it has to do with the items in the safe. Or my whole interaction with Varunn. Or because I can't help feeling what's happening now is somehow connected to the past.

Or maybe I still feel guilty for my role in what happened back then.

– Private Journals of Akran

CHAPTER TEN

Once upon a time, the Pandavas lost their kingdom, themselves and their polyandrous wife in a game of dice. The Kauravas decided to publicly strip Draupadi as she was now their slave and couldn't object to their version of a gender reveal party.

Seeing her five husbands impotent and helpless, Draupadi prays to Krishna to protect her. Instead of smiting the villains down, Krishna decides to cover her with endless layers of clothing, thus frustrating the voyeurs in the hall and giving the entire episode a PG rating at best.

Draupadi then curses the Kauravas. Her curse is accompanied by meteors, flashes of lightning, a solar eclipse, a minor earthquake and the howling of jackals, vultures and, inexplicably, ravens as well.

The sound-and-light show terrifies Dhritarashtra, who returns the Pandavas' possessions. A fragile peace is restored until they are invited for a second game of dice, in which they lose once again and are sent into exile for thirteen years.

There's only one problem with this fantastical tale.
It never happened.

There was no single original text for the Mahabharata. Nothing survives over two thousand years without going through substantial edits and retellings. Somewhere along the way, an aspiring poet seeking to make a name for himself decided that the animosity between the siblings was too flat—they needed a more visceral hatred between both parties. A highly charged incident that will serve as a character-defining moment for everyone involved. Hence, the first game of dice with all the hair pulling, thigh slapping, oaths involving blood drinking and said thighs breaking, stripping the 'smoking hot' princess, magical clothing etc—all very melodramatic but extremely unlikely to have happened.

Don't believe me? Look at the evidence. The people themselves. Every person's behaviour in that hall is a sharp contrast to how their characters are portrayed in the rest of the epic. Karna is the epitome of virtue throughout the story—but here he acts like a dick. Duryodhan is jealous of the Pandavas and clearly the villain, but except for this incident, there is not a single instance of him molesting a woman or even being disrespectful to them in any way throughout the rest of the epic. Bhishma is renowned for his wisdom, virtue and strength of character, yet here he sits silent, without making even a token protest.

Secondly, would such blatant disrespect to a daughter of their household be something the Kuru dynasty could afford to allow? Draupadi and the Pandavas were visiting guests in Hastinapur, protected by the laws of hospitality. The people in the hall were all of the Kshatriya class—sworn to uphold and protect those weaker than them. A public humiliation of Draupadi would do more harm to Duryodhan than good. Kings depend on the goodwill of their populace. It would *be different if any of the rulers in the epic were portrayed as tyrants, but almost every one of those present in the hall during that fateful dice game is seen as a chivalrous warrior outside of this one scene.*

Keep in mind, she wasn't a nobody. Draupadi was the princess of Panchala, arguably the most powerful kingdom in ancient India after Hastinapura. Panchala had already defeated the Kaurava incursion once and was a semi-hostile neighbour, thanks to part of its kingdom having been annexed. Stripping the Panchala king's daughter and humiliating her husbands – the only warriors who were able to defeat Panchala in the first place adds another layer of incredulity to the tale.

And then we come to the Pandavas. Are they all really such dumbasses that after losing the first dice game, they meekly go back home, and when invited a second time, they accept the invitation again? How colossally stupid would they have to be to do this?

The only way this narrative makes sense is if the first dice game never happened. It was inserted later to shape the theme of the Kauravas as villainous monsters and the Pandavas as the underdogs.

Here's something else to think about. Throughout the epic, Yudhishthir comes across as the most sanctimonious, holier-than-thou preacher in all the land. Would someone so attuned to dharma and duty put up his brothers and their wife as collateral on a dice game? Himself, possibly, maybe even his brothers, given that they were fairly spineless when it came to questioning their mother or eldest brother. But tossing their wife in there like a stack of poker chips—especially without her consent—not only did that go against any sense of justice, it was also plain stupidity.

It's been argued that Yudhishthir's belief in dharma made him naïve. Even if that were true, here are some of the ways in which Draupadi is described by the people of that era.

> *'Of deep, plump and graceful breasts.'*
>
> *'Of beautiful, well-developed and well-rounded bosoms without any space between them.'*
>
> *'Slender-waisted like a wasp with thighs fair and round.'*
>
> *Even ignoring the weirdness of comparing someone's waist with that of a wasp, it's evident Draupadi was like the Kim Kardashian of the ancient world. Someone who as intelligence goes, might have been head and shoulders above the rest of the Kuru clan but nobody paid attention to anything above her shoulders. Yudhishthir, for all his faults, wasn't an idiot. He should have known that the Kauravas weren't urging him to put Draupadi on the block because they admired her mind.*
>
> *The most compelling evidence of all? Draupadi praying to Krishna to save her. Krishna was not worshipped as a god during the time of the Mahabharata. If people knew he was a god, both sides would be tripping over themselves to not go against his wishes. Why would anyone want to risk battle when you have a god batting for the other team?*
>
> *Krishna being worshipped as a god is first referenced nearly seven hundred years later in a treatise on grammar called the Panini Ashthadyayi. Prior to this, in the sixth century BC, he was revered as a wise sage and preacher (referenced in the Chhandogya Upanishad) but divinity wasn't ascribed to him.*
>
> *Of course, I knew he was a god back then as well. But hardly anybody else did.*
>
> — Private Journals of Akran

The meeting with Virach was to take place at his house, a palatial mansion on Malabar Hill. Every instinct I had strongly advised me to walk away from this invite. It was too damn convenient.

I am not a suspicious person by nature but … actually, who the fuck was I kidding? I didn't trust anyone. You don't live for so many centuries by inviting people to your abode after meeting them once. Ergo, he needed a quiet spot to have me killed or captured.

Well, that was fine. I had my own secret weapon.

'You are still carrying your little bow and arrow, aren't you?' I asked without turning around. K had gone invisible, but I could feel him looming behind me like a large shadow.

He gave a snort of disgust. 'It was never a little bow. It was a longbow. A little bow is what that silly Greek fellow in a diaper used to use.'

'Fine, whatever. Are you carrying it now?'

'Of course not, I've moved ahead with the times. I'm carrying a crossbow now.'

There were quite a few choice replies I could make, mainly that a crossbow qualified as a little bow and that using one did not mean he had moved ahead with the times. I settled for rolling my eyes. K could be a sulky bitch if he felt insulted. I already had more than enough drama in my life.

'What happened with Deanne after I left?'

He grinned. 'She told us a few stories about her life as a Valkyrie. Judging from her stories, you were lucky she didn't disembowel you for insulting her.'

I nodded sheepishly. The first thing I did after I got home the previous evening was search for information about Valkyries. They were the shield maidens of Odin himself. Fearsome warriors who revelled in bloodshed and battle, and who were also responsible for guiding the souls of fallen warriors to the feast halls of Valhalla.

From what I had learnt, some of these old-world pantheons consisted of fewer gods with a lot more domains under their purview. That made them batshit scary and powerful if you ever crossed them. Freyja, for instance, was a Norse goddess of beauty, sexuality and fertility, but she was also the goddess of sorcery, war, wealth and death. Not to mention, she rode in a chariot pulled by cats.

'Did she say what she was doing this evening?'

'She said something about putting on her armour.' He smirked. 'Do you think it will take her as long as it normally takes women to put on make-up?'

I ignored him. I was too busy worrying about my safety to get distracted by his brand of humour. Hastily, I did another quick check of my possessions. A half-useless sword on my back? Check. Insulated gloves and boots? Check. Sense of impending doom and bone-crushing pessimism? Check.

Yup, I was ready.

'Alright, K, this is it. Any last questions?'

K had a thoughtful look on his face. 'Actually, I was wondering about something.' He briefly launched into a description of an elaborate battle scene from a show he had just watched and how the protagonist narrowly escaped by the skin of his teeth.

I counted to five before I spoke again.

'K, I meant did you have any questions about the meeting with Virach?'

'Oh, that! No, I'm good.'

I sighed. 'Okay, what is your question about this random scene that you saw on television and felt was important enough to bring up at this time?'

K grinned. 'During the Mahabharata, wasn't there a battle formation or something that was impossible to counter?'

I had a feeling I knew what he was going to say next. 'No formation is ever impossible to counter.'

'But there's one that comes close, right? The Chakravyuh?'

The Chakravyuh was a military formation designed by Drona on the thirteenth day of the war aimed at capturing Yudhishthir. It was a multi-tiered deployment of seven concentric circles with the toughest warriors in the centre. Over time, the formation had taken on mythic proportions in Indian folklore. In my personal opinion, it was also something that only someone with no clue about military strategy would describe as 'impregnable'.

'The Chakravyuh was a terrible idea. Even a semi-competent general today would easily destroy that formation if it was deployed.'

K frowned. 'That doesn't sound right.'

'Forget about how it sounds. It makes no sense when you think about it rationally. For one, it's a massive sink of resources aimed at trapping one or a small group of warriors. The obvious counter to this is to never penetrate the formation. Why would you deliberately enter a maze of enemy soldiers? Stay on the outside and snipe away at them from a distance. There were enough archers and chariots to quite liberally pepper the defenders with arrows and turn them into pincushions. Breaking into the centre isn't even necessary.'

'Breaking it will allow them to kill the leaders,' K pointed out.

'K, the first rule of combat is to strike with your strongest forces at the enemy's weakest line of defence. That's how you turn a battle into a rout. A formation where your strongest warriors are inside leaves the weaker, more inexperienced, ones at the front. They are the ones most likely to break and run away. The opposing army can concentrate their most heavily armoured troops at one point on the outermost circle and break through that setup while the rest of their troops stand around impotently.'

'Secondly, the soldiers in the Chakravyuh weren't advancing forward. It was a battle that started at dawn and ended at dusk. That's a twelve-hour period under the hot sun, in full battle armour while being attacked by enemies. If you don't want to collapse from the heat or from thirst, you can't maintain a static defence position out in the open. You need to close in with the enemy. By standing there and waiting for the Pandavas to attack them, they gave up their mobility. There were no trenches, palisades, earthworks—no defensive stockade of any kind. Just a sea of human soldiers standing closely together.

I was warming to the subject. 'And consider this. The Kaurava army was supposedly over two million soldiers. Let's assume that number is exaggerated by a factor of ten and they have suffered losses until then. You are still looking at around two hundred thousand soldiers on the field. Maintaining a complex formation like that would require everyone to know their parts and follow instructions at all times. With banging drums, soldiers screaming, horses neighing, war conches being blown and elephants making a racket, you would barely hear the instructions being yelled at you from a few feet away. Yet the Kauravas and their allies were all able to come together into this super-secret military formation and maintain cohesiveness for the entire day, which stretches the bounds of credulity.' I paused. 'That isn't even the main challenge.'

K shot me a questioning look.

'The Chakravyuh was a circular formation in the middle of an open field. Again, basic military doctrine—don't expose your flanks or the enemy can just roll them up. There's limited flexibility to retreat, which is a terrible idea when drawing up an order for battle. The last thing you want is to be encircled completely in a pincer movement. If that happened, your entire army would get annihilated in the course of a single day.'

'Exactly what happened in "The Battle of the Bastards,"' said K with an awestruck look on his face.

I had no idea what he meant so I pressed forward hurriedly. With K, it was only a matter of time before he got sidetracked. I didn't have the mastery over pop culture that K did, but weapons and military tactics were topics I actually knew a great deal about.

'Also don't forget, less than a quarter of the army was actually fighting ... the concentric circles meant there were a great many soldiers who were twiddling their thumbs in the formation's inner circles while the outermost defence layer was bearing the brunt of the entire opposing army. This negates the tactical advantage of the larger army if it chooses to adopt a defensive posture. A smaller force can destroy a much larger army in this way since, at any point in time, only the outermost soldiers are able to grapple with the enemy.'

While he was disappointed, I preferred he knew the truth rather than believe in an idealistic fantasy.

K looked deflated. 'Why is it then lauded as …'

'Because it makes for better storytelling. To believe that life in ancient times was much more scientifically advanced, people lived longer and were smarter despite all the evidence to the contrary. If it truly was so fabulous, then some record of it being used outside of the epics would exist. Instead, it's only mentioned in the story of the Mahabharat.'

'If this formation was really so terrible, surely Drona wouldn't use it?'

I grinned. 'Drona used that formation because he knew that aside from Arjun and Krishna, the other Pandava leaders were completely clueless when it came to strategy. He deployed it while Arjun was distracted in another part of the battlefield. Yudhishthir and the rest of the Pandavas saw a big circular formation and immediately decided the only way to combat it was to get to the centre. That's what the real tragedy of that day was. They could have shortened the war by five days and saved millions of lives.'

K gave me a sombre look. 'You realise you've just destroyed another cherished belief of mine?'

I sometimes forgot that K was older than me. He had spent most of his life sowing wild oats and not really experiencing the epics like I did. A long life didn't always make you wiser. Your experiences were what mattered.

'Mythology isn't literal, K,' I said gently, to take the sting out of my words. 'You aren't expected to believe word for word all the fanciful tales people make up about us or what happened in the past. You can't honestly believe we could transplant an elephant on a human body or even have a decapitated head watching the entire battle and still talking, do you?'

'OMFG!' Kama exclaimed, clutching his head. 'Now you are telling me Ganesh isn't real?'

I sighed. 'No. He is real. He just doesn't have the head of an elephant and the body of a man. It's again a story that defies logic. You want to preserve your son. I would assume everything that makes him who he is, his brain, his personality, all of it resides in his head. Why on earth would you preserve the body instead and use the head of the first animal you saw? More to the point, if you really had the capability to sew an entire head back on after it had been decapitated, why not use the original head?'

K blinked. That question had never occurred to him.

'These stories were never meant to be taken at face value. They were oral retellings of wisdom and learnings enshrined in a story. What matters is what they were trying to teach. They helped humans rationalise things they had no control over—be it the seasons, the weather, or death itself. Somewhere along the way we've lost the plot. A message about ego, hasty actions and repentance has been interpreted as a true story about plastic surgery.'

'We should tell people the truth then,' K began half-heartedly but I could see from his face even he knew what a dumb idea it was.

'Tell people their most cherished beliefs they've clung on to for thousands of years aren't real? Some of them might listen,' I conceded. 'But they aren't the ones I worry about. The ones who claim Sita was the first NRI and we have chariots that fly between planets—those are the crazy ones. They will cheerfully murder you rather than listen to a worldview that contradicts their own.'

I shook my head. 'They need to question people in power instead of worshipping them as gods. To learn how to reason critically instead of committing violence on those they have a difference of opinion with. The only way they will learn is when they stop bragging about science, history and philosophy from thousands of years ago and instead start educating themselves in science, history and philosophy today.'

K gave me a glum nod.

'We can talk about it later. For now, let's go inside.'

I knocked on the door and Virach opened it, looking more nervous than ever.

'Come in, come in.' Besides his nervous twitching from the last time, he had also acquired a facial tic.

'You said you may have acquired the jewel?' I asked, getting straight to the point.

Virach nodded. He took out a pouch from a drawer in his desk and loosened the drawstrings. I peered inside. It was the ruby, all right. The sheer brilliance of it hadn't dimmed over the centuries.

'Where did you find this gem, Virach?'

Virach grew a little more animated. 'Remember that earthquake in Latur a few years ago? It damaged a lot of buildings and property, but it also opened up an underground cave that had been sealed. Inside were hundreds of manuscripts sealed in earthen jars—a treasure trove of them. All were from the Dwapara Yuga.'

'I've never heard about this.'

Virach giggled nervously. 'Some of my friends and I managed to hush it up.'

By friends, he meant other Nagas. Well-connected individuals who would then take a cut of anything they would find.

'Most of the contents were mundane—trade receipts, bills of lading and the like. We had a small auction and I ended up bidding on most of the items because of my fondness for relics from that era.' He goggled at me like an earnest puppy.

'Get to the point,' I snapped impatiently.

'Yes, right. So, there was one scrap of paper in there that was interesting. It was a letter from an innkeeper to his wife. A guest of his had left a package with him for safekeeping. It was meant to be a gift for someone, but he had taken ill on the road and feared it would be stolen. He left it behind with instructions for someone to come and collect it later. After a couple of months, the innkeeper decided the guest wasn't coming back and opened it. Inside was, as he described it, the brightest gem he had ever seen in his life, and a letter.'

'What did the letter say?'

'That the gem was cursed. Its spell could only be broken if it was thrown into the Ganges from the highest point of the Ram temple at Rishikesh.'

I felt my gut clench. When I had first been cast out, I spent a lot of time on the banks of the Ganges near Rishikesh. At that time, the water was blue and crystal clear, treated with genuine regard and respect. A stark difference from what it was today.

Being the holiest river in India, the Ganges was a pilgrimage destination. People from near and far would come to visit, for a dip in its holy waters was said to cleanse you of all sins committed in this life. It was customary to also throw an offering into the river. Most of the time, they were flowers and packets with incantations scribbled on the leaves. But ever so often, someone wealthy would come along and throw slightly more valuable trinkets into the river. Chains, ornaments, gold coins, precious and semi-precious stones. These would sink to the bottom and be buried in the silt. I had amassed a small fortune from locating those gems. It was how I had survived in the beginning, friendless and alone, selling some of those coins for food after I had been cast out.

Was the gem supposed to fall into my hands? Had I missed it while searching? That was hard to believe. Its glow was too bright for me not to have noticed, and I had trawled the riverbed quite thoroughly on more than one occasion.

'Unfortunately,' Virach continued, 'the innkeeper decided to keep it for himself. Maybe it was cursed after all since the whole area was buried under tons of rock in an earthquake. It was only recently that this second earthquake unearthed the documents. And the gem.'

'May I hold it?'

Virach reluctantly handed me the jewel.

The gem dazzled as the light refracted over it. There was something hypnotic about the way it gleamed. I could almost feel it whispering as I reached out to touch it.

It felt cold to my fingers. I turned it over in my hand, looking for a flaw. Was there something on its edge that looked like a speck? I brought it closer to my eye to take a look.

And like a bolt of electricity, something shot through my arm and into my mind. A sensation unlike anything I had ever experienced before—a feeling of falling backwards into a bottomless pit.

Except the pit was in my mind. Another flashback. I was back again in the gardens of Dwarka.

'But I am the one in charge of the weapons. How can I let them get taken?'

'You will find a way, Akran.'

I bowed.

'It shall be as you say, master.'

'What will you say when they question you? When they ask why you betrayed your most sacred trust?'

What the fuck! I had never seen any of this before!

I could see Akran, the younger, hesitating.

'Perhaps you could block my memories, master? Make sure that they cannot be discovered?'

I had volunteered to be lobotomised? What the bloody hell was going on?

The man smiled indulgently. Or at least I think he did, because I still couldn't see him, but his voice sounded like he approved.

'As you wish.'

'You know the terrible burden that I place on your shoulders, don't you, Akran?'

Akran, the younger, nodded.

'This is necessary, is it not?'

'It is as it is meant to be. When you are ready, you will know more.'

The vision disappeared as abruptly as it had appeared, with Virach waving his hand in my face to get my attention.

'Are you alright? You zoned out back there.'

I was too shaken to speak. Something had just happened. A slew of memories I didn't know were locked within the inner recesses of my mind had just come flooding back.

I quickly placed the ruby back on the table. My hands were clammy with sweat. Was the gem creating false memories? Setting me on some dark path? Or was it really able to dispel any spells that bound the mind?

Shukra, Sars and a couple of others had investigated the magic amnesia I was afflicted with at various times in the past. It was significantly more powerful than anything they had ever encountered or experienced. The identity of the person I was speaking to was completely hidden away. This particular memory was better concealed. Even after so many millennia, I had never seen any trace of it before. How many more such memories were there?

Virach was still rambling on about something. Reluctantly, I focused my attention on him.

'So, I gave it a lot of thought and decided I wouldn't want to be party to anything illegal. I will be happy to give you the jewel.'

I tried not to let my relief show. After that last experience, one way or the other, I was planning to take that jewel, even if it meant clubbing Virach on the head. It was too dangerous to let him keep it.

'There are two conditions I must insist upon. First, I still need some collateral. This is a business, and despite your assurances, I need something of equal or greater value.'

This was, more or less, in line with what I had expected. I extracted the sword from my back and handed it to him.

'This is made from the original iron mace used by the Yadavas to kill one another. It can also be used against celestials though I can't guarantee this one will kill them since it has been used already.'

His face assumed a stoic mask. He was too shrewd a businessman to let me know how valuable he thought it was. But I could tell from the way he held it, almost reverently that it was definitely of interest.

'Second,' he continued, 'I'll have you know I spoke to the other buyer last evening as well. He said that the whole thing was a misunderstanding; he was not involved in any kidnappings or any other such activities. He is, in fact, a model member of society and has contributed to many charities and enterprises.'

'Contributing to charity makes you a good person as much as owning a pet goldfish makes you a marine biologist,' I said, my face stony.

Virach tried to process that statement, failed and gave me a blank look.

I suppressed a sigh. 'He's obviously lying.'

He looked offended. 'Surely not. I have a sense about these things, you know.'

After only one meeting with him, I was convinced, that this 'sense' he was claiming was nonsense.

'Besides,' he added, 'he has in his possession another rare gem—it allows one to be without fatigue, hunger or thirst. I researched the provenance of the gem, and it definitely belongs to him. He's offered it to me as well with similar conditions: he will permanently give up all rights if he can possess the Syamantaka for a few days.'

Something about this gem he was describing sounded familiar. I was sure I had seen it before. But where?

He gazed owlishly at me. 'You have to admit that is a far better deal than this sword you are offering.'

'I might be able to offer something similar,' I said, placing the earrings that I had recovered from the warehouse on the table.

Virach's eyes widened. 'And what are these?' he asked. He tried to appear casual, but I had noticed the gleam of recognition. He knew what they were.

'These earrings belonged to Karna. Indra knew that Arjun would never be able to defeat Karna as long as he had these and the armour on, so he disguised himself as a mendicant and asked for them as alms. They are made of Amrit and can prevent disease and ageing.'

His eyes shone with greed. 'And you will give this to me permanently in exchange for a few days with the jewel?'

I shook my head. 'You can have the earrings, but only after two days. If my guess is correct, they need both the jewel and the earrings for the yagna. I mean to keep them both in a safe location, temporarily. Once the auspicious time is over, you can have them both back.'

Virach nodded, but he still looked suspicious. I knew what he was thinking.

'Examine the damn things all you like; they are real. You can sense the power emanating from them.'

'Why would you give these up?'

'Because I don't care about any of this. I don't hoard gold or magic. These were never entrusted to my care. I just want to stop whatever this is from happening and then be left alone.'

This answer seemed to please him. Not that I cared about his opinion, but it was the truth. These items were lost an eternity ago. Having them locked up in the vaults of a private collector wouldn't give me sleepless nights.

I had my nightmares for that.

'Here's what I've decided,' he said. 'I think it's best that we all meet up and discuss this in a nice, civilised fashion. I've also invited the buyer here, and he would be happy to meet. It was his idea, actually.'

Crap on a stick! I knew this idiot would screw things up!

'You called him here?'

'I did. I'm sure you all know each other from aeons past. Here he is now.'

On cue, he walked in. He was dressed like a businessman in a suit, but seeing his face reminded me of an earlier time—when he wore armour and rode a chariot.

No, no, no, hell no! Not him!

He recognised me instantly. It was too much to hope for that he would have forgotten. His smile, as he looked at me, was warm and genial. Like a cat pleased to see the mouse that had been tormenting him for so long, finally trapped with nowhere to go.

'Akran! I'm so glad you could be here.'

I wasn't fooled, not by a long shot. I could see it in his eyes. Cold, blistering hate. And malicious triumph. Here I was, trapped in a room with him, and he was going to kick my ass.

I smiled weakly. 'Hello, Ashwatthama.'

CHAPTER ELEVEN

I am sooooo fucked!
— Private Journals of Akran

Cards on the table. I did not see this coming. And this was bad. As in, epic, video game boss level bad. On a scale of one to ten, with one being screwed in a light, gentle, almost pleasant prod and ten being the worst experience ever, I can safely say I was at around a hundred. Of all the people or celestials I've met in this long and chaotic existence; this one was probably the scariest.

I had imagined Narakasura to be a problem, but that was a vague, formless dread. A possibility that could be avoided. More importantly, Narakasura didn't care who I was.

Ashwatthama, on the other hand, cared. He cared a lot. He was both, a freaking Maharathi—one of those grandmaster warriors of another age with knowledge of all weapons and combat skills—and a Chiranjivi—though, unlike others, his immortality was because of a curse.

At over eight-feet tall, he was built like an ox. I had forgotten how tall everyone was in the Dwapara Yuga, as compared to now. Ashwatthama was, by those standards, slightly below average height. Here, he filled the room with his presence.

A tense silence followed. Beside me, K was also frozen with fear. The last time he had been so outclassed, his body had been burnt to a crisp. I wouldn't be surprised if he curled-up into a foetal ball on the floor.

The years had been good to Ashwatthama. I had seen him once after he had been cursed, with blood and pus seeping from his wounds. Now, he seemed healthy again with well-toned muscles and a luscious mane of hair, like a Victoria's Secret model. The curse was meant to last at least three thousand years. Time flies when you are having fun. Or if you are immortal. Now, he had recovered and looked completely normal. Except for the height, of course.

'You are looking well,' I managed to say. It came out as a croak.

He gave an expansive smile as he cracked his knuckles, making a clear popping sound. I couldn't help but wince as I heard it. 'I've missed your sense of humour, little Yaksha,' he said, chuckling. 'I can't wait to hear more of your trite observations.'

A lot of other things clicked into place. An alliance between Yakshas and Asuras? It would take serious balls to negotiate that. Someone who wanted to end the Kali Yuga early? Yup, I could understand that as well. But most importantly, the sheer power needed to raise a long-dead demon? When you are shunned by society for millennia, you end up spending a lot of time by yourself.

Do you know what most men did when they were all by themselves in an era with no television?

No, not that. Get your minds out of the gutter, humans! This is serious.

They would spend their time meditating, accumulating boons for their devotion and penance.

I already knew whom Ashwatthama would have been praying to. Lord Shiva. The one god in the Trinity who handed boons out like candy to demons and humans alike.

Want to guess what Shiva is also known as?

The Destroyer. When you pray to someone with a nickname like that, you know you aren't asking for cuddles or world peace.

I could sense the waves of energy rolling off him. He was bursting with power. There was a casual arrogance to the way he stood and looked at me. He knew I was no possible threat. Even if I could access my mana, I doubted I could stop him.

Virach finally seemed to realise that things were not as hunky-dory as he had imagined. 'Is something wrong?' he asked anxiously, addressing both of us. 'I know you all didn't see eye to eye during the Great War, but surely that was a long time ago.'

Ashwatthama ignored him as he continued to stare at me.

'Are the rumours about you true, then?' he asked. 'Did you really kill Krishna?'

He did have major pent-up rage issues against Krishna—what with the curse, the leprosy, the pus and all. A wild thought struck me that he would probably think we were on the same side, given I had inadvertently killed the person he hated most.

But no. I didn't see that happening. I was too high on his shit list.

'Of course,' he continued, 'I wasn't all that surprised when I heard. I knew you weren't much for following the code of Dharma, were you?'

Yeah, I knew he was going to bring that up.

My little feud with the man mountain had begun during the Great War. Ashwatthama had fought on the side of Duryodhan and his own father, Dronacharya. He was a skilled warrior who had grown up beside the Kuru princes and harboured a deep affection for all of them—Pandavas and Kauravas alike.

As a celestial, I couldn't interfere directly in a human war. There was a code of conduct that had been discussed and agreed upon, prior to hostilities being declared, that was binding on all humans, yakshas and demons alike. Supernatural beings were only allowed to kill other supernatural beings. Mortals were off-limits to us. All the rules officially broke down after Abhimanyu, son of Arjun, was dishonourably killed, and Ghatothkach, the demon son of Bhim, joined the battle. But that's a tale for another day.

By the fifteenth day of the war, Drona was on a rampage. There was no way for the Pandavas to win unless he was eliminated. It had been prophesied that Dhrishtadyumna, the brother of Draupadi, would kill Drona but looking at the sheer destruction Drona was causing, it seemed impossible.

Deciding to show some initiative, I went to Indravarman, the chief of the Malvas and asked him if I could rename one of his elephants Ashwatthama. He thought I was crazy to come forward with this odd request in the middle of the battle, but my connection to Krishna was well-known. I took the newly christened elephant to Krishna and told him what I had done. We were in perfect sync at the time and he figured out almost immediately what I intended. I still remember how a smile played on his lips as he called Bhim to his side.

'Kill the elephant,' he instructed. 'And tell our allies to celebrate joyously as if we have killed Drona's son Ashwatthama.'

Bhim did as he was asked. My friend, being the shrewd tactician he was, knew what Drona would do to verify the truth.

It happened exactly as we had expected. Knowing that Yudhishthir was a firm believer in dharma, Drona drove his chariot up to Yudhishthir and asked him if it was truly his son who was dead. Of all the people on the battlefield, Yudhishthir was the one person who was completely incapable of lying. As a baby, if you stuck a finger in his mouth and urged him to bite, he would likely refuse because it went against his dharma.

'Yes, Ashwatthama is dead,' said the eldest Pandava.

To be precise, that is part of what he said—the only part Drona truly heard.

For at that moment, I committed the second part of the dastardly deed.

Yudhishthir was the son of the god of truth and justice. He couldn't lie to save his life. So immediately after offering this confirmation, he felt compelled to add a disclaimer.

'Maybe it's an elephant. Maybe a man,' said the eldest Pandava.

Dronacharya heard none of that. For at that moment, I blasted a conch shell right near his ear.

B-school grads from elite schools whose tuition might cost as much as owning a small apartment might describe this as 'exploiting a market opportunity'. A slightly cruder school of thought would describe this with a vivid picture involving a bamboo and a very tiny portion of your anatomy. It loses some of its elegance in translation, but the point remains. Deafening someone with a conch shell wasn't forbidden, but it probably should have been

This tiny act changed the course of the war. Hearing those words sealed Drona's fate. Losing the will to live, he laid down his weapons and sat down to meditate right in the middle of the battlefield. Dhrishtadyumna, Draupadi's brother, saw him sitting down and severed his head with a clean stroke of his sword. And the rest is history. Or myth. Depending on what you choose to believe.

Ashwatthama was deeply attached to dear old dad. That incident began his downward spiral into madness. Until that moment, while he continued to side with Duryodhan and his father, he kept urging the Kaurava princes to reconcile. Drona had trained him together with the Kuru princes. He looked at all of them with equal affection. Purely out of his devotion to his father, he had joined the ranks of Hastinapur. But deep down, he believed that the Pandavas were just and truthful. This deed shattered his idealistic fantasy.

After the war was over, in a night attack, he destroyed most of the remaining army of the Pandavas, killing Dhrishtadyumna, Shikhandi and the sons of all the Pandavas with his own hands while they were sleeping. This by itself was a heinous crime since, by the rules laid down at the start of the war, a warrior was not permitted to slaughter someone sleeping and defenceless.

But Ashwatthama wasn't done. His goal was to ensure the Pandava line was permanently destroyed, and to that end, there was one final successor—the unborn grandson of Arjun. Using a divine weapon—the Brahmashirsha from a blade of grass—he directed it at the womb of Uttara, the pregnant wife of Abhimanyu.

Angered by this attack on a civilian, and a baby no less, Krishna cursed Ashwatthama. For three thousand years, he would roam the earth alone and guilty, with ulcers, blood and pus oozing out of his injuries, praying for death but unable to find release. No human would be able to heal him or ease his suffering.

One would expect that a curse like this would sap away at your will and leave you a broken husk of a man.

It's a pity my friend underestimated the depths of hatred that a half-crazed monster could hold on to after all these years.

Pretty much everyone he hated from that time was gone. Except me.

All of this ran through my head in that long minute as I gazed at him warily. Ashwatthama looked completely relaxed. With good reason. He had nothing to fear from me.

'Cat got your tongue?'

I should have let sleeping dogs lie. There's no point in goading someone who's already imagined a hundred innovative ways to kill you. Yet I yearned to wipe that smug insufferable look off his face.

I beamed at him. 'How have you been, Ash? Tried killing any more babies in their wombs recently?'

The tightening of the skin around his eyes was the only sign that he had taken offence. He continued to maintain that empty psychopathic smile on his face.

Virach cleared his throat nervously. 'Now, now, there's no need for this. Let bygones be bygones. We can all sit down and discuss this in a friendly, civilised manner.'

'Is that the gem?' Ashwatthama asked, pointing at the pouch. Virach gave a very slight nod.

'Virach,' I spoke slowly and clearly, without taking my eyes off Ashwatthama, 'you are a fool. Ashwatthama isn't here to make deals. He is going to kill you. He doesn't have the gem that he spoke about. He surrendered it a long time ago, and I watched Krishna destroy it with my own eyes.'

Virach turned to face Ashwatthama, fear gathering in his eyes. 'No, he is a man of honour. He wouldn't—.'

Before he could finish, a lightning bolt shot out from Ashwatthama's hands, incinerating Virach on the spot. He had a moment to produce an agonising shriek before his charred remains tumbled to the floor.

There was no time to think or even breathe. Even as Virach had been transitioning from medium rare to well done, I was moving. The cards were out of my hands and flying towards Ashwatthama as I called out the incantations, hoping against hope that at least one of them would hurt the son of a bitch.

'*Halahala.*'
'*Agni.*'
'*Hima.*'
Poison. Fire. Frost.

His eyes lit up at the prospect of battle, although his reactions were languid and uncaring as if we were just two friends out strolling on a summer day.

The green poison cloud dissipated into mist, filling the room with an unearthly fragrance. The fire spell began to bloom, then choked out suddenly as if an invisible hand had cut off all the oxygen it needed to feed on. The frost turned into a puddle of water at his feet.

My three best spells, and he hadn't even blinked.

Even as he countered my attack, he raised his other hand and pointed it at me. The bastard was ambidextrous as well. Was it too much to hope that the universe would cut me some slack?

A red bolt of fire shot out towards me. I managed to throw a shield card at it, hoping it would suffice, while I grabbed the earrings. I would have preferred to have taken the jewel, but it was just out of reach.

'*Kavacch.*'

The card took the full brunt of the blast and disintegrated as I leapt towards the door. I heard K's footsteps right behind me. Discretion was the better part of valour. There was no shame in admitting we were completely outmatched.

I had fled into Virach's study. I had a moment to slam the door shut and hope it was well-shielded before a massive fireball slammed into the door, turning it into kindling.

I didn't know what other magical properties the earrings had, but every little advantage would help. I should have thought of wearing them earlier when I expected this to be a trap.

Please let them be clip-ons ... please let them be clip-ons ...

Fuuuucccck!!

There goes that plan.

Frantically I shuffled through the remaining cards. Spells of confusion? Despair? Sleep? None of those would even tickle him. I needed something quick, and I was running out of options. A little voice in my head was screaming at me to prostrate myself and beg his forgiveness.

Fuck that! I'd rather go down fighting than just roll over for him.

He stepped through the door slowly and unhurriedly, like he had all the time in the world. There was something sinister and frightening about the way he moved, like a panther stalking its prey. The bastard was toying with me.

I pulled out the demon cards—a Dakini and a Dasa. Dakinis are female imp demons, the size of a toddler. They are malevolent little harpies with horns and claws that can transform human flesh into ragged strips in seconds. Dasas follow close behind on the hierarchy. Both of these had been imprisoned within the cards a long time ago as part of my last-ditch 'end of the fucking world' game strategy, which I had hoped never to use. I had prepared them in case I was ever beset by assassins from the celestial court.

I threw them both at him, activating the release word for their mystical bindings.

'*Variyas.*'

'*Svatantra.*'

He went for the Dasa first. A flash of lightning incinerated the card even before the demon could step out. He probably assumed it was the stronger of the two since I threw it a fraction of a second after the Dakini.

It wasn't.

In the space between us, the Dakini exploded out of the card—a hideous creature of terror and fury. She lunged at his throat, snarling as her claws reached for his eyes and ears.

He caught her by the neck as she came within range. The Dakini's fingernails raked across his arm, his face and his chest, drawing long bloody streaks.

His composure faltered for a split second.

I held my breath, hoping against hope that she would break free. The Dakini could inflict massive damage if she got a chance.

There was a sickening crunching sound as she dropped to the floor, her head at an unnatural angle.

A thousand-year-old demon, killed within seconds. And with bare hands.

Not once in those five seconds of battle had he even blinked or taken his eyes off me.

'Come now, Akran, surely that's not the best you can do?' he taunted. 'I am going to make your suffering exquisite. Soon you will wish you could have lived for a thousand years as a leper, rather than experience what I'm going to do to you.'

I stared at him, spent. The last two cards I had thrown had been my best hope. Behind me, K made a little whimpering sound.

'Nothing to add? Well then, let's get started,' he said.

A flick of his fingers sent me flying backwards, crashing into a large ornate bookshelf. Something gave as my back hit the shelf. Ashwatthama was done playing around; the force of the blow snapped a bone somewhere in my back. It wasn't life-threatening since my body would stitch it back together, but it still hurt like hell. I crashed to the floor in a heap, gasping for breath. A bitter, acrid taste filled my mouth.

Ashwatthama chuckled as he ambled toward me. He paused to pick up a book lying on the floor.

'Imagine that. An original copy of *Darkhold*. What a shame I had to kill him.'

I opened my mouth to answer but a flick of his wrist sent me flying upwards towards the ceiling. I felt my skull crack with the impact before I fell again.

'I was expecting you to run away whimpering. I'm glad you decided to make a sport out of it.'

There was something chilling about the way he spoke. Like he had learnt his monologues sitting on Blofeld or Goldfinger's lap. 'No, Mr Bond. I expect you to die!'

'You know how it is. Some of us run, some choose to fight,' I said. 'Some of us even murder people in their sleep, since they are too weak to do it when they are awake.'

If my little jibe hit home, he gave no outward sign.

'It seems you've actually managed to grow a spine. I'll be sure to examine it later, once I detach it from the rest of your body.' He laughed at his own wit.

It might have been his delivery, but I really didn't think it was funny.

His eyes gleamed as he caught sight of the earrings still held tightly in my hands.

'You think those will help?'

I said nothing. Not because I couldn't think of a witty rejoinder but more because I had the salty taste of blood in my mouth.

'Crawl over to me on your hands and knees and beg for forgiveness and I might let you live.'

I spat the one loose tooth out. 'I'll pass, thanks.'

He laughed and gestured with his fingers. The pouch with the earrings flew into his hands.

'I should take you back with me. Keep you in the hold with all the others and make you watch as I kill them.'

'You will get a front-row seat as your world crumbles and everyone that ever mattered to you dies. Your friend Shukra, that pretty young goddess you hang out with … all of them back in the mud where they belong!'

I winced as I struggled to sit up. I had just one card left, a slow burner. It was like a short fuse grenade, absorbing mana from the air around it before it overloaded and detonated.

'Go fuck yourself!' I whispered as I ran my thumb over the back of the card before flicking it to the side. It slid next to a pillar beside him, a support beam for the ceiling. Once activated, the card would absorb mana greedily until it reached full capacity and then explode.

I didn't think he would hear me, but he did.

His eyes shone with malice. 'Defiant till the very end. We should carve that on your tombstone.'

I was grasping at straws but had nothing else left. I could feel multiple bones in my left arm had cracked from the force of that last throw. They would knit back together slowly with some judicious use of my mana. Didn't make it hurt any less, though.

'K, I need help,' I whispered urgently.

'What can I possibly do? You want me to shoot him with a few of my arrows?'

Hell, no. The last thing I wanted was for Ashwatthama to be overcome by lust while I lay unable to move. It probably wouldn't work on him, but would you really want to take a chance and find out?

'Can you make me invisible?'

Silence. K wasn't a coward. He was an elemental, shaped by people's beliefs across the centuries. Millions of awkward adolescents, stumbling through their first love, had left their mark on K. The feeling of trepidation when putting yourself out there and taking a chance at rejection and pain manifested in his personality as someone with a healthy fear of the unknown. Besides, he was traumatised by his past experience with wrathful beings of immense power.

The fact that he had remained by my side instead of bolting away the first chance he got meant a lot to me.

'Can you do it or not?' I rasped. After a while, he whispered, 'Yes, I need to let you into my aura.'

'Wait for my signal.'

I looked up to see Ashwatthama staring at me. 'Talking to yourself? Gone mad finally, have you?'

His eyes narrowed. 'Or is there someone else in the room?'

He threw the book to one side and began to mumble an incantation. I recognised the spell. The eye of all-seeing would dispel any magic of cloaks, shadows and invisibility in a fifty-foot radius. I needed a distraction. And fast.

'Hey, Ashwatthama! You know why your father deserved to die, don't you?'

Even back in the old days, Ashwatthama was known to be hot-headed. Three thousand years had done nothing to change that.

He broke off his chanting to glance sharply at me.

Good job, Akran. Piss off the guy who can murder you with a wiggle of his eyebrows.

'What did you say?' There was a dangerous edge to his voice, warning me to be extremely careful with what I would say next. Clearly, major daddy issues were at play here.

'He was so jealous of a sixteen-year-old stripling that he broke the rules of war and ganged up on him with all the other Kaurava leaders. He killed Abhimanyu with them. What a grubby dishonourable fellow he was!'

Beside me, K gasped in horror. 'What is wrong with you?' he whispered urgently.

A low guttural snarl emerged from Ashwatthama's throat. He moved forward in two quick steps, grabbed me by my neck and lifted me off my feet. The image of what he did to the Dakini a couple of minutes ago popped into my mind.

'You are going to regret that last comment of yours, Yaksha,' he hissed.

'Does the truth really hurt so bad? Would you like to have a good cry on Daddy's shoulder?'

A little vein on his forehead began to throb as his grip around my neck tightened.

'Oh wait, he isn't here. Is he, Horseface?'

When push comes to shove, I can be as eloquent as an Indian politician promising to fix potholes with glitter and rainbows if you vote for him. Yet, here I was with pedestrian little taunts like 'horseface'. Why would I do something like that? It was so beneath me.

Except that particular little insult held a lot of meaning to Ashwatthama. His eyes glinted dangerously.

'Any further pearls of wisdom you would like to share before I tear out your tongue?'

Despite the pain, I smiled. He had given me an opening on a platter. 'Yes. Three words, actually.'

Remember what I said at the beginning of this yarn about magic needing three elements?

A mystic. A binding. And an anchor.

I was the mystic, calling out the necessary words of magic. The card I had tossed was the anchor, the focus that allowed me to channel the spell.

That left the binding. A sympathetic connection between the anchor and the mystic.

I had used up my limited mana pool. Every time I flicked a card, I was using mana. Prodding it toward my intended target. Making sure it exploded at the right moment. Healing myself from the damage he was inflicting on my body.

Ashwatthama had no such limitations. He had never known what it was like to be mana-deprived. Starved and parched, holding on to every last scrap for survival. He had a massive ocean of mana at his disposal and was throwing it around like rice at a Christian wedding. The very air around us was crackling with raw power. It served as a crude but effective binding.

All the damage he had caused my body had left me running on fumes. What I needed was a spark to ignite that little powder keg he had built around himself. I had less than a spark. The barest smidgen of power still left that I had painstakingly hoarded, ignoring the multiple wounds on my body that were screaming to be healed.

In my weakened state, I couldn't do jack shit with him at a distance.

But him holding me? That completed the fucking circuit.

The card I had dropped began to glow. Ashwatthama's mere proximity to it had filled it to the brim. All it needed was the trigger phrase.

He had a full second to figure out why I was smiling. I did have something I was itching to tell him. Pure coincidence, it was also the trigger phrase.

Pearls of wisdom? Alright, here they were.

'Go fuck yourself!'

Cued to the trigger phrase, the card exploded. It was the most spectacular conflagration I had ever seen—the card was packed to the brim with all the excess energy it was leeching off his presence. Converting that into heat and fire with him taking the full brunt of the blast was delightful to behold.

No matter how powerful he was, he could still feel pain as keenly as anyone else. The blast shredded the skin of his back into ribbons, causing him to howl in agony as he let go of me. But that was merely the icing on the cake. Of far more importance was the supporting beam for the roof it blew up, causing huge ungainly chunks of plaster and tile to collapse all over him.

'K—now!'

I felt K grab me in an embrace as the roof collapsed. There were a brief couple of seconds where my pathetic aura tried to wrestle with that of K before it fizzled out and rolled over. His aura was considerably stronger than mine, shielding us from falling debris while keeping us invisible.

Ashwatthama was not a celestial being, just an immortal, thanks to a curse that probably hadn't been thought through carefully enough. He didn't have an aura like ours, but his powers protected him. Watching him burn had set my heart singing—you could see bleached bone from the back of his skull as the flesh seared and dripped away like hot grease on a boiling pan.

I do not ordinarily delight in the suffering of others, but this was a joy to watch. I fervently hoped it would take him a long, long time to recover.

Under normal circumstances, when Krishna laid a curse on someone, it was backed by the force of his own divine will. It would be impossible to break.

Except three thousand years had passed and the curse had ended. What Ashwatthama was now living on, was his massive storehouse of power.

There was a chance, a faint one, mind you, that this would have stopped him. We watched silently as the sickly smell of burnt bacon wafted through the air. It reminded me of Peppa Pig.

If only the Universe didn't hate me!

In front of our eyes, his body began to stitch itself back together. New flesh enveloped the glistening bone of his skull, stitching itself back like nothing had happened. Even his hair began to grow back, sprouting across his head like a fertile wheat field.

The chunks of falling stone all around him were merely an irritant. Ashwatthama shrugged off the debris and looked around, staring briefly at the roof and then all around him. There was too much dust in the air, but that didn't seem to bother him.

We held our breath as he glared furiously all around, trying to discern where we were. My breathing was ragged from the exertion of fighting him. I needed a distraction.

The explosion had created a hole in the ground. Noticing a stone lying on the floor, I waited till his back was turned, then flung it in.

Ashwatthama whirled at the sound. He stepped closer to the hole, still looking around suspiciously.

I had never been to Virach's house before. But I know Nagas. They prefer to bury their loot underground. The room below was a storeroom where he had his private collection of curios. If magical weapons were in the house, they would probably be there.

Ashwatthama had the same thought. He bent down on his haunches and peered into the storeroom. It was pitch dark in there, but one word from him and a ball of light flew below, lighting up the whole place.

Far in the distance, we could hear the sound of sirens. I hadn't offered any prayers to the heavens in over three thousand years, but I was willing to start now if it would make a difference.

K and I crouched quietly, not daring to move. Or even breathe. The slightest sound might alert him to where we were hiding.

After what seemed like an eternity, Ashwatthama turned away. He still needed to collect the Syamantaka jewel before the cops came to investigate. An incantation from him brought another ton of rubble into the room below. He was not taking the chance that we might find something in there that we could use. The room was well and truly sealed.

The exit to the room that we were in, had been covered with rubble from the explosion. Without breaking stride, he blasted a hole right through it and walked away while we collapsed onto the floor exhausted.

For a minute, neither of us said anything. K was the first to break the silence as he broke into hysterical laughter. I watched him for a moment before joining in. We had lost the jewel and the earrings, and gotten Virach killed, but we had gone head-to-head with the most dangerous man alive and survived. It felt like it was worth celebrating.

Eventually, we stopped, partly because it wasn't really all that funny and more because it hurt too much to laugh. My ribs felt like they were dancing a jig inside my body.

'Horseface? Really?'

I grinned. The name Ashwatthama meant 'horse-voiced.' They chose it because when he was born, he cried like a horse. I always suspected naming a kid something like that would leave them scarred with deep emotional issues.

'What do we do now?' K asked, wiping tears from his eyes.

It was a good question. For the first time in my life, I had no answers.

'Let's go back and warn the others,' suggested K. He looked like he was in desperate need of a drink. I couldn't blame him.

It was as good a plan as any. Something had been bothering me, though. Something Ashwatthama had said while we were fighting. Because of the adrenaline-soaked terror I had just experienced … some things weren't coming back to me.

It was only when we reached Creeda that I finally remembered.

'You will get a front-row seat as your world crumbles and everyone that ever mattered to you dies. Your friend Shukra, that pretty young goddess you hang out with …'

He knew about Shukra being a friend of mine. Our little act at the library hadn't fooled him.

We stared at the smouldering ruin wordlessly. The café had been gutted. It looked like a trio of suicide bombers had attacked the place. Fortunately, there were no patrons inside when it happened.

The common wall between the café and the library had been blown apart. A quick check inside confirmed my worst fears.

There was blood on the floor.

And Shukra was gone.

CHAPTER TWELVE

*R*estoring a woman's virginity is a classic example of patriarchal values inserted into a tale to make it fit with the times. Chastity was seen as an essential virtue among 'good' women, and Draupadi being married to all the five Pandavas directly contradicted that. A workaround was inserted about her virginity getting restored every year, thanks to a sage's blessing, each time she visited the next brother in the queue. It sounds like the brainchild of an adolescent male and would be seen as a blessing only by a man.

While Draupadi was the most well-known beneficiary of this insertion, it is a common trope in the Mahabharat. Vyas offers it as a boon to Draupadi, Sage Parashar offers it to Satyavati and Surya offers it to Kunti.

Given that in two out of three mentioned cases, it is being offered to a woman by men looking to get laid by said woman, one can't help but wonder if this was an actual magic trick that sages learnt early on when they were

looking to get lucky or simply an elaborate con from the Vedic pickup artist playbook to dupe gullible women.
— Private Journals of Akran

'What are we going to do?' K demanded, a note of hysteria creeping into his voice as he repeated himself for the fifth time.

I shook my head wearily. Two eyewitnesses claimed they saw a couple of men dressed like gangsters throwing fireballs at the café. They concluded it was some sort of newfangled rocket launcher—the human mind will often rationalise what they see to fit their understanding of the world.

Shukra's kidnapping had shaken us all. More than anything else, it was the sheer disregard for every protocol the celestial court had set up. Our existence was meant to be a secret from the mortal world. We had assumed that their distribution of heavenly music was an accident. But a broad daylight attack on Creeda was a gauntlet being laid down. They didn't care anymore.

Fortunately, the Tea Room was secure. For now, at least.

We briefed Sars and Deanne at the Tea Room immediately after leaving Creeda. Deanne had never been there before and Sars had been in the Tea Room since morning working on her ley line program.

While Shukra had put up many enchantments to protect his precious books, the library itself had not been as heavily warded.

I was pissed off. And wracked with guilt. Shukra and I had spoken about it a few hours before we had left for Virach's place. Bringing back a dead demon required the Sanjivani mantra. He was the only one who knew it. We should have locked him securely in the basement until the auspicious time for the yagna had passed. Instead, we went out there like fucking amateurs and had our asses kicked.

'How much time do we have?' I asked Sars.

'The auspicious time for the planetary alignment is in eight hours.'

She too looked shaken by the news of the attack. Sars and Shukra enjoyed each other's company. They were like-minded in their thirst for knowledge and had spent many hours together, discussing topics only of interest to them.

Eight hours! My knuckles had turned white as I clenched my hands into fists. I knew Shukra. He would do his damnedest to resist.

The problem was, I also knew Ashwatthama. With a deadline fast approaching, he would skip the interrogation stage and directly begin brutalising him.

Deanne spoke up. 'We will get him back, don't worry.'

I didn't know enough about Valkyries other than them being fearsome warriors. And she certainly dressed the part. She had walked into the café wearing a blue knee-length dress, which she discarded once we were inside, revealing a bronze armour that gleamed like burnished gold.

A sword as long as my arm and an ancient warrior helmet were also placed on the table beside her. I suspect she was itching to get out of that door and start decapitating heads or whatever Valkyries did. At any other time, I would have been amused by her excitement. Now, I was terrified.

'Deanne, you don't know this guy. He is insanely powerful. It's like going up against a god.'

She cocked her head.

'He can bleed, can't he?'

Reluctantly, I nodded. 'He can bleed, but …'

She snorted. 'Then stop selling so hard. I told you I'm in. The bards will be singing ballads about this battle for ages.'

I stared dumbfounded for a moment. Valkyries are crazy! Anything I said would only make her more eager to fight.

'Any luck finding out where Ashwatthama and his gang might have taken him?'

Sars pursed her lips. 'Sixteen possible locations. I've checked all of them on the parameters you gave me. Factories, mills, warehouses, even abandoned buildings and parking lots. Nothing.'

'Ignore what I said last time. Widen the net. Look for any locations in a two-hundred-mile radius.'

'I widened it already. It covers all of Mumbai. No luck.'

I could feel the blood pounding in my head again, so loud that it was impossible to think. Was it even possible for a celestial to have a heart attack? I was feeling breathless, my palms were sweaty and I was struggling to stand upright.

This was my fault … I should have just … just …

'Stop!'

I was hallucinating. Someone who looked just like me was standing in front of me, with arms akimbo glaring furiously. A vein on his head was throbbing.

We stared at each other for a moment. The voices of the others in the room had faded into a dull buzzing.

I had a million questions and I was expecting profoundly disappointing answers. In all likelihood, I was simply going crazy.

'Not the fucking time to have a meltdown. Solve this now, grieve later!'

As far as apparitions go, it was at least dishing out sensible advice. It wasn't something random like a dancing baby.

I opened my mouth to speak but a wave of dizziness engulfed me, leaving me unsteady on my feet.

There was a tiny popping sound in my ears. I blinked. The apparition was gone. Judging from the others' reactions, nobody else had seen anything strange.

'Akran, are you okay?' K reached out a hand tentatively. 'You seemed to have spaced out for a minute there.'

'I'm fine.' Whatever that hallucination was, it was right. Now was not the time to fall to pieces.

'What about that other program you were running?' K interjected suddenly. 'The one with the ley lines?' He gave Sars a hopeful look.

Sars looked like she had bitten into a lemon. 'I need more time. It's like finding a genuine Nigerian prince—there are too many false echoes to filter through!'

I slumped, dejected. We didn't have time. No point in saying it. We all knew the clock was ticking.

'What can we do?' I was grasping at straws here. Find me something to punch or kick and I would do so. This was not my area of expertise.

'I need something to narrow it down. Did Ashwatthama say anything during the fight? Any place that he mentioned?'

I tried to recall. Between him slamming me into walls and trying to rip my head off, I was too focused on staying alive.

'K, anything?'

K gave me a pained look. 'I was too busy wetting myself at the time.'

I turned to Sars. 'He might have mentioned something but since he was also actively trying to kill us, I can't really recall.'

Sars gave a frustrated sigh. 'I can't pinpoint a location. There are too many variables!'

'What about that company buying all that stuff? ANDOR?' Even as I said it, it struck me. Son of a bitch! 'He even named it after his father. ANDOR is an anagram of DRONA.'

'It doesn't take a genius to figure he's still got serious daddy issues,' K muttered.

She tapped a few keys on the laptop in front of her.

'I already cross-referenced with all listed Andor assets and holdings. Nothing!'

Deanne looked doubtful. 'Are they really that stupid? Doesn't it make more sense to keep a low profile and not leave a trail of clues?'

I shrugged, then winced as I did so. I was still sore from the beating I'd gotten. Too much strain on my limited trickle of mana.

'You need to look at it from their point of view . They think they are smarter than everyone else. They aren't going to put their assumptions on hold just because of a few minor setbacks.'

'It's also a matter of pride,' Sars added. Skulking in the shadows under an assumed name is something Ashwatthama's ego wouldn't allow.'

'Hold!' K exclaimed. His face had turned red with excitement.

'Hold what?'

'That's what he said. He was going to put you in the hold!'

'Sars?' I said quietly, feeling a sudden, desperate flicker of hope.

'On it,' she said, tapping at her laptop keys again. 'I'm assuming he meant a boat. A large one. A yacht or something.' She peered intently at the screen and then groaned as a bunch of names rolled across. 'There are at least sixty-seven names.'

'All Andor?'

'Not necessarily. A lot of these maritime corporations have lease agreements. They outsource tankers, small ships, etc. to other conglomerates during non-peak season. So, they could be partnered with a legitimate business.' She slammed her hand on the table in frustration. 'It's going to take too long!'

'We'll just search each one manually, then. Wait …' A thought struck me, 'Sars, cross-reference any ley line intersections in the sea around Mumbai with the coordinates of these ships. See if any of them are in the same place.'

Sars was already nodding her head. 'It's a good idea. That will take a few minutes. I'm not looking for natural phenomena anymore, but if I extend these in a pattern that ley lines normally stretch, account for the curve …' she continued mumbling as we all watched.

'There are three likely spots where they will conduct the yagna. Assuming they choose to do it on the ship itself.'

'I don't think he is going to risk moving them, so close to the time of the planetary alignment. Too many things can go wrong—he might get discovered, somebody might notice the missing girls being transported—I'm betting he chose a location close to wherever he plans to conduct the yagna and has stashed the rest of the girls there. In all likelihood, Shukra has been taken there as well.'

Sars made a small sound of frustration. 'Unfortunately, it doesn't help. None of them are near any of the three likely locations I was hoping to find.'

'Maybe they'll move there later, closer to the yagna?' K suggested hopefully.

'That still leaves us with no way to act before that. Unless we have a stake-out for each of those locations.'

I kept staring at the screen. Rows with ship names and details, most of them in green.

'Sars, why are some of these marked in red? They don't have a name or location listed next to them.'

'Those are decommissioned ships. They are still in the registry but they will all eventually go into the yard. Let me see …' She opened a new screen and began punching numbers.

'Hmm. Four of them. Chathrand, The Weary Mother, Kamakhya, Naglfar.' She frowned. 'Where have I heard that last name before?'

I felt a sudden thrill of excitement. 'Kamakhya. That would be it. The name is tied to a local legend about a goddess and Narakasura lusting after her.'

I turned to Sars. 'Using her name is one more way for them to strengthen the bond when opening the gate.'

I rose to my feet and then collapsed as my knee gave way. All three of them rushed forward to lend me a hand.

'How bad is it?' Sars asked.

I winced. It was pretty darn bad. I had muscle pains in places I didn't know I had muscles in. Fortunately, I continued to look stoic, as if I was merely dizzy and not half dead.

'I'll be fine. Let's find Shukra and then I can sleep for a week.'

Deanne shot K a worried look. 'You are in no condition to fight,' she said to me. 'Stay here and K and I will go and get him.'

K shot out of his chair. 'Umm ... I will?'

Deanne glared at him, and K flopped back, defeated. 'Okay, yes, of course, I'll come.'

I shook my head. 'I'm glad to hear that but I'm coming as well. Ashwatthama is my responsibility.'

No one argued, though they all looked like they had plenty to say. Whatever. We were not going to be able to convince each other, and we were short of time.

Sars spoke up. 'You don't need to do this. The celestial court will intervene. We need to tell them exactly what's going on.'

'Haven't you already tried before?'

Sars gave a sheepish look. Her association with me had made her a black sheep as well. The words of an exiled traitor were not to be trusted, nor anyone else who hung out with him.

After living with a stick up their ass for over three thousand years, the celestials were unlikely to suddenly become more flexible in their thoughts and actions.

'We just need to keep trying.'

I shook my head. 'They can be counted upon to debate what needs to be done right until the yagna is over. The court is long on talk but short on action. We need to do this ourselves.'

'With the human authorities crawling all over the attack on Creeda, couldn't we just provide an anonymous tip?' K asked.

'No. At this point, he will slaughter everyone who tries to stop him. They attacked Creeda in broad daylight. They are not going to hesitate to indulge in more murder and mayhem if anyone gets in their way when they are this close to completing their precious yagna.'

'Besides,' I added, 'this is Shukra we are talking about. He's one of us. I will not leave him in their hands for any longer than necessary.'

I turned to Sars. 'If we fail, you might be our last hope. Keep pushing the court, and let's hope they recognise the threat we are dealing with.'

Sars nodded. 'Get to the docks. I'll find a yacht operator online and get him to meet you there.' She hesitated. 'There's still a couple of hours left. I know you want to save Shukra, but there's also a good reason why Ashwatthama chose that location. If you approach it directly, you'll be sitting ducks.'

'What do you suggest?'

'Take the boat and drop anchor a little distance away from them. Not too close, just enough to spot them at a distance. Ignore them for the next six hours or so. Once it gets dark, you can attempt to board. It will also give you some time to heal.'

I didn't want to wait any longer than necessary, but there was no escaping the logic of what she was saying. Besides, I was practically useless at the moment.

I turned to Deanne. 'Coming?'

She grinned as she stood up. 'Thought you would never ask.'

CHAPTER THIRTEEN

During the unending wars between the Asuras and the Devas, Shukracharya and his knowledge of the Sanjivani mantra made a massive difference. Realising that the Devas needed an advantage, Indra convinced Kacha, the handsome son of his guru Brihaspati, to become Shukra's disciple. Before long, Shukra's daughter, Devayani, became infatuated with Kacha. The Asuras, suspecting that Kacha was working with the Devas, had him murdered on two separate occasions. Each time, at the entreating of his daughter, Shukra brought him back to life. The third time, however, the Asuras killed Kacha, burnt his body, mixed his ashes with wine and served it to Shukra.

Shukra learnt an important lesson that day, namely there was no such thing as a free lunch.

He was now faced with a quandary—saving both his and Kacha's life would require him to teach the boy the Sanjivani mantra.

> *It's ironic that Shukra, despite being regarded as one of the smartest people in that era, didn't choose the obvious solution i.e. teaching the mantra to his daughter, a grim reminder of how deeply ingrained prejudices can turn all of us into idiots.*
>
> *Through his stomach, he taught his disciple the mantra, and Kacha emerged, tearing open Shukra's belly like an 80s horror film rendition and killing him in the process. Kacha then recited the hymn and brought Shukra back to life.*
>
> *Why did Shukra not teach his daughter the mantra instead? Maybe because the attitude towards women back then could be summed up in three words.*
>
> *Bros before hoes.*
>
> – Private Journals of Akran

I was still a bit uncomfortable about having Deanne accompany us. Not that I thought she was incapable. I had gotten my ass kicked by enough female celestials over the centuries. But this felt different. I was taking someone I was romantically interested in into a warzone. That felt fundamentally wrong on several levels.

After the tongue-lashing she had given me, I couldn't dream of broaching the subject with her again. The temperature drop from the last time was still fresh in my memory. All the others had felt it too. Consciously or not, she had an elemental ability to lower a room's temperature when she wanted someone to feel her displeasure.

My reading of Norse myths had indicated only one other person with similar powers—Skadia, goddess of winter hunting and mountains. When I asked Deanne why she wasn't referenced in any Norse mythology, her face had clouded over.

'My tribulations aren't too far from your own,' was all she would say on the subject. Clearly, she had an interesting past.

If the world didn't end, we would have a lifetime to discover each other's secrets.

'Why exactly is this happening on a boat?' K asked again to no one in particular. I started explaining for the umpteenth time and then gave up. K just liked to hear the sound of his voice as he complained.

There were two primary ways for celestials to traverse realms. Portals were the most popular method among the more powerful gods and demons. They were complicated pieces of magic, not entirely dissimilar from a summoning. They usually required a highly experienced or specialised expert to craft a portal spell.

The alternative was to use ley lines.

Humans tend to think of heaven and hell in a very linear fashion with heaven being above and hell being below.

Shukra explained this to me once with an analogy about three tennis balls bouncing inside a washing machine. Intersections of ley lines are spots where the balls meet. If you are a flea, bouncing about on one of those floating balls, then at the moment of impact, you can piggyback from one world to the next. It's not a great example because the intersections last for several hours instead of seconds and these alignments aren't random—they follow trajectories that can be plotted using star charts and higher order mathematics, but honestly, this Eli5 version was the only thing I could recall after listening to him drone on for two hours. I would take that as a win.

Ashwatthama had found a suitable spot for his yagna, where the earth's ley lines intersected, and anchored his ship there. What he was essentially aiming for was to open a passage between the living world, as we knew it, and the nether realm, and then call Narakasura into being through a combination of the magical hymn and the items in his possession.

The tanker lay exactly where Sars had predicted it would be. It was an ageing bucket of rust and bolts, but there was something soothing in the way it bobbed gently in the water.

Our boat was anchored a quarter mile away. Deanne had insisted that the last leg of our approach would have to be silent. She followed up on this statement by diving into the water before we had a chance to protest. Despite her armour and the sword on her back, she swam like a shark, silent and swift, with long powerful strokes.

K and I came up behind her reluctantly. We were less encumbered than she was but also in far worse shape. The six hours of waiting had done me a world of good though. The crippling incapacitating pain and dizziness were gone. All that was left was pain from a hundred minor sources. But I could power through those for Shukra's sake.

It's funny how your mind tends to fixate on the most nonsensical things right before you go into battle. Like your brain is trying to shed everything unimportant and get it out of the way so you can maintain razor-sharp focus after. Right now, as I looked at that floating tanker in the middle of the sea, all I could think about, oddly enough, was how Shukra, Sars, K and I seemed to have spent most of our time together, yet had never once discussed living together under one roof. We only seemed to meet up for meals, or at the library or the Tea Room and the occasional bar. Maybe after all this was over, we could all just live together.

Crazy, right? Especially when we were about to raid a murderous villain's lair and could all end up dead.

It was a moonless night. We clambered onto the deck, dripping wet, yet unnoticed. Both K and I were gasping and heaving like we had just run the marathon. Deanne, on the other hand, looked like she could be doing this all night.

'I expected you to be rusty,' she said, smirking, as I flopped onto the floor. She glanced at K. 'But you? Aren't you supposed to be a fertility god? Where's that fabled stamina and vigour I've heard so much about?'

K made his best effort to look dignified. 'I don't know how it's done in your part of the world, but a god of love is not required to use his arms and legs much. We are judged by our ...'

'It's fine,' I interrupted. 'You are right, Deanne. We aren't as fit as we should be.'

'For the record, I was going to say we are judged by our silver tongue and skill at wooing women,' said K in a hurt tone.

'Oh okay.' I really hadn't thought that's where he was going with it. 'I apologise. I didn't realise ...'

He grinned. 'Of course, our tongues also have a great many purposes they can be used for.' He waggled his eyebrows suggestively.

I growled softly and he subsided, still pleased with himself. Deanne, as always, found him amusing instead of annoying.

'Tell me about it later,' she whispered. 'For now, we've got a job to do.

There were about a dozen human guards patrolling the deck. They were the usual motley crew of villains for hire, just what you would expect, armed with large guns, six packs, and walkie-talkies. The ship was also bustling with other armaments. There were two anti-aircraft guns, one on either side of the ship. High atop a raised makeshift platform, a machine gun nest was also visible and pointed towards the city. Clearly, Ashwatthama was not willing to take a chance that we would find a way to launch a full-borne air or sea assault.

K whistled softly through his teeth, 'That's going to be a bitch to deal with.'

Silently, I agreed. There was only one way to get to it, and that was up the steel ladder guarded by four men below. The nest had a bird's-eye view of the ship. If it wasn't for K's aura, we would all have been spotted already.

'Let me deal with them.' Deanne's eyes glowed with excitement as she extracted her sword. She threw me a scowl of irritation as I grabbed her by the arm.

'What are you doing?' she hissed.

'Playtime is later,' I whispered back. 'First we rescue Shukra.'

Her forehead creased with annoyance. 'That is what we are doing. These people are in the way.'

'They can be avoided. We need to get below the decks first. If you attack them now, it will alert everyone.'

She smiled, showing sparkling white teeth. 'They won't know until it's too late.'

Before I could protest further, she had slipped out of my grasp and disappeared into the shadows. I bit back a curse. There was nothing to do but wait. I trusted her tactical skills in assaulting an armed fortress far more than my own, but I couldn't help feeling her motivation was the joy of battle. Mine was the joy of surviving with all my friends alive.

I watched as she identified her first target—a large, broad-shouldered, muscular goon who clearly spent most of his time in the gym. She moved lithely and silently across the deck, closing the distance between them until she was right behind him. The hilt of her blade struck him hard on his head, causing his eyes to roll back as he collapsed. Grabbing him before he fell so as not to alert the others, she dragged him behind a heavy canopy and several coils of rope, before moving to pursue her next victim.

'You know,' K said conversationally, 'you've got to admire a woman who sets her sights on what she wants and goes out and gets it. No hesitation, no mewling by her pathetic boyfriend about how it's not safe, yadda yadda. She's a role model for women everywhere. They should make a movie about her.'

'Are you quite done?'

He grinned. 'For now.'

'Good.' We sat huddled together in the shadows, the darkness settling around us like a shroud. I snuck a glance at the watch on my hand. It was one of those fancy Swiss pieces, handcrafted to perfection without a single electronic component within. It showed two hours until midnight.

'Akran, look.'

I glanced up to where K was pointing. One of the guards had lit a cigarette, and its glowing tip stood out in the darkness of the night sky. Behind him, almost wraith-like stood Deanne. Her hand snaked around his neck, and the man struggled briefly before collapsing to the floor.

I blinked. She seemed to have moved rapidly from one guard to the next without any rest or pause between her actions. At least four of the guards were down already. And the rest still hadn't noticed.

I nearly jumped out of my skin as she suddenly appeared next to me.

'Well, what do you think?'

'You are amazing.' I meant that with all my heart. 'But you can't leave a job unfinished. One of them will notice that people are missing if you stay here and talk to us.'

She shushed me. 'I was just making a point. Don't worry. I made sure to take out the moving patrols first. Now, all we have to deal with are the static guards.' She cocked her head. 'In my culture, raiding an enemy camp together is the equivalent of a third date.' She grinned broadly. 'With everything else that implies.'

I kept my face blank. Beside me, K made a strangled sound as if he were choking on his own laughter.

'While I am delighted to hear that, I think we need to split up. You can continue up here—I'm going to find Shukra.'

Deanne nodded. 'That's a fine idea. It leaves more enemies for me to deal with. Besides, you would only get in the way.' She gave K a quick glance. 'Take care of him.'

'I will,' we both replied automatically before turning to glare at each other. Deanne laughed and then disappeared into the shadows.

A narrow staircase led us into the bowels of the ship into a long passage. We split up—K heading towards the stern while I made my way to the helm. It seemed safe enough since there didn't seem to be any other people on board.

Sars had a saying for situations like this. 'Something smells rotten in the state of Denmark.' I always figured it had something to do with fish, but it's an odd phrase to use when you live in a city full of pungent smells like Mumbai.

That phrase felt appropriate here. The hold had the gloomy depressing feel of a tomb where puppies came to die.

The inside of the tanker had been completely repurposed, and a large room was set up for the yagna. Ashwatthama sat in the centre, meditating in front of a fire. Inside the room, I could also spot a dozen or so young girls lying on makeshift pallets, all in a deep sleep. They were also tied up.

One of them was definitely Anna, the girl I had been sent to find. I let out a tiny breath of relief I didn't realise I had been holding. Part of me had resigned itself to the idea that we may never find her or that she would already be dead.

On a table nearby lay multiple objects. I recognised most of them without even looking. Varuna's umbrella. Mother Aditi's earrings. The Syamantaka. A large meat cleaver with dried, crusted blood on the edge.

K made his way back to me. 'I found him,' he whispered urgently. He led me down a passage where Shukra lay bound and gagged. The chains around his arms and waist were made of silver. He was bleeding profusely from a gash on his forehead. A silver arrowhead had been stuck deep in the wound, leaving it open and unable to heal.

He was in bad shape.

K retrieved a water skin from one corner of the room. Untying Shukra in a matter of moments, he offered it to him. Shukra grabbed it and drank greedily, spilling almost as much as what passed between his lips.

'Easy, old friend, easy,' I whispered.

'I tried,' he said, his voice hoarse. 'I told him I would not give up the mantra.' He shuddered. 'He just laughed and placed his hand on my head. I fought him off, but it was like swimming against the tide. He forced his way in, sifting through my memories. There was no way to stop him.'

I felt a rush of sympathy for him. Indra had once tried a similar brute-force attack on him to extract the Sanjivani mantra from his head. He had failed. Shukra was no slouch, particularly when it came to mental defences. Yet, what Indra and all the other gods lacked was Ashwatthama's sheer force of will. The grand old patriarch, Bhishma, had once said that Ashwatthama was part-incarnate of Shiva himself. And Shiva, like the other two members of the Trinity, was in a separate class when it came to power.

'How long before he is done with the yagna?' I asked.

'He started about twenty minutes ago,' Shukra whispered. His voice seemed hoarse as if he had been screaming. Listening to him made my gut clench. I would make the bastard suffer for this.

'He needs about forty minutes, I think. The last ten minutes are crucial. That's when he will kill the kids, throw the magical items into the fire, and break open the seals that close off the underworld from this one.'

I nodded. 'One problem at a time. Let's get you out of here.'

With the removal of the silver arrowhead and a couple more silver pieces embedded in his legs, the colour began to return to his cheeks. We helped him stand, one arm around each of our necks as we brought him to the stairs. Once there, I turned to K.

'Get him out of here quickly.'

'What are you going to do?'

'I'll be right behind you. Hurry!'

K hesitated. 'You know that you'll be seen, right?'

'I'm going to be okay, don't worry.'

He looked at me, conflicting emotions washing across his face.

'Now, K!'

He shook his head once and then disappeared.

I moved back to the main room, no longer invisible. Ashwatthama was lost in his chanting. His back was towards me as he mumbled his incantations.

Something about the room had disturbed me profoundly the first time I'd seen it. I hadn't been able to put my finger on it then, but I could see what it was now. The floor had little channels on it to collect blood. They started at each pallet and met together at the centre of the room into a makeshift trough. They were going to kill the kids as they slept and let the blood flow into the yagna.

I did not think of myself as a highly principled person. Like I've said before, exile has a wonderful way of making you reconsider your principles. I would happily indulge in piracy (online, not the seven seas), jaywalk when I was in a hurry and indulge in a great many vices in K's company.

But if there was one thing that defined who I was, my personal line in the sand, it was this: I would gladly give my life if it meant protecting those that were worth saving. In this case, a bunch of kids.

There had never been a moment when I saw more clearly the difference between right and wrong.

My job was to stand between them—the innocents on one end and those who wished them harm on the other. Murdering psychopaths, infernal legions, even the goddamn heavens if I had to.

If it was the last thing I would ever do, then I would hold my ground, look them in the eye and kick them in the nuts before I went down fighting. They might snap me like a twig but they would also not be able to walk without limping for years to come. That's what being a yaksha was all about. Heroic last stands and desperate battles against overwhelming odds.

The chanting had taken on a droning hypnotic quality. The rhythmic repetition of words, seemed to echo across the room. The shadows around him writhed of their own accord, twisting into unnatural shapes resembling creatures this world had never seen. I could sense the metaphysical seals breaking between this world and the demon realm. The room itself seemed to darken even further like a malevolent presence had made an entrance. Something whose presence cast its own weighted shadow upon the world.

A huge crowbar stood propped up against one wall. I picked it up with both hands and tested the balance. It felt fine, a heavy, sturdy weapon. Let's see what it would do to Ashwatthama's head.

I crept closer as he added a laden spoon of ghee to the fire, causing the flames to glow brighter and fiercer. The moment felt like it deserved an appropriate wisecrack.

From one angle, his head did look like an elongated ball on a scrawny neck.

Fore? Nah, only geriatrics played that game. Something baseballey? Perhaps, but I always associated it with spitting, bubble-gum and crotch grabbing. There was really only one perfect choice of words here.

Gripping the crowbar firmly in both hands, I swung as hard as I could, yelling 'Howzat' and imagining a stadium going wild as I did so. I half hoped his head would go flying off like it did in those Looney tunes cartoons.

Three feet from his head, the crowbar did a funny thing. It bent out of shape, as if it had hit a force field of some sort. The shock of the impact travelled up my arm, making me drop the crowbar to the floor with a metallic clang that reverberated through the room.

Stupid of me to think it would have been that simple.

And behind me, I heard chuckling.

It was a trap. And I had walked right into it.

***

They were on the deck, forced to take a breather, given the extent of Shukra's injuries. Deanne's plan to eliminate the hostiles first had been the right call after all. She was clearly the better tactician. They could rest for a bit.

'Are you all right?' Shukra asked as he looked at K's face. It had gone pale, and he looked like he was having a hard time breathing.

'I'm fine,' K mumbled. 'Shukra, we have to go back in.'

Shukra gave a wan smile. 'I don't think I can go anywhere.'

'Yeah, okay. You stay here, but I have to help Akran.' K had a haggard look on his face as he dry-heaved over the edge of the railing and into the sea. 'There were kids in there, Shukra. We can't leave them to die!'

People often assumed, as a fertility god, that K was only the god of lust. That wasn't true, though it certainly was a large part of his existence. He was the god of love. Period. The love of a parent for their child, the infatuation of a first crush, the tender love of a kid for his first pet, the affection between siblings, the starry-eyed love that daughters hold for their fathers or what little kids everywhere feel for their moms—all of this made him what he was. He lived through their experiences, their sorrows, their joys and pains. The sheer madness in harming a child—those who trust and look up to you to take care of them and protect them from the cruelties of the world—affected him on a more fundamental level than it did for any of the rest of us.

Being there in the bowels of the ship watching the kids bound and helpless and knowing what was in store for them had hit him where it hurt. Being in close proximity to the malice inherent in this act physically assaulted the essence of who he was.

Shukra nodded. 'I'm not going anywhere. Do what you must. Help Akran!'

***

They stepped out of the shadows, adorned like the last time, in way too much gold. I had half expected to tangle with them in more casual clothing—shorts and a T-shirt, perhaps, but instead, they had decided to make this a formal affair.

Suited me fine. I hadn't exactly gone commando for this operation either.

They had one more companion with them—a giant demon almost ten feet tall. He had the head of a bull and the body of ... well, a bull again, except that he was impossibly walking erect on his hind legs. Two curved horns and a shock of red hair adorned his head. He seemed not to be wearing any clothes; however, all the naughty bits were tastefully covered.

A wisecrack about the curtains matching the drapes sprang to mind, but honestly, it's wasted on naked demons. He'd probably think I was flirting with him. He shambled to one corner, growling softly. I was guessing he was the backup. The two posturing idiots would want to engage in some banter first.

'We know who you are, Akran,' the younger one announced smugly. He looked pleased with himself. Maybe someone would ruffle his hair later and tell him what a smart boy he was for figuring it out.

'I still don't know who you'll are,' I said. 'And in case you think that was an invitation, let me tell you right now, I don't really want to know either.'

'The first of the Yakshas,' he sneered. 'There was a time when people would quail at the sound of your name! Now you are nothing but an pathetic old shadow of your former self.'

'I may be old,' I agreed, smiling. 'Old enough to see all my enemies buried. And the barking of dogs doesn't bother me at all, little pup.'

He reddened, but before he could say anything more, his companion spoke up.

'Quite a reputation you've built for yourself over the years.' He raised his eyebrow enquiringly. 'I'm surprised someone like you chose to back the losing side.'

Mayasura's little black object was still nestled snugly in my pocket. I was going to get only one shot, though, so I planned to keep talking for a bit.

'I wasn't aware there were sides.'

'There are always sides. In this case, it is those who are ready to reach out and take what they want and those who are sheep.'

I pointed a finger at Ashwatthama. 'You know he is crazy, right? Once he is done with this, he'll probably kill you all just for fun.' I then thumbed a finger at the demon who was standing in one corner watching us with a disinterested glare. And you are cavorting with a demon! Do you not get how wrong that is?'

'You still think of demons as our enemies. We are united now. It's us vs the sheep. Celestials vs humans. We all want the same thing.'

'You really think so? The entire court is supporting this? Because it goes against every law of dharma that's ever been written.'

The older celestial looked at me like I had grown three extra heads since he last saw me. 'You are standing against us because of some misguided attachment to these humans?'

'A child,' I answered.

'A human child,' he retorted. 'Kill one and ten will take its place. They are a blight on this land. They prey on this world like locusts and devour everything it offers. They cannot see beyond their own personal gain. Why would you risk your life for vermin?'

I had heard this argument over and over again, over the years. It never failed to sting because clichéd and tired as it was, it held a grain of truth. There were a great many idiots out there who were multiplying and they happened to be the most vocal. Chlorinating the gene pool almost sounded like a good idea. Almost.

They would think me naive to believe in the innate goodness of humans. The rot reached all the way to the very top. Millions of them filled with hatred and pumped up on a vicious cocktail of fear mongering, xenophobia and a fundamental lack of education.

'You are right!' I said at last. 'They aren't perfect! But when has that ever mattered? Why are we judging them for their faults instead of how far they've risen? Look at how much they've accomplished in the past hundred years alone without our help.'

'Even a monkey can compose a song on a sitar if you give it sufficient time,' he sneered. 'All it means is that he is aping what he has seen. He doesn't understand or appreciate the music.'

'And you'll never know if they are capable of appreciating the music, as it were, if you end their lives now.' I pointed at the sleeping girls. 'You aren't killing one of them today. Or five, or ten. You are killing a thousand possible lives they could have led, a set of infinite possibilities based on the choices they make. One of them might be the greatest mathematician the world has ever seen. Maybe a singer to rival the music of the heavens itself. Or a politician who might bring them together instead of seeking to divide them.'

I paused. 'Maybe that last one is too much to hope for. But every one of those choices will be snuffed out today if you kill them.'

The older yaksha sighed. 'That speech will look pretty on your tombstone,' he muttered as his fingers began to glow.

There were no words left to be said. We would not see eye to eye on this. Their deep-rooted prejudices about the human race were too ingrained for a few words to overturn.

The younger one yawned theatrically.

'Told you he wouldn't listen. Can we kill him now?'

'I killed your friend Varunn not too long ago,' I pointed out. 'He underestimated me as well.'

He laughed. 'Varunn was a fool who bungled something as simple as keeping you under guard. We are going to kick your ass!'

'Hey, so, speaking of asses, does yours ever get jealous of the shit that comes out of your mouth?' I said, with a smirk.

He froze. I doubt anyone had ever spoken to him that way before.

'Was that too subtle?' I smiled mockingly at him. 'Let me break it down for you. Kid, the smartest part of you ran down your mom's leg when you were being conceived.'

He stared at me expressionless. The only clue that my taunts had struck home were his fists, clenched by his side, suddenly lighting up.

Any minute now …

I raised the cards I was holding. They floated in the air above my palm, glowing in a dull shade of orange. Less bright than his wrist, since I needed to conserve my mana but bright enough that there was no mistaking my intentions.

He gave a mirthless laugh. 'You really need a few new tricks. Didn't we just kick your ass when you tried that last time?'

I grinned. 'This one's different. Watch what happens when they land behind you.'

I flung the cards out in this smooth and practised fan-like gesture that was one part panache and three parts bullshit. Both Yakshas immediately raised their hands. Lighting flashed out of their fingertips, incinerating them. It would have stung … if the cards weren't ordinary glowing bits of paper.

The split-second distraction, however, was all that I needed. Mayasura's device came up as I stepped forward, right up close and personal, and pulled the trigger.

Remember how I said electricity and celestials don't mix? Now imagine you are a Yaksha, and a taser gets shoved into your groin.

The tiny little stun gun packed a mean punch. At a little under a million volts, it was not meant for use on humans. And while Mas always claimed the floating cities of Tripura were his greatest achievement to date, it wouldn't surprise me at all to learn this little toy would come in a close second.

I had aimed at the younger of the two shitheads because I didn't really like his face. Or his attitude. Or the fact that he could have fed the population of Mumbai with two square meals every day for a week with just his jewellery.

The electric current exploded through his body, igniting his hair and his clothes. It ripped his aura to shreds, turned his genitals into a smoking ruin, and unclenched his bowels. I couldn't have gotten a better effect even if I had shoved a Brahmastra up his ass. It took all of three microseconds for the power to fully take our man out of commission before the electricity arced forward, searching for fresh targets.

There's a reason I don't walk around sporting a lot of jewellery. Everything silver interferes with my limited powers, and all metals conduct electricity. Especially gold.

The elder Yaksha had chosen to dress like Kubera's bitch. He was adorned from head to toe in gold jewellery, some of which melted straight away into his skin as he howled and writhed upon the floor. For a moment, the electric charge was a live, visceral entity, snapping at both of them and looking around for someone else to attack. It shot between the two of them rapidly, burning the air between them and leaving behind two steaming, charring piles of flesh before finally dissipating.

Barbequed arseholes. The best kind.

'That, shitheads, is why I was known as the first of the Yakshas!'

A slow clapping from behind reminded me that I wasn't finished with all of them.

The demon had shed its bored look and was now appraising me with sparkling intelligence in his eyes. I might have been imagining it, but there was also a hint of respect in there. He dropped to all fours and came closer. Even crouched, he was more than a head taller than me. His breath was fetid as he leaned forward.

'That was well done, Akran, Slayer of Nishika. Now… how exactly are you planning to get past … ME?'

CHAPTER FOURTEEN

The caste system was a rigid hierarchy back in the day. It is the reason why everyone kept calling Karna 'sut putra.' They were letting him know that despite his skills as a Kshatriya, they would always remember his lineage.

But here's the other thing that people seem to forget. You are judged in the end based on your deeds, not which strata of society you were born in. If you acted like a dick but were born into the family of a priest, it didn't give you some sort of spiritual immunity. You still remained a dick.

— Private Journals of Akran

There was a smug, knowing look on the demon's face.

'Do I know you?' I asked.

He yawned. This demon seemed ancient. Before toothpaste was invented—that was for certain.

'I've been around since the glory days of Lanka. It is possible.'

'You are not someone whose parent, sibling or girlfriend I've killed in the past?'

'That has never mattered. Only the strongest survive.'

Great. A Darwinian. Anyone who talked like that would be a bitch to kill.

'And we are engaged in this chit-chat right now because...?'

He snorted as much as a four-hundred-pound minotaur-like demon could. 'Not all of us are as keen to see Narakasura rise again.'

I felt a faint stir of hope.

'Are you saying you will help me?'

He chuckled. If you've never heard a massive demon chuckle when he is less than a few feet away from you, I recommend it for the experience.

'You misunderstand me, little Yaksha. We hate your kind. We would never help you.'

'You chose to help those two,' I pointed out.

He stared at me for a moment. 'I didn't mean Yakshas. I meant humans. You are no better than them. I can smell the stench of humanity on you. Frail, naked apes clambering to take their place on the totem pole.'

'Naked isn't really a bad look on some of them you know.'

He shrugged. 'It doesn't matter. They all taste like chicken anyway.'

I was definitely getting mixed vibes here. And the odds of him helping me were vanishingly small.

'Much as I enjoy listening to your culinary choices, can we perhaps get to the point?'

The demon chuckled. 'I will assist by not interfering. Though I will tear you to pieces once the threat is over.'

I hate demons who beat around the bush.

'You are saying I can try and stop him from raising Narakasura, and you won't interfere. But once I stop him, you plan to kill me?'

He smiled, showing a mouth full of yellow pointed teeth. 'Very good, little Yaksha. But just to be clear, I won't just kill you. I'll use your bones to pick your flesh from the gaps between my teeth.'

That was good to hear. Nice that he was so clear about it. Poetic, eloquent demons were the best kind.

I sighed. 'Okay, back away then and give me some room.'

He made a keening sound that I realised was laughter. I picked up the deck of cards and slowly and deliberately turned away from him. I was hoping he would keep his word and not attack once my back was turned, but I had no option but to trust him at this stage. I was running out of time.

Ashwatthama's eyes widened as he saw me. My presence wasn't enough to make him pause or break his concentration. He just glared angrily as he continued to chant. His little trap had been sprung and failed.

My turn, now.

'Hey, Ash,' I waved cheerily at him. 'Did I ever tell you about the animals Drona used to make passionate love to?'

No change whatsoever in his demeanour, aside from the murderous looks he was giving me. I realised that he couldn't hear me. He was fully caught up in the ritual. His ears had probably been shielded as well.

During the Treta Yuga, Ravana had once engaged in a similarly deep and complex ritual. The Vanaras had made multiple attempts to disrupt it, but once the yagna began, you could not move or harm him physically unless he chose to break off from the ritual on his own. Finally, Angad, the crown prince of the Vanaras, dragged Ravana's wife, Mandodari, into the room by the hair. Ravana flew into a rage and abandoned the yagna to rescue his wife.

So, what could I do that could similarly piss off our mendicant here?

K once told me there are three topics guaranteed to piss people off to unholy vendetta-level proportions where they lose all sense of rational thought.

Religion. Politics. And Family!

He would know. He was and always will be the original master baiter.

I thumbed the illusion cards in my hands. The problem with illusions is that they need to be controlled. I need to manipulate the people or objects involved. And I can't do that without mana.

I had enough to last about two minutes. If that wasn't enough, I was out of options.

I knew a little about the etymology of Drona's name. The story was that his father, Rishi Bhardwaj, saw a water nymph and was so consumed with lust, that he emptied his seed into a little pot—presumably, it was uncool to rub one out in the bushes or the river while bathing—and he decided to preserve the evidence. A child was born from that union of man and vessel, and hence he was named 'Drona', which in Sanskrit is a term referring to a pot.

I've heard worse. It's fairly common, at least in the circles I was a part of, for kids to be birthed by gods or rivers or from fire sacrifices or fish and, in one case, from a semen infused kheer poured into someone's ear.

I started with a simple naked apsara dancing in the water. Ashwatthama's eyes widened slightly, but the chanting continued unabated. This was technically his grandmother, though I am pretty sure the version I crafted was at least ten times hotter. Still, it was a very obvious reference that he didn't fail to get, and a little vein began to throb on the side of his forehead, as he watched. A little pot appeared in a corner, out of which popped Drona.

What followed next was a cinematic masterpiece. I couldn't, for the life of me, remember who Drona's wife was, so I improvised with a horse. I led the illusion of Drona through some rapid little gyrations and pelvic thrusts that would have put the king of pop to shame. Ashwatthama's eyes stayed fixed on me, blazing with hatred as he continued to chant.

Drona proceeded to mount the horse vigorously, and a baby dropped out from below. The baby had a face like a horse and made a neighing sound.

He knew I was trying to distract him. A sane person would have persevered and completed the yagna.

Ashwatthama wasn't sane. Millennia of isolation and suffering, as well as his pathological hatred of me, finally got the better of him. With a vicious snarl, he stood up, the yagna forgotten. A dozen bolts of lightning flew from his hands, incinerating me.

Or rather, the illusion of me.

I wouldn't piss off a mad demigod without taking precautions. Even I wasn't that stupid.

To his credit, he knew at once it was an illusion. He whirled around, seeking me with murder in his eyes.

Invisibility was not one of my powers. I could fade into the shadows, letting them envelop me, but that required mana. After that little performance, I had less than a minute's worth remaining.

Ashwatthama chanted softly under his breath before flinging his hand up. A green globe of pulsing energy emerged, hovering in the air for a few seconds before heading straight toward me. It hit my pathetic little mana shield, dissipating it and leaving me out there in the open. All I had was a single deck of cards, and we knew how well they worked the last time.

I smiled sheepishly. 'Hello, Ash. No hard feelings, huh?'

He stepped closer, sneering. 'You think you've won, don't you?'

I did think so. A pyrrhic victory because he was going to kill me, but still, I had triumphed against all odds. Terrified as I was that he was going to kill me in a profoundly unpleasant way, I couldn't help myself from blabbering. Anything that bought me a few more seconds before the end.

'Look, big guy. I killed your dad, you hurt my friend, why don't we call it even and hug it out? Carrying all that anger inside will give you ulcers if you aren't careful.'

He cocked his head, in a curious bird-like gesture. 'Do you actually think I will let bygones be bygones?'

Not even if hell freezes over.

'I'll admit, the chances of that happening are slim. But,' I continued as I saw him glower, 'if you postpone killing me for, say, a day or two, you might come around to my point of view. About the yagna, I mean. Not about your daaaa ...,' I trailed off, as I saw his expression darken. 'Wait, Wait ... Umm, I'll take you to this garage pub called Toto's in Bandra, with music to die for.'

He smirked. I felt an uneasy feeling in the pit of my stomach. It's never a good sign when a villain smirks. Laughing maniacally is still acceptable. It can mean they are overconfident or trying to intimidate you. When they smirk, it means trouble.

'The stars stay in alignment for six more hours. I will gladly restart the yagna from the beginning if it means I can teach you some manners.' He pretended to look at his watch. 'I can torture you for another five hours at least before I need to begin.'

And just like that, my victory turned to ashes.

Despite my admonitions to myself, I winced as he moved closer. I couldn't help it. Was it all for nought? I was about to subject myself to a few hours of unbearable torture, and all I had accomplished was for nothing.

I knew what was coming a split second before he raised his hand, but was powerless to prevent it. His signature move. I felt myself being lifted off the floor and slammed into the wall. A sharp, searing pain in my shoulder told me that it had caught on something jagged.

A cruel grin spread over his face as he watched me bleed. I screamed as he grabbed me by my injured shoulder and threw me across the room.

This was not going the way I had planned.

He smiled maliciously. 'Poor little Yaksha! Trapped and all alone on a little boat. About to find out how worthless your existence really is.'

'He's not alone,' said a soft voice that rang clearly in the silence that followed. Both Ashwatthama and I turned to see who had interrupted his villainous monologue.

Deanne stood there, tall, proud and smoking hot. She looked every inch like a warrior. Ashwatthama would have to be foolish in the extreme to underestimate her. Her gauntlets, breastplate and the metal skirt she was wearing all gleamed brightly like glistening moonbeams. Whatever fight the humans had put up against her on the upper level had also given her face an inner glow.

'I stand with Akran,' she said.

Ashwatthama gave her a disdainful glance. 'I have no quarrel with you, woman. Walk away and I will let you live.'

'I heard you were a great warrior,' said Deanne brightly as she stepped into the room. 'Did you gain that reputation by only picking on those who are weaker than you?' She smirked. 'Or only by killing people in their sleep perhaps?'

Note to self: When you tell a girl you are dating stories about a homicidal sociopath, ask her to kindly refrain from repeating those stories to said sociopath.

A low growl emerged from his throat.

'Three thousand years!' he seethed. 'Nobody remembers or even cares about the wonders I accomplished or the deeds I wrought. A single mistake is what I was punished for. Meanwhile the Pandavas murdered and—'

It's never a good idea to interrupt a villainous monologue but I felt oddly compelled at this point. 'Umm, I hate to interrupt,' I said, giving him my most sincere smile. 'But if you went ahead with this sacrifice, you would be making two mistakes.'

He turned glowering eyes at me, all traces of his self-pity gone.

'And technically, since these two incidents are three thousand years apart, it means you haven't really learnt from your mistakes at all. Which means maybe this punishment was justified …' I trailed off as his eye began to twitch. No, scratch that. It spasmed like a fish out of water.

Akran, breaker of delusions and self-deceptions. If I survived, I would buy myself a couch and nod sympathetically when people moaned about their problems.

A low rumbling sound from behind caused me to turn once again. The large demon raised a paw.

'Allow me to deal with the Yaksha,' he rumbled. 'I have a score to settle.'

Ashwatthama laughed. He was quite mad, I realised, from the fervent gleam in his eyes. He pointed his palm upwards, and a sword appeared magically in it.

'Come then, girl, you want to fight a Maharathi? Let me show you what you've gotten yourself into.' He strode towards her, ignoring me completely.

The Maharathis were like a bunch of dudes in a locker room, bragging about the size of their swords, except instead of actually whipping them out and measuring them, they threw down a number of how many warriors they could fight all by themselves. With these guys, the number was, wait for it… seven hundred and twenty thousand. That's right. That's how many they could supposedly fight. And not like one of those Kung fu movies where each one attacks you, one at a time, while the others shuffle nervously—they could apparently take on all of these dudes simultaneously.

Sure, buddy, and I've got a bridge to sell you.

Here's a pro tip for cutting through all the bullshit you've been told. If someone can't pull off a stunt like that today, chances are, it was just as impossible back then.

At any other time, I would have been insulted to think he didn't find me significant enough to worry about turning his back on me. At this point, however, I felt only relief.

Deanne yelled a primordial battle cry and charged. I wanted to shout out a few words of encouragement, but I didn't dare watch that fight. I was too busy watching the demon.

'What score do you have to settle?'

'You killed my brother a long time ago.'

'What happened to you not caring about any of that?'

He shrugged, meaty shoulders shaking in a gesture of nonchalance. 'I lied.'

'Why would you lie about something like that?'

He smirked. 'I wanted to see how you would handle Ashwatthama.'

He leapt forward as he did so, but I was ready. Two of the cards in my hand were flung out, exploding in his face. They were good, solid explosions and I could feel the heat of the blasts in the confined space within the ship.

They didn't do any good. He shrugged them off and struck at me with a massive paw, which I missed narrowly as I rolled away. I already had a pair of bindings, which I flung out.

'Nibaddha!'

The cards morphed into giant metallic chains that wrapped around his legs. The demon growled; disdain evident in his eyes. With a tug of his arms, the chains tore as if they were made out of paper.

Not good! A demon who, in mere seconds, could break the bindings I had crafted painstakingly over the years, was a level-ten demon, at least. At my current power levels, even a level three demon was too much for me.

Another card turned into a spear which I threw at his face. He caught it between his teeth and snapped it clean.

'Who was your brother?' I gasped. 'I don't think he was this much trouble!'

The demon growled. 'I've lived endless centuries by not talking about my lineage. Better for you to underestimate me as a foe than to learn what a threat I can be.'

'You chose a hell of a day to start.'

He laughed. 'I suppose it wouldn't hurt for you to know who kills you. I am called Shambha-La.'

'Is that like a family name? I still have no clue who your stupid brother was!'

'When I'm done with you, little Yaksha, the world won't have a clue who you are either. I will shred your body into fine strips that I will salt and cure, and feast upon slowly over the next hundred years.'

'That doesn't answer my question … aaargh!'

Even as I spoke, he leaped forward, closing the distance between us. He moved fast, much faster than I could anticipate. Like a blur, his paw slapped the deck out of my hand. One of his claws drew blood from my palm; I tried to roll away, but the demon was faster. Grabbing me by the leg, he flung me across the room and into a wall.

I had a split second to reflect upon how tired I was getting of being tossed around before my head connected with the floor.

Bile rushed up as I dry heaved. Some part of my body was bleeding as red drops splattered the floor. The dizzying agony of my stomach clenching made me feel light-headed, and my vision dimmed. I could see him coming closer on all fours.

'Stop!' I gasped. 'We can discuss this!'

'But I'm just getting started,' he said, as he kicked me viciously.

I felt a couple of ribs crack. A red mist was forming around my eyes.

Shit, shit, shit.

Each new movement brought new pain. It would have been the easiest thing in the world to lie down and slip into unconsciousness.

But not yet.

There was nothing else left. I was running on fumes from the pounding he had given me. The only thing keeping me awake was that people were depending on me to stop the yagna. That, and pride. I'd be damned before I faced the end of the world down on my knees in a pool of my own blood. I would get onto my feet and spit in the face of my enemies, even if it killed me.

Of course, that was easier said than done. My body screamed in protest to lie the fuck down as I gritted my teeth and forced myself to rise. My limbs felt leaden as if weighed down by stones. Still, inch by inch, I rose until I could look him straight in the eye. Shambha-la had taken a few steps back as he watched me get to my feet. Now he clapped his massive paws together.

'Such spirit! I think in another life, we could have been friends.'

'Friends like you make me wish I had more middle fingers,' I muttered weakly. I would like to have said it with more emphasis but the pain in my chest and stomach was making me wheeze.

He laughed again. Which was good. Every moment he spent laughing was a moment he wasn't trying to kill me.

When this was over, maybe I could consider a fallback career as a stand-up comedian. I took a hesitant step backwards, trying to put some distance between us before he closed the gap again. I was out of options. He seemed to enjoy the little cat-and-mouse game, for he matched my pace, leaving me plenty of time to try something else. But what?

The large meat cleaver sat near the ruby and the earrings. I held it in front of me as I swayed unsteadily on my feet. He seemed to think it was funny, for he sat down and howled in laughter.

I doubted the cleaver could harm a demon, certainly not one as big as this one. Maybe if it had magic? But no, it was just an ordinary cleaver, and I had no mana left. It was definitely the end.

So be it. If I was going to die, I would at least learn the secrets that had plagued my existence until then.

I kept the knife aside, picked up the jewel and placed it around my neck.

And watched the world explode around me.

***

'Will you do this for me, Akran?'

They stood together in the empty grove. Dark clouds filled the sky, and intermittent flashes of lightning could be seen in the distance. Akran's companion was draped in shadows.

'First, the curse. Convince Samba that it will be a great prank to pull on all the rishis. They will all be sitting together—Vashishta, Vishwamitra, Narada and the rest. The most vital to the plan is Durvasa. Make sure he is present when it happens. His irascible nature will take care of the rest.'

'It shall be as you say, master.'

'Then, the weapons. For the next stage to take place, they need to be lost.'

'But I am the one in charge of the weapons. How can I let them get taken?'

'You will find a way, Akran.'

'It shall be done. I will find a way.'

The stranger cloaked in shadows stepped forward, and I finally saw the face of the person who had tormented my thoughts all these thousands of years.

It was Krishna himself.

CHAPTER FIFTEEN

Despite the more obvious lessons the Mahabharata teaches us, there is one subtle but major learning that is often overlooked. About shooting your mouth off before thinking through the consequences.

Or more precisely making terrible vows.

There is an art to them of course. Draupadi vowing to leave her hair untied unless washed with Dushasan's blood was strictly minor league. Except for the larger hygiene concerns, it impacted nobody except herself. Similarly, Bhim vowing to drink Dushasan's blood had no long-term consequences. Except perhaps for Dushasan.

The more dangerous ones, of course, were those whose repercussions everyone else would feel.

Bhishma's oath of celibacy can be pointed to as the root cause of the eventual conflict. Karna vowing never to turn away someone who asks for alms is another. It allowed Indra to deprive him of his most powerful defences. Arjun threatening to kill himself if he couldn't kill Jayadratha was

> *a narrowly averted disaster thanks to Krishna's intervention. Under-promise. Over Deliver. It's a pretty simple life lesson.*
>
> *Yet thousands of years later, humans are still doing the exact opposite.*
>
> – Private Journals of Akran

As I looked closer, I realised I was wrong. It was not the Krishna I knew.

This was an aspect I'd never seen before—an older Krishna, one with white hair.

I knew then why I called him master. This was a different Avatar of Vishnu, one that the rest of the world hadn't been privileged to see. I was being honoured exclusively, and I felt undeserving.

'There's a reason why I am doing this, Akran. My time on earth is over. The Kali Yuga needs to begin now. But until I return, I need to entrust you with looking after my flock.'

'Why like this, lord? Why not, like in times past, where you die peacefully, instead of in this cruel, needlessly violent manner?

'It is as it needs to be, Akran. The Kali Yuga does not begin or end placidly. The events are so shocking that centuries later, people can still point to the date and say, "That was when it began."'

I nodded. The memories were clearing up. I felt like a fog had been lifted from my mind. For the first time, I could feel something like sunlight filtering in, bringing thoughts back to life.

'You will spend a long time without your powers. It will help you understand the people you will save better. And when the time is right, the jewel will grant your memories back.

'What will you say when they question you? When they ask why you had betrayed your most sacred trust?'

'Perhaps you could block my memories? Make sure that they cannot be discovered.'

'As you wish.' The older Krishna looked sad, almost contemplative. 'You know the terrible burden that I place on your shoulders, don't you, Akran? Do you accept this charge? Being condemned by everyone? Being cast out of the heavens?'

I nodded silently in lockstep with Akran the younger. I could feel his emotions exactly as he was feeling them. The conviction that he was doing the right thing. The knowledge that he would be ostracised. The resolve to see this through, no matter the cost.

'When you are ready, you will know more. The gem is the key, Akran. Wear it sparingly. Its power can consume you if you aren't careful.'

'All of this is necessary, isn't it?'

'It is as it is meant to be. Your role here isn't done. An ancient evil is returning to the world. I trust you to help stop it.'

'What is my role after that?'

He smiled. 'Whatever you choose it to be.' His voice seemed to be coming to me in waves, fading in and out.

My eyes snapped open. I awoke feeling light-headed. Less than a few seconds had passed as I dreamt. Something had changed within me. Something was not the same. A wicked, gravity defying feeling was pushing through my insides.

First, a trickle, then a gurgling stream, and finally like a biblical flood, the power rushed back in. It swelled up within me, bursting forth in a massive wave, a feeling I had not experienced in well three thousand years. I could feel every hair on my body stand as I rose a few feet above the ground and began to glow. Still, the power continued to build up. More and more until it felt like I would burst.

It was akin to finding an oasis after you have wandered through a desert, dying of thirst for weeks on end. That's what it felt like. Unbridled exhilaration. A sense of completeness.

I looked up at the demon who was watching me, wide-eyed with fear. He should have killed me when he had the chance, instead he had wasted an opportunity toying with me and being sadistic. My thirst had been quenched but the flood of mana refused to be contained. It was spilling out like I was a leaky faucet.

It was time to put it to good use.

I pointed at the demon. A blast of blue lightning from my fingers tore his right hand apart. The demon growled in anger as he charged forward—a savage hulk of teeth and muscle. Maybe he was hoping I needed time to charge up between attacks.

He was wrong.

I forced my will into his mind, freezing him as he reared on his hind legs to leap. His face contorted and he clawed at his head, ripping out big chunks of flesh as he tried to shut me out. It didn't work. I no longer needed to lock eyes or even be close to him to get into his head.

There.

I clenched a mental fist deep inside his skull, and the demon's head exploded, gore splattering all over the floor. The terrible Shambha-la, a demon who had survived thousands of years through his raw cunning, lay dead before me. It was a worthy addition to my title.

One down, one more to go.

I spun on my heel to watch what else was going on. K showed up quite clearly in my sight. Despite him being invisible, our auras had connected, and I could see him. He was watching the battle between Deanne and Ashwatthama with a slightly worried look on his face.

A real sword fight is nothing like the competitive fencing matches we see today, with everyone being polite and restrained as they seek to score points. A fight where both opponents are seeking to kill the other is truly a sight to behold—both frightening and heroic at the same time.

Humans tire easily. Their battles turn into slow, plodding matches since stamina usually makes the critical difference. An actual honest to god fight among celestials is a joy to behold. Deanne and Ashwatthama fought like a pair of snarling, hissing cats, each seeking to break through the other's guard, neither asking nor giving any quarter.

The fight had not been going well for her. Despite her strength and skill, her armour was already damaged, and there were deep gashes on her arms and legs.

It turned out that Ashwatthama was pretty decent with a sword. But that wasn't the deciding factor. He could heal much faster than her. Even as I watched, she struck him thrice, on his arm, on his face and his shoulder, but his wounds healed instantly. Every hit that he landed, however, took her much longer to heal. She needed help.

She broke from her last attack on him, and they both stood a few feet from each other, glaring. Deanne was panting hard. I didn't think she had fought someone quite like Ashwatthama before.

I stepped forward next to her. 'All going well?'

She snorted, then glanced at me and did a double take. 'What have you done to yourself?'

'Got myself an upgrade. This is the real me!'

'Uh-huh. Can the real you stop posturing and lend a hand?'

Ashwatthama opened his mouth to speak, but I ignored him. Banter during battle was just plain stupid.

A powerful blast of lightning flew from my hands and engulfed him. He staggered back in pain before raising his hand to counter it.

I waved my hands again, and once again, lightning shot out, but this time, Ashwatthama matched it with his own. The two bolts struck each other in the centre of the space between us before they both fizzled out.

Right. Maybe this is how banter started. It's because someone realised that, despite their best efforts, they had been hopelessly outclassed and the least they could do was to say something clever before the battle ended.

'You've gained back your powers,' he spat.

A master of the fucking obvious. 'You must be a Yogi,' I deadpanned. He continued to stare blankly. I hate it when sarcasm bounces off people.

'It is over, Ash man. You can't beat both of us together.'

'Would you like to pick a weapon?' he mocked. 'Even at full power, I'm more than a match for you and your friend here.'

Yakshas didn't use conventional weapons. We had no need for them, and it would be stupid to engage with a Maharathi, anyway. Still, what he said gave me an idea.

The jewel had cleared my mind of everything—the memories that were hidden, the block on my powers, and something more—the location of the sacred weapons.

I reached my hand out tentatively and found the dimensional fold in space where they were hidden. There were quite a few of them. The Sudarshan Chakra was particularly powerful but way too complex for me to wield. The same went for the plough of Balaram. There was one weapon, though, that felt appropriate.

I extracted the long-curved blade. It gleamed with a dazzling blue light, looking just like it did when it made its first appearance on the mortal plane over three thousand years ago. The Blade of Shiva. The sword that guaranteed you victory if your cause was righteous. The Chandrahas.

I handed the blade to Deanne. Between the two of us, she was clearly the better warrior. All she needed was something to even the odds.

'Use this sword. Any cuts made will slice through his magical shields. Every blow you strike on his flesh also adds poison to your attacks. They will force him to heal slowly, like a human.'

Deanne gave a feral smile as she took the proffered blade. Ashwatthama cursed again as he assumed a defensive stance. Deanne rushed forward, pressing her attack while I used some of my mana to heal her wounds and remove her fatigue.

She feinted at his shoulder, at the last second twisting her arm to strike him above his knee. The effect was instantaneous. The sword was imbibed with Halahala, the blue poison that Shiva had swallowed during the churning of the oceans. Ashwatthama's curse kept him alive, but the poison countered his natural ability to heal. The gash her sword had opened up on his leg began to bleed.

Ashwatthama screamed as he launched a blistering counterattack, forcing her to back off. For a few seconds, he had forgotten about us. His rage was entirely focused on her. It was time to end this.

'Are the kids okay?'

K had stepped forward quietly to stand by my side.

'I removed their bindings. They are still unconscious. We can take them up together once we are done.'

'Let's do this then.'

K reached out and grasped my arm. There was a momentary crackle as his aura adjusted to my new power levels before our auras intertwined and melded into one. I tugged at his arm, and we ran straight at Ashwatthama.

We might have looked pretty stupid running arm in arm if we hadn't been invisible.

I couldn't penetrate Ashwatthama's defences through magical means. The only way to strike at him was with physical contact, through his aura.

We reached him a split second after he knocked Deanne off her feet with a blow to her jaw, using the pommel of his sword. He raised it upwards, preparing the killing thrust, just as we smashed into him.

Our combined auras proved to be enough to neutralise him. There was a spasm of pain that shot through all of us as our auras forcibly connected. For a few brief seconds, we were able to physically grapple with him.

It was the perfect opportunity for me to land a punch on his face. It felt like I was punching granite.

To his credit, he barely blinked at the surprise attack. He simply stepped out of range of Deanne's sword, grabbed me by the neck, and began to choke the life out of me. He didn't realise until it was too late that K had stabbed him in the chest with three of his little love arrows.

Physical weapons, other than the Chandrahas, couldn't hurt him. His body was able to heal rapidly. But K's arrows weren't physical. They were embodiments of his own power as a god of love. And if the mighty Lord Shiva of the Trinity could be affected by them … well, our boy-wonder here had no chance in hell.

The change was instantaneous. He was still staring at Deanne, but now his jaw dropped open, and he looked slack-eyed. As he lowered his sword arm and fell to the floor, an idiotic grin took shape on his face.

Deanne stared at him dumbfounded.

'What the fuck is wrong with him?'

'He's in love.' I grinned. Ashwatthama looked like a love-struck puppy. Despite my amusement, I knew it wouldn't last. The spell couldn't hold him for long.

'How do we kill him?'

'You can't. There's nothing we can do to stop him. All we can do is slow him down.'

She jabbed her sword into his neck. It was a hard stab, a mortal wound on anyone else but it only pierced his neck slightly. Enough that only a tiny trickle of blood emerged.

'No harm in making an attempt, then.'

'Deanne!' I spoke firmly.

She turned to me with a half-annoyed, half-challenging look in her eyes. 'What?'

'Let it go. It's cruel to kick someone when they are down. Especially when it is not going to do an iota of good.'

She gave a disgusted snort. 'Where I come from, we don't leave an enemy alive.'

I was too tired to argue the point, but I did it anyway.

'He is meant to stay alive until the next Yuga. There's no getting around that. You can stab him, burn him, drown him—it doesn't matter. It will cause him pain but the boon he received will keep bringing him back to life. You can't kill him.'

She gave a snarl of frustration and stormed away. Ashwatthama stared at her retreating backside with that same goofy grin on his face like a teenager discovering his first *Playboy*.

The water inside the ship had reached ankle level already. Together, K and Deanne assisted in carrying the unconscious children upstairs. I used the same chains they had used on Shukra to bind Ashwatthama as he lay on the floor.

This was it. My final chance to talk to him. Part of me still felt responsible for the state he was in. Everything that happened to him was directly because of my actions.

'Ashwatthama, I'm sorry. This apology comes three thousand years too late but here it is. There are a lot of things I regret, chief among them being my role in the death of your father. He was a good man, and I had nothing but respect for him.'

A slight change in his breathing was the only clue that maybe my voice was cutting through the fog in his brain. I pressed on.

'But it was war. We all did things we weren't proud of. The gods know you have more than enough reason to regret your actions after the war.'

'What I never intended is for my actions to have set you on this path. To make you feel so much hatred for me and the world, that you were willing to burn it all down. If I had any inkling of this, I might have intervened with Krishna on your behalf. You have a destiny beyond this Yuga as one of the world's greatest sages. That will only happen when you relinquish all desires, including ones such as ending the Yuga early and killing billions of people in the process.'

He gave no sign that he had understood or even heard me. Still, I paused as I climbed up the staircase to look at him one final time. The water had already reached knee level. Soon, the entire ship would be submerged.

In that moment, I pitied him. I knew what it was like to wander the earth, alone and friendless, hated by most of those who had previously loved you. After the initial stage of fear, there was anger. A white-hot desire to inflict pain on all of those who had brought you down. The only difference was that having friends like K, Shukra and Sars had pulled me back from the brink. Thanks to them, I had been able to claw out of the despair and blinding hatred at the injustice of the hand I had been dealt. Ashwatthama had been unable to forge those bonds of friendship with anyone. That was what led to his downfall.

I couldn't kill him. Or even rehabilitate him. He wouldn't listen to reason. Especially not from me. There was too much raw hatred, pain and suffering in there.

All I could do was hinder him. I would keep doing that every time he resurfaced.

EPILOGUE

ONE WEEK LATER

We sat together in Creeda. All five of us. It had been an interesting few days.

The library and the café had been fully repaired. Things were finally back to normal. On the surface, at least.

'What's the news from upstairs?' I asked Sars.

'The celestial court is in turmoil. They finally figured out you just saved them from a catastrophe.'

She hesitated.

'You can tell me the truth, Sars. I won't be offended.'

She made a face. 'They are also blaming you for it. Some of them are saying you engineered the whole thing to curry favour with the court. The only reason nothing's happened yet is that nobody up there quite knows how to deal with the fact that you've gained back your powers.'

I rolled my eyes. The politics of the court would go exactly as I predicted. Nothing had changed in the past three thousand years.

'There's talk of hauling you back and reinstating your punishment.'

I smiled. Part of me was hoping they would try. I had never felt more alive than I did now. I suspected I was a lot stronger than any of the other celestials and was looking forward to testing that theory.

'They overstepped their authority and committed the biggest travesty of justice ever,' said K. 'They would all be happier if you were to conveniently disappear.'

'Maybe I should have a chat with them,' Deanne suggested.

Deanne and I had started seeing each other. As promised, she had taught me plenty of new tricks that I didn't know before. At least a couple of times every night so far.

I shook my head. 'Back when I was powerless, all I cared about was how to get back to being part of the celestials again. Now, I don't care anymore. I've got everything I need right here.'

There was a moment of silence.

'Any word on the demon I tangled with?' I asked Shukra.

Despite the trauma of having been kidnapped, Shukra was looking well. I suspect that he even enjoyed the little adventure we had just gone through. It was a quintessentially human trait—time healing most wounds.

'As a matter of fact, yes. Shambha-la is—sorry, *was*—a demon prince. Killing him is a pretty big deal.'

'Big enough that I might have other demons coming after me?'

Shukra nodded.

'Good. I'm looking forward to it.'

Sars spoke up again. 'It wasn't supposed to be this way. The celestial court was supposed to be protecting the human realm instead of preying on it. If they did their jobs, we wouldn't need to clean up their mess every time.'

Shukra cleared his throat. 'I was thinking perhaps we could do something about that.'

'What do you mean?'

'All of this started when you decided, out of the goodness of your heart,' he ignored my mock glare and continued, 'to help someone in need. Why not do that more often?'

I considered the idea. 'What do you have in mind?'

'Every one of us here has abilities. And all we've done is squander them away. Some of us in hiding like you, some because they choose to live a hedonistic lifestyle,' he glanced pointedly at K, 'some like myself who grew weary of the politics of the court. But when someone like Ashwatthama comes along, whose plans impact everyone, we can't wait for the celestial court to act.

'What I propose is that we take matters into our own hands—we take on the challenges nobody else wishes to solve. Rescue the innocents that this city has lost. We work on our own terms. And we make a difference. A real, tangible difference.' He glanced at Deanne. 'You're one of us now. This is open to you as well.'

She smiled. I could see that his words had pleased her.

'You think there is a need for this? As in, you think this was not a one-time thing that just happened?'

Shukra took a moment to reply.

'Do you remember how I told you once about the realms and how they move?'

'The tennis balls in the washing machine?' I hazarded.

Shukra beamed. 'Exactly! Ashwatthama's yagna was like a giant hand closing in and holding the three together, long enough for someone like Narakasura who had been disembodied, only to be resurrected and gain passage into our realm.'

I gave a wary nod. I understood the mechanics of what he was talking about but was unsure of where this was going.

'Except instead of just the three realms, he's picked something else up as well.'

I shot a quick glance at the others who appeared just as mystified as I was.

'What do you mean something else?'

'I didn't notice them before, because they are not in a geo-synchronous orbit with the rest.'

'What are they?''

'Soap Suds'.

'Soap suds,' I repeated.

K raised a hand. 'You might be taking your analogy a bit too far,' he said mildly.

Shukra nodded. 'Fair enough. There is something out there. Not realms like ours inhabited by lots of people, more like smaller pockets or rifts in inter-dimensional space where theoretically other entities could live.

'You've never noticed them before?'

He leaned forward, his face grave as he spoke. 'They are all heavily concealed and cut off from the other realms. About half a dozen or so. There is no way to traverse from there to here or vice versa. Ordinarily, when Swarg-Lok, Earth, and the underworld move about, their trajectories always intersect. Not these. They seem like self-contained bubbles, always floating about, just out of reach.'

I leaned back to think about what he was saying. 'Why is this relevant?'

'Ashwatthama's yagna snagged one such bubble.'

'By accident?'

He shook his head. 'On purpose. It looks like he deliberately ensnared that particular sliver of a realm and forced it to align with the others.'

'But why? Everything he did until that point, the hostages, the items, etc, were all geared towards bringing Narakasura back.'

'There's no doubt that was one of his goals,' Shukra said. 'But clearly he also had something else planned that none of us noticed until now.' He hesitated. 'Crossing back from the land of the dead to the living would send a ripple through the realms. That ripple might have been intended to pop the bubble and release whatever was in there.'

A grim silence greeted his words. 'I take it you don't know what was in that pocket realm?'

'Not a clue'.

'But you think it could be a real threat!'

He smiled but said nothing.

'Do you want to see my research?' Shukra asked.

'No need,' I said. 'You are right Shukra. We have been purposeless for a while. Maybe this is what we are meant to do.'

'Yeah.' K pumped his hand in the air. 'Like the Avengers, except we eliminate threats proactively. The Threat Terminators? The Hazard Hunters? The Crisis Crushers.'

'We can workshop the name,' Sars assured him, as usual amused by his enthusiasm.

I glanced around at the group. K was strutting around pretending he had a cape. Deanne and Sars were both smiling. Even Shukra looked like he was having fun.

It sounded clichéd, but of all the pop-culture references K had fed me over the years, the one sentence that stayed with me was from some animal-themed trilogy involving a lizard and an octopus. The line was simple and heartfelt... it resonated with me even back then, but only now did I truly understand its meaning.

'With great power comes great responsibility.'

I had lived with humans for a very long time, never quite belonging, always living on the sidelines. In large part, this was because I wanted nothing to do with them. I was content, without the weight of their expectations. I was free to go anywhere, to do anything, or be anyone. It was liberating.

It was also selfish. And I had had enough.

There was a vague, formless evil out there that threatened everyone and everything I cared about. All of a sudden, the life I had led until this point seemed meaningless. I could not be a spectator anymore.

K sidled over, while the others continued talking excitedly among themselves. He had an uncanny knack for knowing exactly what I was thinking.

'No regrets?' he asked.

'No regrets,' I answered, finding to my surprise that I meant it.

'Because if we do this,' he continued, 'our idyllic life is at an end. No more living in the shadows. We need to step out into the spotlight. Paint a big target on our backs if we need to. Let those who worship evil's might, beware our …'

'I'm with you,' I agreed before he could launch into another comic-book monologue. 'It's time I stopped playing nice.'

He gave a mock gasp of horror. 'All along, this was you being nice?'

I smiled. 'Trust me, K, this is just the beginning …'

'Admit it,' K said. 'The reason you were taking this case personally was because it reminded you of someone in the past. A cowherd, perhaps?'

'Not a cowherd', I said slowly. 'A prince. Of Ayodhya.'

THE END ... FOR NOW

THE MYTHOLOGY BEHIND THE SERIES

I love the Mahabharata. At 1.8 million words, it is four times the size of the Ramayana and ten times the length of the Odyssey and Iliad combined. Not only is every character painted in shades of grey, but the sheer size of the epic means that every re-read provides a new perspective or insight into something you hadn't thought of before.

Like many tales that are orally passed down from generation to generation, over time, certain elements have become more fantastical. There is also the human tendency to embellish stories, particularly when dealing with certain subjects such as faith. It is akin to saying there are many truths to a tale, and we choose which truth works best.

Akran is, of course, fictional. According to Hindu scriptures, the Kali Yuga began when Krishna left this realm. The length of the yugas is almost certainly an exaggeration—4,32,000 years is the number that gets thrown around most often because a day in heaven was equivalent to one year on Earth.

If we instead assume that time remains constant across realms, then instead of 4,32,000 BCE, we get the much more reasonable 1183 BCE (4,32,000/365) as the approximate date when Krishna died and the Kali Yuga began.

Why do I call this a more reasonable date? Because frankly, despite several jingoistic narratives about how the

Indian civilization is hundreds of thousands of years old, reality does not stack up.

Yuval Noah Harari makes a compelling case in Sapiens that by around 9500 BCE, agriculture was still not widely practised in the world and sheep herding had just begun in Northern Iraq. The late stone age is supposed to be between 50,000 and 39,000 years ago. An advanced civilisation 432,000 years ago has no basis, in fact.

To put the likely date of 1183 BCE into a wider historical perspective, the Mayan calendar counts time from this point (1100 BCE). It was a period of turmoil across the world's fledgling civilizations – the end of the Shang dynasty in China, the likely date for the fall of Troy (1184 BCE), the collapse of the Hittite Empire (1180 BCE), the end of the New Kingdom in Egypt, the end of the Mycenaean era and the beginning of the Greek Dark Ages. In India, the decline of the Indus valley civilization happened right around this time. This led to the Indo-Aryan migration to South Asia from Central Asia which led the Harappan's to migrate South. If there was ever a point of time in Indian history where a massive battle took place that might have changed the geographic map of the kingdoms of India, left a collective imprint on the psyche and consciousness of the people of that era, this would be it.

Those interested in understanding how I arrived at these dates can visit www.rohanmonteiro.in for a more detailed explanation.

When we say Devas, we are, of course, referencing the portfolio gods, excluding the main Trinity (Brahma, Vishnu and Shiva). The Samhitas, the oldest layer of text in the Vedas, list thirty-three such gods. On the other side are the Asuras, or the Demons. What I found interesting while researching this novel is that in ancient Persia, during the Achamenid Period (550 BC–330 BC), which has undoubtedly had an influence, Azurha is the god of Zoroastrianism (possible etymological root for the word 'Asura') and Daeva is the term for a demon. Maybe all the stories of gods and demons being told were rooted in folklore/tales about early civilisational clashes between Persia and India, and each side demonised the other.

- Nick Furry is a real cat who lives with a friend of mine, along with eleven other cats. He is blind in one eye, hence the name.
- The Board Gaming café, Creeda, in Churchgate really existed. It was an amazing place, ahead of its time, served the most delicious Maggi noodles and had a very friendly owner. Other locations mentioned in the book, The Tea Room, Doodally's, and so forth, are also real though Covid did end up decimating several small businesses (The Tea Room has shut down as of December 2021). Doodally's makes excellent craft beers and has fun quiz nights.

I replaced the name 'Bar Stock Exchange' in Bandra with Sensex, since I thought it sounded cooler. The dishes I mentioned are amazing and must not be missed.

- Shukra identifying forty kidnappings as unusual is entirely for the purpose of this story. In reality, according to 2021 data by the NCRB (National Crime Records Bureau), on average, eleven kidnappings take place every hour in India.
- The problem with the traditional view of Dharma was that it determined roles based on caste. Thus, there was no

upward mobility possible and no matter how talented you were, you could not become a merchant if you belonged to an untouchable caste.
- Over time, as roles and society evolved, the interpretation of Dharma also began to change. A friend who is also a teacher at ISKCON in Mayapur, Vinod provided one interpretation that I found the most meaningful. In his opinion, freeing oneself from the cycle of birth and rebirth and becoming lovingly associated with the lord is the ultimate reward for fulfilling your dharma. You can achieve this by maximizing your unique strengths/talents and if doing so leads to a betterment of society as a whole. Thus, if your passion is to sing, then sing. If it is to write, then write. In many ways, this is more about following your heart and doing what matters to you rather than being bound to a rigid inflexible stratum of society based on your birth. Pro tip : If you wish to tease an ISKCON devotee, don't ask him why he has only one wife while Krishna had 16,000. It doesn't work. They have a very dry and detailed answer on the subject.
- The sacred weapons that went missing are mentioned in the Mausala Parva. Several dark omens were witnessed, including the disappearance of the Sudarshana Chakra, the conch and chariot of Krishna and the plough weapon of Balarama. One explanation for this is that the celestial weapons had fulfilled their purpose on earth and returned to heaven. Arjun also experiences this phenomenon later, when he is defending the women of Dwarka from barbarian invaders. His celestial weapons do not appear when he calls for them, and his inexhaustible quivers of arrow shafts get exhausted.

For the purposes of this story, I mentioned that the snake who stole from Uttanka was Virach. According to most sources, the snake was named Takshaka, and he goes on to play a role later in the Mahabharata as well. However, there is an in-universe explanation of why Akran assumes it was Virach. Something that will be revealed in Book 2 of the Celestial Chronicles.

- Prince Ram, adhered to the Brihaspati Neeti i.e. the means to achieving an end must be righteous. Krishna focussed on the end goal—the Shukra Neeti—which proclaimed that the ends justified the means. The challenge with the Shukra Neeti is that unless you are a god, it is a slippery slope distinguishing between that and the Kanika Neeti. People can justify just about anything to themselves by believing in the righteousness of the end goal.

Akran's words about how he would refuse to condone the harming of a child are inspired by the work of a short philosophical fiction written in 1973 by Ursula K. Le Guin titled *The Ones Who Walk Away From Omelas*. It is the story of a land of great prosperity that depends on a single child's perpetual misery. Many people can rationalise the gift and say that one evil deed for such a plentiful bounty is acceptable. Those who walk away are the ones who refuse to accept that the ends justify the means.

There are no references to the Chandrahas after it was handed over to Ravana by Shiva. It has been speculated that he used it to kill the eagle, Jatayu. Since the act was not righteous, the sword returned to Shiva, but there is no official source to confirm this.

The Ganges is still the most sacred river in India. Unfortunately, it is estimated that more than three million litres of untreated sewage from towns along the Ganges are pumped into the river daily.[1]

When it reaches Varanasi, the untreated sewage (or most of it) gets pumped into the waters and turning it into one of the most polluted rivers in the world.[2]

Besides the literal 'child in the basket' examples, there are plenty of other stories of children being abandoned (in the woods, if not in a river) who go through a transformative journey before inheriting the throne. The Persian king, Cyrus (6th century BC), the Greek heroes Perseus, Jason and Theseus, and even the Trojan prince, Paris, are all examples. In Japanese mythology, there's the tale of Momotaro, a boy discovered by an elderly couple floating down a river and raised as their own.

If you had the misfortune of not being abandoned at a river at birth and still sought to link your name with divinity, you have a few other options available. Emperor Augustus commissioned a poet (Virgil) to spin a glorious tale about his ancestor, the Trojan prince and hero Aeneas escaping the sack of Troy and founding the city of Rome.

Kunti claiming that her kids were the children of the gods is not unique. There are several recorded instances across the ancient world when women who got pregnant, either outside

---

[1] Stuart Butler, "The Ganges: River of Life, Religion and Pollution," Geographical, March 21, 2024. https://geographical.co.uk/culture/the-ganges-river-of-life-religion-and-pollution.

[2] Kanchan Lal, "12 Most Polluted Rivers In The World — Sea Smart," Sea Smart, February 1, 2024. https://www.seasmartschool.com/blog/2022/2/17/12-most-polluted-rivers-in-the-world.

of marriage or while their husbands were away, claimed it was due to the gods. It was a convenient explanation for inconvenient pregnancies. Among the Greeks, it was usually Ares who visited—in the guise of the husband—while the men were at war. Zeus also had a similar reputation, which Alexander used to his advantage by claiming he was his son (a claim fully supported by his mother Olympias, which understandably strained relations with his biological father Philip II of Macedon). I would highly recommend Valerio Massimo Manfredi's three books series to learn more about Alexander). Norse women usually blamed Odin, who came disguised as a bard or a handsome merchant. And, of course, this is one of Christianity's founding myths.

Was Duryodhan seen as a bad king? By most accounts, no. He was popular among his subjects and had opened the royal coffers to the people in a time of famine, as chronicled in the epic. His two biggest character flaws were his jealousy and his pride. Yet, there were a lot of traits in him that were seen as the hallmarks of a good ruler. His sense of fairness and justice was well-known. He raised Karna to be the prince of the Angas even though he was the son of a charioteer. It may have been for his own selfish reasons, like tweaking the noses of the Pandavas, but judging people by their merits instead of their caste and birth was a bold move, even for a prince.

Also, among the Kuru princes, Duryodhan had no equal in mace fighting, with the exception of Bhim. At the end of the war, when offered single combat with anyone of his choice, Duryodhan chose to fight Bhim—the one person against whom his victory was not certain.

I feel compelled to add at this point that the Pandavas had just won the war. They wouldn't risk endangering everything they had fought so hard for to gain in a single one-on-one battle. It's likely that Duryodhan wasn't given a choice of whom to fight. And who is to say, if he had won, maybe he would still be exiled or killed.

The temple dedicated to Duryodhan, the only such temple in India, is located at Edakkad Wada of Poruvazhy village in Kerala. The story goes that a woman gave him water (or possibly toddy) when he was thirsty. She belonged to a class of untouchables and offering him water from her hands would have ordinarily been a death sentence. Duryodhan, however, thanked her for putting his needs as a human being ahead of her own life and giving him water. He also prayed for the well-being of the people and gave away land to the village out of gratitude.

When the people of the village heard the tale, they decided to build a temple in his honour—it was the first experience they had with someone of the Kshatriya class treating them kindly. The woman who gave him water became the priestess of the temple and her descendants and other members of her community continue to maintain the temple to this day.

Duryodhan's actions may look progressive today, but his behaviour then was considered a grievous breach of social norms. The strong-willed prince cared little for the opinions of the people he ruled, focusing instead on ensuring his vision for the future was realised. That put him at odds with the rigid caste system of the day. At the very end of the epic, Duryodhan is seen in heaven by Yudhishthir. His adherence to his duty as a Kshatriya and a king, despite his many flaws, granted him a place in heaven.

In contrast, Yudhishthir, while portrayed as one of the good guys, shows a weakness for gambling and puts his own kingdom and his wife/the wife of his brothers up as stakes in a gambling board. While he did have a clear and legitimate claim to the throne, once he put it up on the gambling board, he should no longer have had any right to demand it back.

Like the Mahabharat, the Ramayana, India's other great epic also has a scene where a deer is being shot by a royal: King Dasharatha.

It's tempting to think of the deer/human confusion to be nothing more than a convenient literary trope. However, according to a quick Google search, multiple hunters have mistaken humans for deer even as recently as 2019 (South Carolina) and 2023 (Malaysia), so we shouldn't be too hard on Pandu or Jara or Dasharatha.

The earrings of Ma Aditi being the same as the ones given by Surya to Karna was creative license on my part. They could certainly have been two different earrings.

- The Star Wars sandwich is where you watch movies four, five, six, then one, two three and four, five, six again. You've thus watched the movies in order of release and chronologically on the same day. So, congratulations. You are officially a Star Wars nerd. If you want to achieve legendary status, watch it on May 4th (May the fourth be with you) and persuade someone who's never seen it before to watch it with you.
- The story of Kamakhya is a local tale in Assam. Narakasura wanted to marry Kamakhya Devi. When he proposed, the goddess challenged him to build a staircase from the bottom of the Nilachal Hill to the temple within a

night, before the cock crows. Narakasura was almost about to accomplish the job when a cock crowed. Kamakhya Devi had strangled a rooster and made it crow untimely to give the impression of dawn to Naraka, which might actually be the world's first and only literal example of cock-blocking. Duped by the trick, Naraka thought it was futile and left it halfway through. Later, he chased after the rooster and killed it, which, given the circumstances, is understandable. The place where this occurred is known as Kukurakata, situated in the district of Darrang. The incomplete staircase is known as Mekhelauja Path.

Naraka Chaturdashi is celebrated in West Bengal as Bhoot Chaturdashi. It is believed, that on the eve of this dark night, the veil between the two worlds is thinner, and the souls of the deceased come down to earth to visit their dear ones. It is also believed that the fourteen forefathers of a family visit their living relatives, and so fourteen candles are placed all around the house to guide them homeward and especially to chase away any evil and unwanted spirits.

- Not to get technical but Madri sleeping with the Ashwini twins and then delivering twins is perfectly plausible. The medical term is heteropaternal superfecundation. I had naively assumed the 'super' was tagged on because it was an impressive feat, but that's not actually the case.
- As most students of military history will know, no battle formation is impregnable. The Mahabharata states that only three people knew how to break through the Chakravyuh, but that seems implausible. A circular formation like the one described is vulnerable to a

double envelopment, which is precisely what Hannibal used against the Romans in the battle of Canae 216 BC.

Saladin, Alexander, Genghis Khan, Suleiman and Nadir Shah all used similar tactics to encircle and destroy enemy armies.

Game Of Thrones fans will recognise exactly how the double envelopment manoeuvre is executed in the 'Battle of the Bastards' where the majority of Jon Snow's soldiers are unable to fight because the circumference of the outer circle is being pushed inwards.

I had the pleasure of corresponding with Dr Roel Konijnendijk, a Dutch historian, author and Oxford professor who most people might recognize from his YouTube videos on Ancient Warfare tactics.[3] He confirmed my opinions on the Chakravyuh as a 'tool of storytelling and not as a reflection of any real historical situation'. In his opinion, the Chakravyuh is similar to the Eight Gates Formation from the Chinese Romance of the Three Kingdoms. Both formations are meant to demonstrate the peerless tactical skill of the commanders who use them and deliberately construed to be beyond the ability of any human general or army.

- Halahala is a poison that emerged from the sea when the Devas and Asuras decided to churn the oceans to gain the nectar of immortality. The airport in Bangkok has a set of statues depicting the scene. To save the realms, Shiva drank the poison, which turned his throat blue and

---

[3] Insider. "Ancient-Warfare Expert Rates 10 More Battle Tactics In Movies And TV | How Real Is It? | Insider." YouTube video, 18.54, October 26, 2021. https://www.youtube.com/watch?v=DPMiWwqX4wI.

henceforth, he is also known as Nilakantha (the one with a blue throat). The Chandrahas adding a poison attack is inspired by fantasy and has no basis in Indian mythology.
- While Kacha did learn the Sanjivani mantra, he was unable to make use of it. A curse by Devayani (when he refused to marry her) rendered him unable to remember the mantra when it was needed. It's a theme that repeats itself regarding knowledge gained through dishonest means. Near the end of the war, Karna, who had learnt the use of divine weapons through Parashurama by pretending he was a Brahmin (Parashuram had vowed not to train Kshatriyas), also forgot how to use them. Parashurama had cursed him that it would forsake him at a crucial point when he needed the knowledge.

According to myth, Dronacharya popped out of a vessel called Drona, hence the name. He also learnt how to use Parashurama's weapons and their knowledge and was the teacher of the Pandavas and Kauravas; hence the title, Acharya (Teacher).

Babies appearing like dominoes in thirty minutes or less isn't restricted just to Kunti. Satyavati's son Vyas also popped out, in his prime, through same-day delivery.

It is interesting to see how heroes were perceived in ancient times. They were not meant to be ordinary humans thrust into greatness—instead, their birth itself presaged that these would be characters whose stories would continue to echo through time.

Satyavati was conceived from a fish, which was supposed to explain her unusual body odour (there might have been a simpler explanation for that, particularly for a fisherwoman in a time before soap was popular). The Kauravas emerged from a hard piece of flesh broken into a hundred pieces and placed into pots full of oil. Bhishma was born from the river Ganga. Hanuman was born of a particularly potent fertility kheer, which makes him sound like quite a handful (it's also incidentally a story that has completely turned me off eating kheer in general).

Makes you wonder if ordinary humans have been doing it wrong all this time.

Deanne is a character I made up—a cross between the Hellenistic Diana, the Huntress and Wonder Woman. It was tempting to choose an Indian goddess, but the story I am envisioning at this point will involve stretching out across other mythologies over time.

Thank you for reading my ramblings, and I hope you enjoy and recommend *Shadows Rising* to all your friends.

NOTES ON THE CRAFT

I am a pantser, not a plotter.

It's a term I learnt during the course of writing this novel. Some writers outline and know the plot of their story before they even begin. Some fly by the seat of their pants and the story reveals itself to them as they write.

At the rate of about a thousand words a day, it was about a week and somewhere near the end of the third chapter that I finally began to have an inkling about what the story would shape into. At the end of Chapter 3, when Akran walks away from the gangsters thinking he now knows the kidnappers' identities, at that moment, he doesn't actually have a plan. There's a process of free-form association where I write what I am thinking and try to explore a particular path. It often means several written words need to be discarded, since traversing down a one-story path results in a dead end and I need to backtrack.

For those wondering, the process for me is typically a thousand words a day when I am in the mood to write. I wrote *Shadows Rising* in 2018 during a two-month break between jobs. It was 30,000 words in length. It wasn't very good, although I was really proud of it.

I loved the way the story sounded in my head, but I intensely disliked the way it read when I converted it from thoughts to pixels for the first time. Excited, I sent it out to lots of people, all of whom rejected it.

Less excited, I then spent six months revising, editing and tweaking the subject matter. It increased the length to nearly 50,000 words. By this point, it looked substantially better than the first draft but still no publisher was willing to touch it (and I still hated the prose).

Most of them never returned my emails, one of them said she liked my writing but there was no market for fantasy in India. One even suggested I add elves and dwarves in there to make it more 'fantastic'.

I decided to ignore the wilder of those suggestions and keep writing. *Shadows Rising* remained on my laptop, occasionally being brought out for a little polishing every time I thought of something.

Along the way, I had the opportunity to include many of the myths. These are the tales that often get missed—the side stories in the epics—the stories of Uttanka and the earrings, Kama and Shiva, how Ravana obtained the Chandrahas, how Drona got his name, etc. One of the things I hoped for with *Shadows Rising* was, besides telling an original story, to illuminate a few of the other interesting gems that exist in Indian mythology.

Finally in 2022, I decided enough was enough. I quit my job one more time and dedicated my time to writing. I had a vague couple of ideas for sequels to *Shadows Rising* and I figured I would put them on paper before I lost interest. I had reached 55,000 words by then, had finished writing one of those sequels by July and began to spam every single person in the publishing world I knew—a last-ditch effort before I gave up and self-published.

Except for December that year turned out to be a month of miracles. Sanghamitra Biswas from Westland was the first to express interest. Two days later, a young lady from Penguin, Shubhi Surana, also pinged to say she found it fascinating. And three days later, Mita Kapur, probably the most well-known literary agent in India, messaged me saying she liked the book. And a startup in India offered me a job—all in the same month.

What followed was six months of gruelling waiting while the lawyers crossed the t's and dotted the i's but by the 8th of June, 2023, I finally (OMFG FINALLY!!!!) had a signed contract.

Shadows Rising started as a tale of redemption ... for Karna. He is the boy in the river, the prince who lived as a pauper, the noble warrior, the loyal friend, the villain who suggested disrobing Draupadi, and the tragic hero killed in the end—all rolled into one. A separate book dedicated to him could easily be named 'Fifty-One Shades of Grey,' and it might still not be enough to describe all the different layers that his character displays.

At some point in the middle of the second chapter, I realised I wanted my own character. Someone with a tragic backstory and who is fundamentally flawed but who is unencumbered by a past they cannot change. With Akran, I could tune his history to make him have all sorts of interesting mythological roles. He could make appearances in the Ramayana if needed. Or possibly have enemies among the Asuras or even some of the Devas. That's how Akran was born, a foul-mouthed Yaksha who, like myself, is highly introverted, doesn't like people except for the friends he already has and most importantly, is very fond of good food in Mumbai (the last bit may not have come out quite so eloquently, but I shall fix that in subsequent books).

I was concerned that Akran's use of profanity might turn people off. However, I counted, and his choice of colourful language seems mild compared to most people I hang out with. In a spread of roughly 75,000 words, he only says or thinks 'fuck', or some variation of it, for a maximum of eighteen times. Throw in slang for illegitimate kids, male reproductive organs, female dogs, poop, the behinds of donkeys and a few other possible words that might classify the book as PG-13, and it's still well under fifty words—that looks like a pretty decent number to me. Either that or I've been hanging out with people who cuss a lot all my life.

K happens to be my favourite character, much more than Akran. The irreverent thoughts that keep popping up in his head very much reflect the inner recesses of my own mind. I wrote a short 2000-word story about him hitting on two women in a bar—it's rude and unprintable at the moment but I hope to someday share it with all of you.

Sars also doesn't get enough love in this book. As a character, I find the idea behind a rebellious goddess of knowledge fascinating. In part, she represents a nostalgic memory of India in the '90s—when I first got the Internet, and the world exploded in terms of suddenly having access to millions of new ideas right at our fingertips. That's who I imagined her to be—a hacker/polymath/savant who can function as the knowledge board for the group. Her skill set, however, is quite similar to that of Shukra. By the time she did make an appearance, Shukracharya was already too deeply engrained in the story, and given his mythological connection to the Sanjivani mantra, she ended up being only a side character in this novel.

Sars and Kama will both get far more love and attention as the series progresses.

ACKNOWLEDGEMENTS

As always, this book was only possible with the help of some very important people.

My wife Sharon—struggling authors need hardworking spouses in the background to keep a roof over our heads. I am especially grateful for all her efforts in supporting and encouraging me to pursue my dreams while she puts food on the table. She also fended off everyone who expressed shock at my pursuing such a dismal career by patiently explaining that we should all be encouraged to follow our passions.

My daughter Zarah, who is six at present, recently wondered when I would write a book with her picture on it. I dedicate this to her and truly believe she will be even cooler than Akran in a few years.

My son Zach, who is eight, loves the idea of underpowered demi gods battling demons and tossing magic and fireballs around. I'm not going to let him read this until he is older, but I hope he will someday have as much fun reading it as I did writing it.

My copyeditor, Jessica Pegis from Girls with Glasses. This is our third manuscript together, and I can see my writing improve each time, so I am grateful for the feedback.

Sanghamitra Biswas from Westland, who took a chance on this book and made it a reality. Shubhi Surana from Penguin was incredibly amazing in providing feedback, even after I signed with Westland. Mita Kapur from Siyahi, who did all the heavy lifting as far as negotiating the contract goes.

The amazing authors who took time out of their busy lives and agreed to read this manuscript and provide a quote if they liked it, even though they had never heard of me before I reached out. As an Easter egg, I included the names of three ships in the book, each of a different author I had initially planned to include Sword of Albion from the excellent post-apocalyptic Koli series by Mike Carey but settled on Naglfar instead (from the Prose Edda and one of the most influential comics I've ever read—Lucifer). Chathrand is from Robert Reddick's four-part series about a gigantic ship. The Weary Mother is from Sam Sykes's *Seven Blades in Black*, which also happens to have the wittiest, snarkiest female lead in any fantasy (IMHO).

Closer to home, Anand Neelakantan wrote a book in 2013 called *Ajaya: Roll of the Dice*—a story from the POV of Duryodhan. I wrote to him back then as a curious fan and was able to reach out to him again 10 years later to request a blurb, which he has very kindly provided.

Ashok Banker was also extremely kind—another author that I had reached out to in 2003 as a reader. He remembered me and was kind enough to provide a blurb. Not only that, he also took time out of his busy schedule to answer a few of my queries. I had the pleasure of exchanging several emails with him, and when I expressed worry about how the story sounded so much better in my head VS what it looked like on the page, he had a very profound observation to make: 'No book ever achieves perfection, only publication.'

In alphabetical order, I also wish to thank Kevin Missal, Koral Dasgupta, Saksham Garg, Sidin Vadukut and Trisha Das

ACKNOWLEDGEMENTS

for reading and providing blurbs. Scott Lynch, Manu Pillai and Samit Basu were busy, but they took the time to write back and explain that it would not be possible. Thank you for that!

Special thanks to the beta readers—Ashwin, Ceto, Kailash, Vivek, Sumeet, Namratha, and Nikitha.

A special thanks to my mom who was so excited after hearing about my first book, that I felt motivated enough to write a few more. 2024 is the year of her 75th birthday and my parents' 50th wedding anniversary; so I am very glad the book will get released this year.

To my dad whose moral code of right and wrong has stood as a beacon for me and my siblings when it comes to living our lives.

And finally, a big heartfelt thank you to all of the readers—even you downloaders, pirates and freeloaders. I've been on your side of the fence with too many books I want and too little money to spend. If this book actually gets pirated, it's likely a sign that it is successful and that would be a good thing. Unless you are very talented or very lucky, writing is one of those callings that is endlessly frustrating because you believe deep down that the story you wish to tell is wonderful; but somehow, the teeming millions all around you cannot see it.

It takes dedication and commitment to read a book from cover to cover and if you have reached all the way to the very end as I ramble on, then I am definitely grateful for your support.

Thank you once again. This journey is only beginning.

May 2024
Rohan

www.ingramcontent.com/pod-product-compliance
Lightning Source LLC
LaVergne TN
LVHW010155070526
838199LV00062B/4362